The Season of Risks

AN ETHICAL VAMPIRE NOVEL

Susan Hubbard

Simon & Schuster Paperbacks

NEW YORK LONDON TORONTO SYDNEY

SIMON & SCHUSTER PAPERBACKS
A Division of Simon & Schuster, Inc.
1230 Avenue of the Americas
New York, NY 10020

First Simon & Schuster trade paperback edition July 2010

SIMON & SCHUSTER PAPERBACKS and colophon are registered trademarks of Simon & Schuster, Inc.

For information about special discounts for bulk purchases, please contact Simon & Schuster Special Sales at 1-800-506-1949 or business@simonandschuster.com.

The Simon & Schuster Speakers Bureau can bring authors to your live event. For more information or to book an event, contact the Simon & Schuster Speakers Bureau at 1-866-248-3049 or visit our website at www.simonspeakers.com.

Designed by Jacquelynne Hudson

Manufactured in the United States of America

1   3   5   7   9   10   8   6   4   2

Library of Congress Cataloging-in-Publication Data

Hubbard, Susan.
The season of risks : an ethical vampire novel / Susan Hubbard.
p.   cm.
1. Vampires—Fiction. I. Title.
PS3558.U215S43 2010
813'.54—dc22   2009051618

ISBN 978-1-4391-8342-7
ISBN 978-1-4391-8711-1 (ebook)

In memory of Steven Garfinkel

There is a two-fold Silence—sea and shore—
Body and soul. One dwells in lonely places,
Newly with grass o'ergrown; some solemn graces,
Some human memories and tearful lore,
Render him terrorless: his name's "No More."

—EDGAR ALLAN POE, "SILENCE"

To watch the birth and death of beings is like looking at the movements of a dance.

—BUDDHA

The Season of Risks

Preface

There are some things I know for certain.

I am half-mortal, half-vampire. Some call me a hybrid, others a half-breed.

I was born in Saratoga Springs, New York, fifteen years ago. But this year, I turned twenty-two.

I'm a synesthete, apt to see words and numbers in color and texture.

The two friends closest to me both were murdered.

My name is Ariella Montero, and I know a secret. Telling it will change everything.

~

Once I had a friend named Kathleen. Although she was in my life for less than a year, I thought that she knew me better than anyone.

Sometimes we played a game called Anything in the World. Kathleen invented it. "If you could have anything in the whole world, what would it be?" she'd say.

The first time she asked me the question, I said, "I have no idea."

We sat in the belvedere, the summerhouse in our family's gardens in Saratoga Springs. It was June, and the air felt heavy with lavender, layered with the scents of white and yellow roses.

"Come on, Ari." Her face showed her disappointment—particularly her eyes, streaky grey, the color of water. Not *gray*. That was a stronger shade, more opaque, like lead.

I shook my head. "I can't think of a thing."

"Then you ask me." She lay back, relaxed as a kitten, against the cushioned seat.

I repeated the question: "If you could have anything in the world, what would it be?"

She pretended to think hard. She creased her forehead and stared across the room.

But I heard what she was thinking. The thought swelled so loud that it drowned her words, which said something else entirely: she wanted to be me.

Kathleen is gone now.

But years ago I saw her ghost in our garden, beckoning me to join her. Even now, sometimes at night I hear her voice, thin as water, silver as mercury, calling to me from a place I've never been, a place I can only imagine.

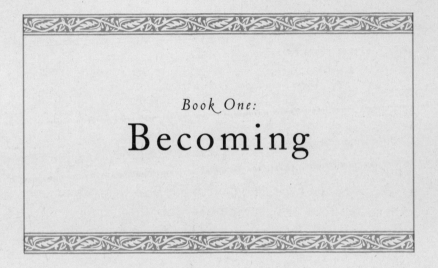

Book One:

Becoming

One

The season of risks began with the summer of love. That was my name for it: a time of strong feelings that changed quickly, from bliss, to embarrassment, to anxiety.

Those feelings came with the smell of coconut oil, worn by others to tan but by me as perfume; the sharp green scents of the ocean, always nearby; the surf sounding bass notes for wavering songs played on some distant radio; and sand damp-soft between my toes, gritty on my clothes, and on my lips the taste of salt from the sea or from tears.

My mother and my father sat facing each other in wicker chairs under an awning in the backyard of our rented cottage. We were on Tybee Island, near Savannah. They wore wide-brimmed hats and loose-fitting clothes made of unbleached linen. I saw them from my bedroom window when I awoke; they probably had been up for hours and might have just returned from a walk on the beach.

The sounds of their voices woke me, his as measured as music, its inflections blending the places he'd lived: Brazil, Virginia, England, even a tinge of southwest Ireland, where he had traveled the year before. Her voice was liquid Savannah: a soft drawl that made me picture young women lazily discussing their beaux as they primped for a ball.

But she was talking about ghosts.

"No, it was September," Sara said. Sara is her name, but I call her Mãe, the Portuguese word for *mother;* she told me she liked the sound of it better. Her hair is as long as mine, but hers is reddish brown. Mine is dark, like my father's. I've been told I have her eyes. I can't clearly see my reflection in mirrors, but I hope that it's true.

"It couldn't have been September." Raphael's voice never sounded irritated or emphatic, but managed to be speculative and a bit remote, even in disagreement. He prided himself on his long-term memory. "By September I had arrived in England. When you told me the ghost story, I was still at school in Virginia. It must have happened earlier."

My father had told me that ghost story. A young man killed in a duel in 1815 had shown up in Mãe's apartment in Savannah—or rather, his apparition had. After a few visits, my mother decided that her visitor was the ghost of someone named James Wilde, whose grave she'd seen in Colonial Cemetery, across the street.

My mother bent forward to pick up a tall glass of Picardo, one of the blood substitutes that provide the nutrients and oxygen we need to keep us from drinking mortals' blood. The dark red liquid glowed as she lifted the tumbler to her lips, then set it back on the table. "But I remember the way the air smelled. Like dead leaves."

"The odor came from him. From James." My father turned his head, and I glimpsed his face—sunglasses, narrow nose, upper lip curved in a bow and lower lip turned down at its corners. I'm told my mouth has a similar shape. "Remember, I was with you the last time he appeared."

"The green smoke in the room." Her voice was low, and I had to strain to hear her. "I'll never forget that night. But it was cold and damp. It must have been September."

He looked off at the century plants edging the yard. "The cold and damp—they came from James."

The words made me shiver, although the morning air felt warm and already humid, hinting of afternoon rain. Poor James Wilde, killed in a duel at the age of twenty-two because a friend had called his honor into question.

Then I began to think of my own ghost story: the night two years ago when my friend Kathleen had appeared outside my window, although she'd been killed a month before. The way she called my name. And I said nothing. I sat watching her, too numb to respond.

I pushed the memory away. I wasn't ready to revisit it yet. But for the rest of that sunny summer, I grew more and more aware of cold patches of shadow all around me, cast by nothing I could see.

～

"*Please* don't tell me you're eavesdropping again." Dashay swung into the room before I could move from the window.

"Please *do* come in," I said in my most formal voice. Dashay was my mother's best friend, and probably mine, too—but I valued my privacy, particularly when invading others'.

"Already here." Dashay dropped onto the foot of my bed. She wore peach today—a pale shirt and darker cargo pants, an apricot-colored scarf woven through her hair. She glanced toward the window. "What are they up to?"

"Disagreeing about the past," I said. "About when things happened." My parents had recently reunited after several years apart. My father had raised me on my own, until I ran away to find my mother. Using dreams and hunches to find her in Florida, I managed to bring them back together again. Exactly how together, I couldn't tell yet.

"Facts don't matter to memories." Her voice had darkened.

She shook her head, as if to clear her thoughts. "I'm going back to Blue Heaven today. Check on the horses and the honeybees, take care of some business. Want to come along? Leave the lovebirds on their own to figure out *what* happened *when*."

Dashay talked too fast, I told myself, and I needed time to think about her question. "I'm still waking up."

Already I felt torn. Blue Heaven meant home—the farm she and my mother owned in Homosassa Springs, Florida. A neighbor had been taking care of things while we were away on Tybee. I missed the house, the horses, the bees. Most of all I missed Grace, our cat. But I didn't feel ready to leave my parents. Yes, I wanted to eavesdrop some more. I wanted to know if they were in love.

And to be more honest with you than I could be with myself at the time, I wanted to decide if I might be in love myself. His name was Neil Cameron.

"I think I'll stay here," I said. Strangely, Dashay looked relieved—only for a second, until her mouth reshaped itself to an expression of regret.

When she left, I turned to look out the window again. They still sat there, talking, their voices now too soft for me to hear.

~

The week before, I'd gone sailing for the first time. Cameron had a sloop called *Dulcibella*. He'd sailed it up from St. Simons Island and docked at a marina on the Intracoastal Waterway between Savannah and Tybee Island. It was our first meeting alone together.

I'd met Neil Cameron the previous spring, when one of my college classes took a field trip to a caucus of third-party candidates in Savannah. From the moment I saw his dark blue eyes, watched him move, and heard him speak, he charmed me, and since then he had charmed a large percentage of the

American public in his campaign for president. They might not have been so charmed had they known he was a vampire.

How can one vampire identify another? That's a common question mortals ask. I'd found out the most obvious way: I noticed that he didn't cast a shadow. But some vampires swear by their instincts; they say they can sense the presence of an "other" viscerally, by a tingle along the spine or scalp. I've felt those tingles, but only when someone or something was secretly watching me. I think many mortals feel them, too. Next time you feel such a sensation, look around. Try to see who's watching you. Even if you see no one, a vampire or spirit might be keeping an eye on you.

Cameron never hid his nature from me—he knew I was *other*, too, the instant he saw me order Picardo. It's an aperitif popular with vampires, too bitter for mortals.

But he did feel a need to hide his real identity from the rest of the world. That was one of the things we talked about, the day of our first sail.

We sailed through tidal marshes, seeing no other beings except the occasional long-legged shorebird, half hidden by tall grasses. I sat across from Cameron in the boat's cockpit, watching the muscles in his arm as it moved the tiller. His skin was the color of clover honey; that meant it must have been darker when he was "vamped." Vampires grow paler once they're "declared."

Cameron—that's how I thought of him, not *Neil*—looked over at me and smiled. That's what I liked best about him: the enigmatic smile that made me feel as if I mattered to him more than anything, and that I shared his secret, something so important that it could change the world. I wanted him to share my secrets, too.

He wore a beat-up baseball cap, but his dark curly hair escaped at its sides. I felt the urge to reach over and touch it, feel its silkiness, as we rushed through the water.

"Hard alee," he said. As he brought the boat about, we changed places in the cockpit. The sails rippled and flapped, then went taut again. "Are you wearing enough sunscreen?" he asked.

"Plenty." I had coated myself four times.

"I could never give up sailing."

I understood. Seeing land from the water gave it a kind of logic, explained it in ways I couldn't put into words. And when the wind blew strong and steadily, as it did for most of that day, the boat skimmed the waves so lightly that it seemed to fly. But most vampires feared sunburn too much to sail. If my parents had known where I was that day, they would not have approved.

"Isn't it like most risks we take? Preparation makes all the difference." I tightened my sun hat's cord under my chin, thinking of how my father had warned me to always hide my nature from mortals, how my mother had supplied me with a fake ID so that I'd fit in at college. They'd taught me that vampires had to be prepared at all times—to move, to disappear, to reinvent themselves in safer places.

"Preparation works up to a point." He looked sad for a moment. His free hand made an odd gesture—a kind of wave with a twist. I'd never met anyone else who talked with his hands as much as his voice.

"Some risks you can't anticipate," he said. "They're like squalls that come out of nowhere. One moment the water is still; the next, you're awash in the vortex of something you never saw coming."

His eyes moved from the river ahead to me again, and we exchanged a look, despite the veils of sunglasses. I'll never forget that look, or the way his eyes cut through the dark lenses.

"Other storms—you're warned they're on the way. You do everything you can, and sometimes you fend them off. But even with warning, they may turn out to be nothing like what you expected. They may not even pose the same kind of risks."

I didn't entirely understand him. It seemed an odd conversation for such a beautiful day.

We dropped anchor off Oysterbed Island and waded ashore with a picnic basket. Cameron led the way to a flat rock near a clump of wax myrtle trees. He didn't hesitate, and I knew he must have been here before. I wondered who'd come with him.

It might have been Tamryn Gordon—one of his closest aides, who coordinated his campaign strategy. I'd met her at the caucus in Savannah. A tall woman with wavy hair, she wore a red dress that flattered her curves. Her sophistication and style were as dazzling as her face, whose symmetrical features looked as if they'd been carved. But when Cameron spoke, her face flushed and her eyes looked as excited as mine must have been, even though she had likely heard the speech many times before. Yes, Cameron was *that* good.

"He's fresh, but not naïve," she'd said to me without any introduction. Her voice was low pitched, almost gravelly, and its tone sounded matter-of-fact, as if she were checking items off a list.

"Wise, but not complacent," I said tentatively, suddenly ashamed of my faded pink sweater.

Tamryn frowned, as if I'd said something obvious or irrelevant. "He has the potential to be one powerful man." As she walked away, she turned back for a moment, her eyes cold. "Don't you dare ruin things for him."

I'd stared after her, baffled. What had she seen in my face?

Cameron, in the midst of smoothing a rug across the rock, stopped moving. I realized I'd forgotten to block my thoughts. Blocking is the norm with civilized vampires; it takes concentration to generate neural "white noise," but it's easier to do than tuning out the thoughts of others. My mother says that practicing blocking *and* not listening is the best etiquette, but that seems old-fashioned, even prissy, to me. Often, listening to thoughts strikes me as justifiable, sometimes necessary.

"It's okay," Cameron said, his voice gentle. Was he pardoning my jealousy?

He added, "I've been sailing this river for more than a hundred years. And each time, it's a different river."

Something I tended to forget: Cameron had been made a vampire long, long before I was born. "Will you tell me how it happened?"

He knew what I was asking. "Yes, but not today. Let's not let the past overshadow the present." He finished smoothing the rug and began to unpack the food.

Then there would be other days like this. Other chances for me to ask questions, hear his stories. That meant he didn't think me too young or too immature. Or likely to ruin things for him.

～

We talked while we ate the smoked salmon sandwiches and strawberries he'd brought. Like me, and like most Sanguinists—the sect of vampires my father belongs to—Cameron practiced pescetarianism: he ate fish, but no other forms of meat, and relied on blood substitutes to keep strong. The other vampire sects—the Colonists and the Nebulists—prefer red meat and fresh blood. Then there are unaffiliated vampires, who do as they please.

But he was talking about vampires' concerns with nature and the environment, not food. "So you see, Ariella, what unites the sects is far greater than what separates us." As he spoke, he put his hands together, then apart, seeming to forget that one hand held a sandwich. "We need to keep the planet healthy if we're to survive. The differences among us have to be bridged, even if some can't be entirely overcome."

I wanted to agree with him. Identifying with a particular group of vampires seemed antiquated to me and more likely to generate hostilities than resolve conflicts among vampires and humans alike. My mother's friend Dashay didn't see the point of the sects, either; Mãe herself felt ambivalent. But I knew how deeply my father's reservations ran about the Nebulists and the Colonists, and to some extent I shared them.

I thought of the chart my mother had made to teach me about the sects.

SECT	ORIGIN	LOCATION TODAY	CHARACTERISTICS
Sanguinists	England, 12th c.	worldwide	Environmentalists; ethicists; mostly celibate; proponents of equal rights for vamps and mortals; subsist on blood-based sera and artificial blood.
Colonists	Germany, 19th c.	Germany, Latin America, China, and United States (outposts in Arizona and Idaho?)	Use humans for food and sport; favor their extinction through cultivating and harvesting; subsist on human blood.
Nebulists	England, 20th c.	England (Oxon) and N. America (esp. Toronto, Miami, and L.A.)	Proponents of vampire rights; mostly celibate; believe human extinction is inevitable, but prefer to take victims one at a time; subsist on human blood and artificial blood.

Colonists seemed easy to despise, even though I'd never met any. They were known to hate humans, to consider them a blood source—nothing more. Nebulists proved harder to judge. My father's oldest friend, a vampire named Malcolm Lynch, was one of them. He claimed to want what was best for all, but clearly considered vampires intellectually and physically superior to mortals.

Only the Sanguinists favored equal rights for vampires and mortals. And now here came Cameron, telling me that position was "too idealistic."

"You can't have equality if one group is essentially invisible," he said. "I saw a poll last week that claimed forty-five percent of registered voters believe in vampires. The question was designed to identify ignorant voters—that is, anyone who believes in vampires must be a fool."

"But it's possible some of those voters *do* believe. Some of them might even be vampires."

I knew it was a weak argument. No one kept official records or census numbers on the vampire population in America. But there were abundant rumors among the mortals that vampires existed—rumors that grew and spread sporadically when something gruesome happened that humans couldn't explain. And sometimes rumors led humans to hunt suspected vampires, set fire to them, or try to hammer stakes into their hearts. Horror movies and books reinforced the stereotypes that vampires were all bloodthirsty, soulless fiends who needed to be eradicated so that mortals could live in peace. I tried not to let the stereotypes upset me, but they made me feel sick sometimes.

"Yes, it's possible." Cameron took a sip from his glass of wine, a fine red made with pinot noir grapes and laced with Sangfroid, another blood substitute. "In any case, it's pretty clear that America isn't ready to elect a self-proclaimed vampire as president."

I set down my plate and leaned back on my elbows, watching an osprey soar high overhead, a silver fish dangling from one talon. Cameron's points made sense. But how would things ever change unless vampires openly declared themselves?

There were a few isolated cases of vamps "coming out of the box," as it was called, but they were dismissed by the general public as acting, or at worst, behaving psychotically. Yet if you searched the Internet, in less than a minute you'd find hundreds of thousands of blogs and postings from self-proclaimed vampires. Were they all liars or lunatics?

Until more real vampires came out of the box, nothing would change. Most would continue to live in secret, moving periodically or having surgery to conceal their agelessness.

Cameron sensed my disappointment. He held out both hands like parentheses. "Ari, whether the voters know it or not, if I come to be elected, I *will* be the first vampire president. I'll be able to shape policies to protect our interests and build a future that benefits all of us."

I resisted the urge to say, *But that sounds too idealistic.*

He heard what I thought. "This isn't about ideals," he said. "It's a matter of survival. Vampire factions are in a cold war now—against each other and, to varying extents, against humans. If things get worse—if they flare into full-fledged war—the consequences will be devastating. Worse than the last time."

My father had told me about the Great War. A struggle among the sects for power and influence, it took place in Europe, while mortals were waging what they now call World War I. Millions of vampires were tortured and burned before the sects declared a truce. It took them only six months to learn what mortals decided after more than four years of combat: war was a senseless waste.

Unlike humans, vampires had avoided warfare since then. But disagreements were reportedly growing among the vampire factions.

My father strongly disapproved of war, and the Sanguinists favored peaceful resolutions. I wondered whose side Cameron was on.

He removed his hat, and his dark hair sprang out. He tilted his head and smiled at me. "I'm me, myself, and I."

The downwind sail back to the marina was quiet, except for the occasional cackle of a kingfisher as it darted out from the shoreline. I leaned my back against the deck and looked down at the embroidered tunic I wore over my jeans; it had been a birthday gift a few weeks ago and today marked the first time I'd worn it, hoping that our sailing trip would be a date. *It wasn't a date so much as a campaign stop.* I refocused quickly, blocking the thought.

But those moments when he looked at me, when his eyes told me I mattered more than anything—those weren't campaign rhetoric. They were real. They simply hadn't been enough.

When we docked, we stowed the sails and shut the hatch of *Dulcibella*'s tiny cabin. Cameron would spend the night there and sail home the following morning.

At the edge of the parking lot was my father's ancient black Jaguar, which he'd agreed, after much hesitation, to let me use that summer. Dashay had taught me to drive. Although my style wasn't quite as fast and fluid as hers, it had become more than competent.

Cameron walked me to my car. I unlocked it, and when I turned around, he kissed me. My mind went blank, my mouth burned.

When he pulled away, I moved forward. I kissed him back. This time I had a sensation of red light pulsing behind my closed eyelids, of fire moving through me.

And then we stood apart in the sunlight, both weak, and I wondered, *Is it always like this?*

Cameron shook his head. *No.*

◈

On the drive back to Tybee, I went over what little I'd heard about vampire love.

I knew that Sanguinists and Nebulists had traditionally advocated celibacy; they considered sex a distraction at best, a danger at worst. Mãe had told me that of course there were exceptions: her relationship with my father had been one of them. She'd said sex between two vampires "might be so powerful as to be all-consuming, even violent." But her opinions were based on hearsay—she'd been a mortal when I was conceived. And I wasn't about to ask what *that* experience had been like.

I remembered a conversation I'd had with Dashay.

"Some sects think it's wrong to have sex with mortals," she'd said. "And others think sex is wrong, period."

"But why?"

"They don't want vampires to breed. They all have their reasons. Sanguinists think the world is overpopulated, Nebulists think it's nasty to have sex, and the Colonists want the humans to breed because it means more food. But vampires having children? None of them think it's the right thing to do."

I'd felt insulted, somehow. I decided I needed to talk to Dashay again. She'd had a passionate relationship for years with another "half-breed" called Bennett.

So, yes, I was thinking about sex as well as love.

I turned the car radio dial to the oldies station, rolled down the car windows, and let the breeze and the music blow all my thoughts away. I smelled like coconut oil, I was driving a car down a country road, and I'd just been kissed and kissed back. It was truly the summer of love.

Then my cell phone rang. I turned off the radio and pulled the car off the road before I answered it.

"I thought it was time I checked in on you." The voice belonged to Malcolm Lynch. At one time he'd been my father's closest friend, but he'd never called me before.

Yet Malcolm had been around our family since I was born—and an influence even when he wasn't there. I'd had a conversation with him in Savannah last spring, the same week I met Cameron for the first time. He'd told me more than I wanted to know about the past: why he'd made my father a vampire and why, years later, he'd done the same for my mother. They were too talented to remain mere mortals, he said.

"I don't want you checking in on me." I didn't like Malcolm, didn't trust him. He'd killed my best friend.

"You need looking after," he said. "More than you know."

I looked at the car's dashboard, at the instruments set into burled wood, and in the tachometer screen I imagined I saw Malcolm's face: high forehead, pointed chin, narrow grey eyes, blond hair. The image made me shiver.

"Everything I do is for your own good." His voice had a silky quality that made me listen, though part of me wanted to hang up. "Have you thought about our conversation, back in Savannah?"

I'd tried not to think about it. Malcolm had told me he put Kathleen "out of her misery" when he discovered she was in love with my father. He did it in order to protect me and the rest of the family, because she was about to expose us as vampires. And he'd continued to keep watch over our family since—in order to protect us. Every family should be as lucky as we were, he said.

"You told me I should work with you," I said. "Become a Nebulist."

"Yes, *that*." His voice sounded amused. "But I offered you a chance to contribute to our research. Remember?"

And his words came back to me, as if he'd summoned them: *You're half-vampire, one of a statistically rare group whose physiological traits don't match those of either mortal or vampire populations. As such, you could be immensely valuable to the bio medical community.*

Malcolm wanted me to take part in a series of medical tests. He and his research team wanted to figure out what made me *me*.

"I remember," I said.

"So are you ready to help us?"

His voice was so soothing, so persuasive, that I almost said yes. But something in the dashboard image scared me. "No," I said, trying to keep my voice steady. Then I said it more strongly: *"No."*

"Ari, you disappoint me." The silky quality was gone now. "Well, I'll take that as 'Not yet.'"

My hands were clutching the steering wheel, I noticed, though I didn't remember putting them there.

"We'll talk again," he said. "Meantime, do be careful. Politics is a rough game. You're too valuable to lose."

After he'd hung up, I stared at the phone, wondering how he'd found my number.

Two

I drove back to the cottage as fast as I dared.

After I parked the car, a cold prickling sensation crawled along my hairline, from front to back. I looked around. The empty lane gaped back at me: a tricycle in the driveway of the opposite cottage, an outdoor shower dripping by the garage, a bank of lavender blue hydrangea bushes rustling in the sea breeze. I asked myself: *What's wrong with this picture?*

But I found nothing unexpected. Slowly I left the car. If someone was watching, that someone must have been hidden or invisible.

I stood without moving, only watching, thinking, *Whoever you are, leave my family and me alone.*

~

When the tingling subsided, I went inside.

They didn't ask where I'd been.

My mother sat at the kitchen table, chopping red peppers. She wore a faded flowered apron over her jeans and T-shirt, and her braided auburn hair trailed down her back. Her face—eyes downcast, mouth relaxed—glowed. But the sight of my father surprised me. He stood at the stove, making crêpes, his posture and movements as elegant as if he'd been conducting an orchestra, wearing a tuxedo instead of wrinkled linen.

I'd never seen him cook before. When we lived alone in Saratoga Springs, in upstate New York, he'd sit with me as I ate meals and later have his own privately. He never cared much about food—to him it was only fuel—and seemed to find my interest in it faintly amusing, if not repugnant.

But he took a different tonic these days, a new blend of blood supplements designed to manage his instinctual drives rather than suppress them as his old one had. He seemed a different person in many ways, more at ease with himself and others.

He half turned when I came in and smiled at me. That alone showed the change. In the old days his smile came rarely. Even now it remained shy, an expression of vulnerability as much as happiness, nothing like Cameron's confident grin. But I loved my father all the more for his shyness.

"Well, Ariella has returned to the fold," Mãe said. She pressed her lips together. I knew she wanted to ask where I'd spent the afternoon.

"Beautiful day." I sat next to her. They must have made a pact not to interfere with my freedom. It made sense. In less than a month, I'd be going back to school, and they'd leave for Ireland. They'd decided it was time for them to relocate, reinvent themselves. It was a prudent thing for vampires to do.

I took a deep breath. "I had a sense outside that someone was watching me."

In one fluid movement my father removed the pan from the stove and disappeared out the door.

Mãe went to the stove and turned off the burner. "You didn't see anyone?"

"No," I said. "But my scalp prickled."

Only when my father returned, and shrugged, did the evening resume. He went back to cooking. She continued slicing vegetables. Sadly, we were accustomed to being watched.

"Beautiful day," I repeated, determined to keep it so.

"Yes, beautiful." My mother put down her knife, stretched out her hand, and touched my hair. "Oh, Ari, you should come with us." Mãe could never restrain herself for long. "Ireland is too far away from you."

My father had bought property in southwestern Ireland— an old castle that would serve as home and also house a new laboratory for his biomedical research. My father and I had agreed that I should finish another year of college, at least. And we had made plans for me to join them at the end of spring semester.

"It's far," I said, "but we can write. You can call me."

"I won't call unless there's an emergency." She picked up the knife and slowly began to cut pepper strips. "It would hurt too much to hear your voice and not have you near." She had tears in her eyes, and suddenly I felt miserable, too.

"Mãe, I'll come with you if you need me to." I put my hand on her shoulder.

My father kept cooking and said nothing, but the set of his broad shoulders said, *We've gone through all of this before. We made a decision.*

She noticed. "No, we'll be fine," she said quickly. "I'll write to you, and you'll write back, won't you?" Her blue eyes glistened, blue as lapis lazuli, and I couldn't help but think: Cameron's were two shades darker. His eyes made me think of star sapphires.

I quickly blocked the thought. I wasn't ready to tell them about Cameron.

"Of course I'll write," I said. I patted her shoulder, wondering how long it would be before I went sailing again.

Dinner that night was memorable. Mãe made three different fillings for the crêpes: creamed oysters, roasted red peppers with spinach, and sautéed tofu with garlic, tomatoes, and basil. The crêpes themselves were pale and velvety inside, golden and crisp outside. The fillings complemented the crêpes, and I complimented the cooks. My father seemed pleased.

Then I had to spoil it all by talking about Malcolm.

His words had been on my mind all through dinner. "He's doing research on half-vampires," I said. "He wants to test me."

My father said one word: "Never."

My mother, standing at the sink washing dishes, dropped a knife.

"Malcolm says his work is designed to help vampires and humans live longer, better lives and to protect the future of the planet."

"He's a Nebulist, Ari." My father picked up a towel to dry the dishes. "He bends the facts to fit his schemes. Surely you can see that."

Part of me did. Part of me felt skeptical of Malcolm and all he'd said. But another part wanted to believe that he *had* been acting, continued to act, to protect us. Otherwise, Kathleen had died for no reason.

"Don't we all tend to make facts fit our notions of how things should be?" My question hung in the air between the table and the sink, the words transparent pale yellow, quivering.

But my father wasn't in the mood for debate. "Malcolm has no moral compass and no respect for anyone else's. It's that simple." He dried a plate with a flourish, making it spin on its way to the drying rack.

I wanted to explain. "It *isn't* that simple. As Malcolm said . . ." But I saw from his face that he was close to anger. I kept the rest to myself.

For my father, it *was* that simple: he was a Sanguinist, Malcolm a Nebulist. I admired him, in a way, for holding on to his principles, but that night I found his stubbornness too old-fashioned, even archaic. Wasn't it time for negotiation?

But I kept quiet. I watched him drying dishes. I'd never disagreed with him so strongly, and he'd never been angry with me before. The air felt thick with unexpressed emotions, so dense they made my lungs ache.

The tensions of that night lingered in the cottage for days afterward. Our meals together were strained, with my mother doing most of the talking. My father and I had little appetite.

I spent most of the time alone on the beach, or in my room, practicing being invisible.

Turning invisible requires concentration—and special clothing, unless you walk around naked. I was lucky to possess both the clothes and the concentration. Thanks to our ability to absorb the heat of our bodies' electrons, vampires can, when we choose, deflect light.

My parents considered invisibility a survival technique to be used sparingly, to evade predators; vampires who used it otherwise, they thought, were vulgar tricksters who risked exposing themselves as being *others*. I disagreed. It didn't take much effort to choose a discreet spot to make the change, and in my experience, most mortals weren't particularly observant.

To me, being able to pass through crowds undetected was the ultimate freedom. Of all our special traits, invisibility was my favorite.

So I practiced, even though I didn't dare wear my frayed metamaterials suit outside of my room. I didn't want to risk any more parental disapproval.

Instead of the uniter, I had begun to feel more and more like the outsider in the family.

Thankfully, Cameron called and asked me to go sailing the following weekend.

Saturday was breezy and humid, with wispy cirrus clouds scudding across a slate blue sky. Cameron was already on board *Dulcibella,* pulling a sail out of a canvas bag, when I arrived at the marina. He wore cutoff denim shorts, and I paused a moment to admire his legs: lean and muscular, the color of tupelo honey.

He noticed and gave me a quizzical look.

"I've never seen your legs before," I said.

He dropped the sail, leapt onto the dock, and hugged me. "I've missed you," he said, his voice muffled by my hair.

I leaned back and traced the outline of his lips with my index finger.

I have no memory of boarding the boat, or casting off, or hoisting the sails. But we must have done those things, because soon we were free of the land, moving down the Intracoastal Waterway, under sail. This time I took the tiller. For the first stretch, we had to tack—to periodically change direction. I could feel Cameron watching me approvingly; it was as if the boat told me when it was time to turn its bow into the wind.

The wind was strong and steady, making the rigging jingle and clang. We had to raise our voices against it.

"The weather is unsettled," he said. "We may have to cut our sail short."

But after a while the wind lessened. The boat moved into open water, on what Cameron said was called a broad reach. We were able to talk more easily now.

He asked about my upbringing; he said he'd heard of my father, whose reputation in vampire scientific circles was international. I told him about my homeschooling years in upstate New York and about finding my mother. I didn't say much about Hillhouse and said nothing about the murders of my two closest friends. It wasn't the right time.

Cameron told me about some of the many lives he'd led: stonemason, sailor, horse trainer, student, teacher, lawyer, politician, singer—

"You sing?"

Then he sang to me, in a language I couldn't identify, a song whose melody took root in my brain and played in my head for months afterward.

When the song ended, I asked, "What do the words mean?"

"It's a story song. One of the ways vampires passed on their folklore." He said the lyrics were based on an old vampire tale called "Winter Woman." "Two soldiers lose their way in a snowstorm and take refuge in an abandoned barn," he said. "While they're sleeping, a woman enters the barn. She's draining the blood from one when the other man wakens, terrified. She says she'll let him live, but only if he never tells a soul that he saw her."

He recited the lyrics in English: "'If you ever tell anyone, even your own mother, what you saw tonight, I'll know. I'll know, and I'll come and kill you.'"

I saw the words, icy blue, quiver in the air above us, struggling against the wind.

"Years later, he marries a beautiful woman. They have two children and live together happily. One cold night, the memory of the snowstorm returns to him, and he tells his wife the story of how his life was saved. In an instant, she transforms herself into the Winter Woman, and she kills him. Then she disappears in a cloud of ice."

It took me a second or two to react. "She *kills* him?"

He smiled. "No happy endings in vampire tales." Then he looked away. "Looks like we're going to get some weather, after all."

Cumulonimbus clouds with dark gray bottoms banked the sky ahead of us. Cameron took the tiller and brought the boat about. Sprays of salt water hit us, breaking the spell of the vampire tale. Then we were racing toward land.

Cameron pulled life jackets from the cockpit locker and helped me fasten mine before putting on his.

"I think we can beat the storm." He stretched out his free hand and smoothed back my hair. "Are you scared?"

I looked up at the taut sails and the swirling sky, then back into his eyes, wondering what emotion gave them that gleam. "Maybe a little," I said.

❧

Dulcibella ran with the wind toward the shoreline, barely touching the whitecaps. The air sparked with ozone, and lightning streaked the sky behind us.

"Go, Dulcie!" Cameron said. "That's the way."

He dropped the jib sail as we neared the marina. The boat rounded in the wind and came alongside the dock's windward corner. I sprang onto it with a coil of rope and tied the line onto a cleat, while Cameron wrapped another rope around a post.

"You're a natural sailor," he said, but I barely heard him. Thunder rumbled above us, lightning cracked the sky, and a torrent of warm rain pelted down. We leapt back onto the boat and I nearly fell down the ladder into its cabin. Cameron came behind me, pulling shut the sliding hatch. We stood in the cabin's dim light and laughed. The rain had flattened his curly hair, and his T-shirt clung to his skin. We shed the life jackets and our sandals, and Cameron handed me a towel.

Rain struck the cabin roof, noisy as hail, and the boat rocked from side to side. Wrapped in the towel, I sat cross-legged on a long cushioned seat, leaning against the bulkhead.

Cameron pulled off the lid of an old coffee can and took out matches. He lifted a glass chimney and lit the wick of a tarnished brass lamp that hung above a small table. When he was done, the lamp moved with the motion of the boat, and the smell of kerosene filled the cabin.

Then he came to sit next to me. He took my feet, one by one, and used a towel to gently rub them dry. I pulled my towel free to blot his hair and wiped its edge along his cheek.

His head bent as he dried my legs—first the right, then the left. The tingling sensation spread through me, a thousand times more intense than the sensation I had whenever someone was watching me. I shivered.

The storm made the boat tilt and right itself, over and over again, creaking as it swayed. Our bodies were in charge now, moving together in time with the boat. Our hands and legs entwined, and my fingertips felt swollen. I looked at his throat, had an urge to sink my teeth deep into it. I closed my eyes.

I felt him pull away—first his mind, then his body. I opened my eyes. His mouth was open slightly, and I saw his fangs.

"Why not?" I asked, my voice barely a whisper. My hand pressed the back of his neck, tried to bring him back to me.

He resisted. Shaking my hand off, he sat up on the edge of the berth.

Gently, he pulled me toward him. I pressed my ear against his chest, floating in the rhythm of his heart.

My parents were out when I returned to the cottage. My mouth still felt swollen, and my hair smelled of kerosene. I made myself take a long shower, though I really didn't want to lose the smell. Forever afterward, the sharp odor would remind me of passion, of regret.

It's possible that some trace lingered, because that night at dinner, my parents looked at me as if I were a stranger. Even my mother didn't seem to know what to say to me. I ate quickly and retreated to the safety of my room.

When Dashay returned from Florida a week later, bringing some papers for my mother to sign, I told her I wanted to come along on her trip back to Blue Heaven. I needed a change, I said.

Cameron was back on the road, campaigning. I told myself his absence played no part in my decision. But it occupied my thoughts so much that not until we were halfway to Florida, Dashay driving my mother's old pickup truck, did I notice how quiet she'd been.

I watched her profile: small nose, defiant chin, cloud of cinnamon-colored hair. How lovely she looked, and how sad.

"Tell me," I said, and her hand moved to switch on the radio. I switched it off. "No, tell me."

"You don't want to hear it."

"You know I do."

She took a deep breath. "It's like this. That man's come back to town."

She had to mean Bennett. He'd been part of our family once. When we'd first met, I'd liked him immediately, and I found it hard to stop liking him even when he left her for another woman. Left *us*.

"Did he explain why he left?"

She said, "Hah. He told me how that woman put a spell on him, how there was something in the water—"

"But there *was* something in the water."

Last spring, opiates had been found in water bottled in Miami and distributed across the country. I'd tasted it myself, felt its ability to tranquilize and distort memory.

"I don't care about the water. It's no excuse for the man to take up with a witch like that one." Her right hand pounded the steering wheel, and the truck swerved. Good thing we were taking back roads instead of the interstate.

"You still love him?" I didn't even need to ask. "You do. You love him." I remembered the night I'd seen Dashay and Bennett dancing in the garden at Blue Heaven—I'd thought they epitomized romance.

She shook her head, but her mouth gave her away.

"Then you have to forgive him." I remembered something my father said once, when we were discussing the life of Edgar Allan Poe: *nothing matters as much as forgiveness.*

"He doesn't ask me to forgive him." Dashay stopped the truck at a traffic light, and from her voice I sensed that she'd been crying recently. "He's too confused to know what he wants."

The light changed. We moved on. Dashay said, "Now it's his turn to suffer."

I didn't say anything. I didn't know enough yet to reply. After another few miles, she said, "Funny how folks always like to talk about *love,* when what they feel is something else entirely."

In a way I envied her, for knowing so much more than I did. And suddenly I wished with all my heart that I was older, more experienced, worthy of being her confidante, capable of saying something that might comfort her. Instead I sat in the passenger seat, a silent spectator.

꙰

Homosassa Springs, Florida, is a place even the locals like to keep under wraps. It's home to a manatee refuge, the ruins of a sugar mill, a few hotels, restaurants, and bars—and a large community of vampires, attracted by the mineral-rich natural springs and by the anonymity.

My mother chose to settle there because Homosassa Springs has more *S*s in its name than any other town in Florida. For her, the letter *S* had always been lucky. (If she hadn't left when I was born, my name might have been Simone or Sally instead of Ariella, my father's choice.)

Driving into Homosassa felt like coming home. Down that street was Bennett's old house. I wondered if the new owners had kept the wooden carvings of lizards and birds he'd made that had been attached to the backyard fence. I didn't dare ask Dashay where he was living now.

When we pulled up to Blue Heaven, I jumped out of the truck's cab to open the gate. Grace the cat came bounding down the path from the house. I knelt to pick her up and buried my face in her fur, which always smelled of the dry grass and ferns she napped among.

Dashay sat still behind the wheel, watching us. I sensed that she might be crying again, so I kept my face close to Grace, asking her how her summer had been going, how many mice she'd chased. Finally I carried her with me back to the truck and looked in, long enough to see that Dashay's face was dry, her eyes like stones.

"Say hello to Grace." I set her on the seat and closed the door. Dashay drove the truck through the gate, and I locked it behind us. When I climbed back into the truck, Dashay was talking to Grace in a low murmur, and Grace made the noises, deep in her throat, that sounded as if she were asking questions. Dashay and my mother could communicate with animals in ways I could only try to imitate.

The house loomed ahead, a ramshackle structure built of limestone and wood and plaster, built and rebuilt after successive storms. I paused long enough to drop my overnight bag near the door and raced down to the stables. I talked to the horses, visited the beehives, and noticed that Dashay had added new plants to her Garden of Gloom, which had been leveled by the last hurricane.

Inspired by Victorian mourning gardens, she had planted an array of dark, night-blooming flowers and black bamboo surrounding a fountain shaped like a woman whose eyes trickled black tears. Dashay had been known to indulge her sense of the melancholy from time to time, and I was willing to bet that lately she'd spent more time than usual sitting on the iron bench next to the fountain, meditating on all she'd lost.

Does her brooding give her any comfort? I knew I'd never ask her. I didn't want to think about loss and mourning, much less talk about it, but for a moment, as I gazed at the garden, I thought about Kathleen. Would I ever have a best friend again?

Two Homosassa girls had hung out with me for a while. One of them vanished. The other, named Autumn, had been murdered last spring after she came to visit me at school. Her body was found floating in a swamp.

I sank onto the grass near the fountain, and I let myself grieve for all of my lost friends.

～

When I walked back toward the house, Dashay was sitting outside, as if she'd been waiting for me. She stood up as I approached.

Then something black swooped out of the sky at her, so fast that neither of us had time to react. I caught a glimpse of black feathers and one beady black eye. By the time I could move and ran toward her, it had soared upward and disappeared.

"Are you okay? Did it hurt you?"

She hadn't budged. "Brushed my hair with its wings." She didn't even look scared. "That's my old friend the grackle. He comes to tell me change is headed our way."

I knew about harbingers, creatures that appear to warn us that something important is about to happen. I had one of my own: a blind man. Like Dashay's black bird, he showed up when a major change loomed ahead for me.

"Good change?"

She stretched out both arms, palms up. "Who knows?" she said.

~

The house welcomed us with its familiar scents: sandalwood, cinnamon, wild rose, and white geranium. Mãe used essential oils to clean and polish.

We were finishing supper when Dashay's cell phone rang; she'd changed the ringtone from "Welcome to Jamrock" to some funereal melody that I didn't like at all. She looked at the screen and said, "I don't think I need to talk to that man."

"Of course you do." I would have snatched the phone away to answer it myself if she hadn't changed her mind.

"Yes?" she said in a weary tone.

I left the room to let her talk. My bedroom was a comforting sight; the periwinkle blue walls, the white bed, and the mother-of-pearl lampshade all had escaped the hurricane, although the roof of the house had had to be replaced. I felt a pang that I'd spent so little time here this summer, and that soon I'd be leaving yet again.

Dashay came in. "Look, I'm going to meet that man, talk to him some. I won't be long."

"Bennett?"

She nodded.

"Why don't you say his name?"

"You need to stop asking me questions," she said. She didn't sound angry, merely distracted and eager to be on her way.

I wasn't tired yet, and the house felt warm, so after she left I went outside to cool off. On the house's north side my mother had planted a circular moon garden: angel's trumpets, moonflowers, flowering tobacco, and gardenias—all white flowers that bloomed only at night. That garden, too, had been ripped apart by the hurricane last year and, since then, lovingly restored. A breeze from the gulf nearly always ran through it, making the leaves and blossoms rustle and bob.

I sat on one of four teak benches at the garden's center; brick pathways extended from it like radii, separating the flower beds. When the moon shone, the petals reflected its light; when the moon was full, they took on a near-phosphorescent glow. Mosquitoes hovered, so close that their wings sometimes brushed my skin, but not one bit me—they don't like the taste of vampires.

Tonight a quarter moon cast only enough light to make the flowers faintly luminous. Beyond the garden, pines and mangroves shaded the path that led to the river. I sat listening to the drone of mosquitoes and groans of tree frogs, inhaling the sweet ivory scent of gardenias, wondering where Neil Cameron might be this fine evening, whose company he might be keeping.

And then I saw the cat—not Grace, and not the scrawny tom who regularly stopped by, knowing Mãe would feed him. This was a different cat, strange and yet familiar. Its body had a silver glow.

I rubbed my eyes. The cat still sat calmly, front paws neatly aligned on the brick pathway. Then I recognized it: Marmalade. She'd been a neighbor's cat back in Saratoga Springs. She'd played with me in our rose garden, chased squirrels and butterflies, done all of the thousands of tricks that make cats *cats*. Then, one winter night, she'd been killed by Malcolm. He'd admitted it much later—said he'd done it because the cat annoyed him, got in his way while he kept invisible watch over me.

I have to admit, at times the death of an animal troubles me more than the death of a human, who generally has better options for self-defense against predators. Marmalade had been powerless in Malcolm's hands; he'd admitted he had strangled her and tossed her body against our back steps. At the time, his voice managed to make his actions sound logical, necessary.

In a split second the enormity of Marmalade's death, which I'd pushed out of my mind soon after it happened, came back to me in full force. How could Malcolm—how could anyone—do such a thing? My father had been right. Malcolm should never be trusted, never.

And as I sat there brooding, the silvery cat glided up the path toward me. I watched it come, knowing it was dead, wanting its company yet fearing it. Silently it came, paw by paw along the bricks, and with each step my heart beat faster yet grew cold with dread. I heard my voice say, "Marmalade."

The cat stopped moving.

"Oh, Marmalade, I'm sorry."

The cat seemed to stare at me with empty sockets where yellow eyes once had gazed back with affection, even love.

Then she turned and, just as slowly, walked away. As she went, she began to fade. Her silvery presence dissolved into ground fog, what Floridians call "smoke."

I can't say how long I sat there or how much I wept. Sometime later Dashay's voice called my name, again and again, and brought me back.

I wondered later if I should have tried to follow Marmalade. But then I thought, *Where could she have led me? Only to the land of the dead.*

Three

Dashay made me tell the story twice, and then she asked questions.

No, I said, the cat never touched me. I'd felt scared, yes, but I never thought the cat had come to hurt me.

It had moved the way a normal cat moves. It didn't smell or speak. And yes, I did feel its gaze on me, although it had no eyes.

Finally she seemed satisfied. She sat back on the living room sofa, her eyes bright and alert as if it were morning, not the middle of the night. Grace sat beside her, making small sounds of concern.

"I don't think she meant you any harm," Dashay said. "I do wish I'd been here to talk to her myself, but you said the right kind of words."

Dashay and my mother had some special intuitive power that allowed them to have conversations with animals. My father and I envied them.

"But why did she come here?" I sipped the mug of cocoa she'd made me. *Cocoa, as if I were a child.* But the warmth of the drink calmed me.

She rubbed her palms together. "Could be someone sent her. Or could be she wanted to check in on you, the way a friendly spirit will. Wanted to make sure you're not feeling too sad about her passing."

I'd felt more than sad; I'd felt guilty. Malcolm wouldn't have killed her if I hadn't lived close by, and if he hadn't felt the need to stalk my father and me. But I'd repressed those feelings as much as I could. Now I let my anger against him surge, and I let Dashay hear my thoughts.

She'd never met Malcolm, but she'd heard about him. "What's this fellow look like?"

"Tall, almost as tall as my father. Blond hair, a little long on top, parted on the side. Narrow nose and narrow eyes. I think they were gray. Some people might call him handsome, I suppose. He always wears suits—the tailored kind, like the ones my father wears. And he's very, very smart. When he talks, you believe everything he says."

Dashay listened hard to my description, and I knew she would remember it. "And you met up with him in Savannah?"

"He seemed different there." I set down the cocoa mug. "For a while I believed that he really was our family's friend. He can do that, the way he talks. Make you think up is down, left is right."

"Hah." Dashay didn't like smooth talkers. "Well, Mr. Malcolm better stay away from you now. Or he'll be dealing with me."

I felt so drained that I went to bed without asking her how the meeting with Bennett had gone. But next morning, that was the first question out of my mouth.

"Good morning," Dashay said in reply. She was drinking tea at the kitchen table, wearing one of her embroidered caftans, a long pink scarf wound through her hair.

One of her eyes winked at me over the rim of her cup. I poured myself a cup of tea and sat across from her. The kitchen walls, newly painted a glossy pale yellow, shone in the morning sunlight. There, while we ate toast spread with honey, she told me about Bennett.

"It's like you said," Dashay told me. "He claims he was drugged. The water he drank on the plane where he met that woman, he says something must have been in that water. Because after that he didn't think about me." Her voice sounded neutral, but I sensed emotions ran deep beneath each word. "Maybe it was the woman, not the water."

I thought of the Sirens, whose sweet songs were designed to trap and kill Odysseus, and of Circe, the enchantress who kept him under her spell for more than a year. But Greek myths aren't the only ones featuring femmes fatales; they turn up in Hebrew, Islamic, Teutonic, Celtic, and Polynesian tales, and probably many more that I haven't read. All around the world, women have been casting spells of enchantment for centuries.

"And now, he says, after months and months the spell is broken. He says one morning he woke up with my name in his mouth, and when that happened he came straight back here. And he's been calling me and pestering me for the last week, wanting to tell me all of this."

I couldn't help asking, "So what happened last night?"

She sighed. "I met him down at Flo's Place." It was the local bar-and-grill that catered to the vampire crowd. "He looked—not so good. Thin, you know? Can you picture him scrawny?"

The Bennett I'd known had been a big, healthy man, all muscle. "How can that be? He's a vampire."

She shook her head. "He's a half-and-half."

Like me. And I began to wonder: *how vulnerable am I?*

"Well, that fellow, he's a shadow of his old self. He's lost his house, his business."

I tried to remember what Bennett's business had been, but I wasn't about to interrupt her now.

"He asks me to give him another chance." Dashay had finished her tea. She looked into the empty cup, as if it might tell her something.

· "Then you have to give him that chance." She hadn't asked me, but I felt sure I was right. "You have to try to forgive him. Look at my parents, all they've been through. They're still sorting things out, and they may end up apart in the end, but at least they're giving it a try."

She opened her mouth, but I wasn't finished yet. "Forgiveness means everything."

My voice rang with conviction. *Where did* that *come from?*

Then she smiled at me. "Little Miss Knows-It-All. How old are you now? Fifteen going on forty?"

I didn't mind her making fun of me. It was worth it, to see her smile.

~

We spent that day working around the farm: exercising and grooming the horses, cleaning the stables and the hives, weeding the gardens.

I never minded that kind of work. When I'd first come to Blue Heaven, I wasn't allowed to do chores. My mother had worried that I wasn't strong enough. Children of vampires and humans sometimes suffer from physical weaknesses that full-fledged vampires never experience, and in fact I'd been a fragile child. But once I crossed over—by biting a mortal— my constitution changed, and my stamina grew.

Still, hours of farmwork tested that stamina, and by the end of the day I was thinking of nothing more than a bath and bed.

And maybe a call from Cameron. Sometimes he called my cell phone at night, usually between ten and midnight, to tell me what his life on the road was like. At first the media had ignored him or treated his campaign as a joke; no third-party candidates ever got far, and at best they were considered spoilers, stealing votes from the main-party contenders. But as he made more appearances in more places, people had begun to take him seriously. Sometimes he asked my opinion of a line he planned to use in the next day's speech, and I felt happy to give it, although I wondered why he would listen to someone like me. My experience of the world was so limited, compared to his.

I took my bath early, before supper, and I was towel-drying my hair when Dashay came out from her room, wearing a chiffon dress.

"You're going out?"

"*We're* going out." She twirled to show me the thin yellow panels inset in her dress's white skirt. It reminded me of a wild iris. "I'm taking you to dinner at Flo's."

Flo's isn't a fancy place, but Dashay inspired me to put on a pale green sundress. Twenty minutes later, we were sitting in our favorite worn-leather booth, sipping Picardo. Logan, the bartender, came over to say hello, and some of the locals greeted us. Most vampires aren't overly social, even among themselves. We respect each other's need for privacy and space.

I looked around, half expecting to see Bennett, but didn't find him.

We dined on raw oysters, followed by fried ones—not so healthy, but delicious all the same. Oysters are full of zinc, oxygen, calcium, and phosphorus—also found in blood—which makes them another excellent substitute for vampires who don't bite humans.

It had been a long day, and we focused on the food. At eight Logan turned on a wall-mounted television set. Dashay made a face and began to protest, until she saw what was on: a debate among four presidential candidates. One of them was Neil Cameron.

The first thing I did was block my thoughts, but I knew I

couldn't block my facial expressions. I moved sideways in the booth so that Dashay could see only half my face.

She glanced at me. "I didn't know you had so much interest in this political stuff."

I reminded her about my American Politics course last semester. I'd described it before, but so much had been going on, I said, that she must have forgotten. I babbled on until the debate began.

Cameron wore a dark suit, a light blue shirt, a dark blue tie. He smiled in the early minutes, when the camera was on him, and after that I found it hard to pay attention to anything the others said. What I did hear sounded a bit familiar—a rehash of points he'd made in a speech back in Savannah—but when the questions turned to health care issues, I tuned out the words entirely. Vampires don't need health insurance; they have their own practitioners and their own drugs, and a barter system to pay for them.

Dashay said something, but I kept my face turned to one side, my eyes fixed on Cameron's mouth. Then she waved her hands at me. "Hello!" she said, making an odd gesture with both hands.

"What does that gesture mean?"

"As I was *saying,* he's kind of cool, that Neil Cameron, making Mentori signs right on TV. He's a bold one."

"What are Mentori signs?"

"You don't know?" Dashay enjoyed discovering my pockets of ignorance. "Mentori is vampire sign language. It's a kind of code we use to communicate amongst ourselves. Nice when we can't speak or don't want to share thoughts."

My father hadn't used Mentori, and if my mother had, I'd never seen it. I looked back at the screen. Cameron's left hand extended, palm up, and his right palm met it at a forty-five-degree angle.

"That's the open mouth." Dashay repeated the gesture across the table. "I can't believe your mother didn't teach you this. It means 'time to fix the problem.'"

"Or 'time to bite.'" Logan stood next to our table. "Another round?"

Dashay nodded, and he left us. *"Time to bite,"* she repeated in a low voice. "That's the low-class meaning."

"A sign can have different meanings?"

"Yes, yes. Same way that words do." Dashay looked back at the TV screen. "You see?"

Cameron was talking about the need to strengthen health benefits for the unemployed and homeless. Both palms faced upward now, and he raised them in short bursts, three times. "That means we need to act right now," Dashay said.

Logan set two glasses on our table. "It means 'it's dark outside,'" he said. "'Time to get up!'"

She ignored him, and he went back to the bar. "Cameron is letting the vampires know he's one of them. Risky, but maybe that will get him some of their votes."

I kept my eyes on the TV screen, waiting for the next shot of Cameron. Suddenly the debate ended, the commentators began rehashing it, and Dashay was saying, perhaps for the second time, "Something is wrong with your neck?"

I turned slowly to face her. "It's a little stiff," I said. "I felt a twinge this morning, when I was grooming the horses."

"Is that right." Her voice sounded soft.

I quickly changed the subject. "I thought we might see Bennett here tonight."

"We'll see him soon enough," she said in a tone that finished our conversation.

On the drive home, Dashay promised to teach me Mentori. "Tomorrow," she said. "Wait. Not tomorrow. I have to see a man about buying a horse."

She'd agreed to manage the farm while my mother was in Ireland. In the past, she'd handled most of the horse business, while Mãe managed the honeybees and the herb gardens whose produce was traded for blood supplements and other necessities.

Now Dashay would have to do it all. She'd have her hands full, I thought. Was there a Mentori sign for that?

～

Dashay was gone by the time I got up the next morning. She'd left me a pan of oatmeal and a note: "Back for supper. You cook? Take my car to supermarket. Might be a guest."

I yawned as I reheated the oatmeal. The night before, I had stayed up as late as I could, fighting off sleep while I watched the face of my cell phone, willing it to ring. But Cameron was no doubt busy, while I would be living in a kind of limbo until classes began in September.

I thought about calling him. Instead, I took a shower, then spent nearly an hour staring at my face in the hallway mirror. If I focused hard, I could see my reflection, but it wavered, distorting my features. I saw a flash of blue eyes, a sweep of chestnut-brown hair; but everything always blurred.

That's a curse of vampires: to never have a clear sense of how we look. Contrary to what mortal "vampire experts" might have you believe, we *are* reflected in mirrors, unless we emutate—concentrate and turn invisible. But we can't see our own reflections except for a few seconds at a time. And photographs of us are usually blurred, since the electrons in our bodies instinctively shut down, stop reflecting light, when we're facing a camera. It's a protective mechanism. With disciplined practice, that instinct can be overcome—Cameron had trained himself to do it, but it had taken him nearly twenty years of practice, he'd told me.

What did Cameron see when he looked at me? I studied the mirror, squinting. Then I gave up. Twenty years of practice? Forty minutes was too long for me.

Hours later, as I was leaving the Sweetbay Supermarket in Homosassa, my cell phone rang. Cameron's voice said, "Can you talk?"

I got into Dashay's sedan. "Yes."

"Could you meet me for lunch?" Static and other voices buzzed behind his words.

"Where?"

"Are you in Tybee?"

"No," I said. "Homosassa."

"That's good," he said. "That's better." He gave me directions to a recreation area called Salt Springs in the Ocala National Forest.

As I drove back to Blue Heaven to put away the groceries, I wondered why his voice carried so much tension.

Salt Springs turned out to be a ninety-minute drive. The countryside rushed past me, greener and hillier than coastal Florida, but I didn't notice its details.

I stopped at a booth to pay the entry fee and hung a yellow tag from my rearview mirror. Then I drove into the park and followed Cameron's directions to Salt Springs. In its parking lot were three or four other cars, none of them Cameron's blue hybrid. Then he stepped out of a white compact model—*Of course,* I thought. *He's driving a rental.*

He wore a blue shirt and jeans. I had on jeans, too, and I'd borrowed one of Dashay's shirts: a silk tank top.

He smiled as I walked over to him, but he looked distracted. He made no move to embrace me, and he didn't say hello. "I wanted some time for us," he said, beckoning for me to get into the car.

Once we were inside, with the doors shut, he brushed his fingers lightly across my cheek. Then he started the car and drove down an unpaved road, bordered by tall pine trees, that meandered deeper into the park. Neither of us spoke until we left the car and stepped into the stillness of the forest. Carrying a plaid blanket and a canvas bag, we followed a sandy trail strewn with rust-colored pine needles past campsites and picnic tables. When we reached a clearing by a brook, we spread out the blanket and sat down.

"Hello," Cameron said.

I felt so giddy, so relieved to be sitting next to him, that I felt no need to say a word. He put an arm around my waist and I rested my head against his shoulder, and we sat there, watching water cascade over rocks.

And when he did speak, I wished he hadn't. "I've managed this badly," he began. "The timing is all wrong."

He said the campaign was taking off in ways he'd never expected could happen. "I planned to run as far as I could, to make a point for us, for all of the *others*," he said. "I didn't think I stood a chance with the general public."

The latest poll numbers were proving him wrong, he said. They showed him running neck and neck with the likeliest Republican and Democratic nominees. His campaign team was already at work in the largest states, organizing local workers and making sure prospective voters knew his name. He apparently had the Fair Share Party's endorsement all but sewn up. Political experts were predicting that, for the first time in the history of American politics, a third-party candidate could conceivably win the November election.

Why did all of his good news make me increasingly nervous?

He took his arm away, turned to sit facing me. "Have you told anyone about us?"

"Of course not." I'd kept him a secret from the beginning, without knowing exactly why.

"I hated to ask," he said. "But my staff tell me every part of my life will become public knowledge now, except of course—" He made a quick gesture that must have signaled being a vampire.

"I want us to survive the scrutiny," he said. "I want us to have a chance at a relationship of some sort." He took another deep breath. "That is, if you want one."

"You know I do." My voice sounded calmer and more confident than I felt.

He took my left hand in his. "Then I want to ask you to wait for me. We may not be able to see much of each other for a while, but I hope that you'll be patient. Wait till we know how far this train is going before you decide to get off."

I thought of lines from a Whitman poem: *I am to wait, I do not doubt I am to meet you again / I am to see to it that I do not lose you.*

"What will happen to us if you lose the race?"

He squeezed my hand. "Then you and I can sail away together and never worry about being 'public knowledge' again."

With those words he seemed to relax. He handed me a paper plate and served salad and fruit he'd picked up at a grocery somewhere. He told me he'd been a vampire since the American Revolution, and I thought, *You're more than two hundred thirty years old?*

"Does our age difference bother you?" He knew I was fifteen, masquerading as nineteen.

"Of course not. Does it bother you?"

He shrugged. "It bothers my staff a bit. But a roughly ten-year age difference—that can be managed." Cameron's current biography had him born in Florida thirty years ago. That made him the youngest presidential candidate to date and the first to run since a hotly debated constitutional amendment finally was approved, lowering the age requirement for candidates.

I was curious about his "real" age. "How old were you when you crossed?"

"Twenty-two," he said. "And no, I didn't know George Washington, or Paul Revere, even though I was born in Boston. I was an ordinary soldier in the Continental army. I can't even tell you who made me a vampire. It happened one night when I was on guard duty at the camp. Something or someone came at me out of the dark, bit me and made me bite it, and next morning —well, you can imagine the rest."

Every one of us has a crossover story. In a way I'd been lucky: being born half-vampire, I'd been told ahead of time by my father what the moment and its aftermath were like for him. And as a half-breed, I had never been bitten; I self-declared when I bit a mortal in self-defense. If that moment, or another like it, hadn't happened, I might still be living as a mortal, not knowing my true nature.

The memory of it often came back to me, unbidden, like a bad dream. I'd been hitchhiking, on the road to find my mother, and a driver who picked me up tried to rape me. Without thinking, I'd lunged at his neck. Instinct took over, and when I was capable of thinking again, I realized I'd drunk his blood. And the aftermath of that—the guilt, the recurring hunger—made me feel sick, then and now.

But to cross over without knowing what it meant—that had to be a darker kind of nightmare.

"From which I'm still trying to awaken." He'd heard my thought. "You know the old saying: 'For humans, bad things come in threes. For vampires, they come in seasons.'"

I didn't know it. I didn't know any "old sayings," I realized. My father's lessons hadn't included them, and no written records of them exist. Vampires have a tradition of never leaving evidence that could help mortals identify them. It's part of what I think of as the Vampire Way: a code of behavior designed to keep us hidden and safe.

"For a while I tried to keep on as a soldier, hide what I'd become from the others. I always felt as if I was about to be exposed. So I deserted the army. Ran away to live in the mountains. My family assumed I'd died in battle. Over time I figured out how to live, how to get by without biting humans. I lived on sheep's blood for a while."

The thought made me shudder. I tried to focus on the sound of the brook.

"No, I don't do that anymore," he said. "Today my diet is as pure as any Sanguinist's."

"But you're not a Sanguinist."

"I don't belong to any group." He had a twig in one hand, and he sketched invisible patterns on the rock.

"We saw your last debate on television," I said. "You were making Mentori signs. Isn't that risky?"

"I don't see why." He looked up at me. "Humans don't know about Mentori. No vampire would ever tell them about it—it would ruin its purpose. Mentori has been our secret language for centuries."

"But isn't it dangerous to even let vampires know you're one of us?"

"Just the opposite." He smiled. "I want them to get out and register to vote. Besides, as one of my favorite writers said, 'I shall express myself as I am.'"

I recognized the quote from Joyce's *A Portrait of the Artist as a Young Man*. It was one of my favorite books, too—my father and I had read it together as part of my homeschooling. It made me happy that we shared an appreciation of Joyce.

That afternoon had an odd, dreamlike quality about it. Time simply didn't exist. We listened to the music of the stream running over stones. We looked at each other, memorized each other, because we knew we wouldn't meet again for—months? Years? But what did a few years matter, if we might be together forever?

The dream was disturbed only twice: once, when I heard a rustle in the bushes behind us and dropped my plate; and later, when I thought I saw something in those bushes—merely a shape, a transparent form with no defining features, nestled amid twigs.

My head tingled and began to throb. I tried to tell Cameron what I saw. He went to the bushes, pulled the branches apart. Nothing was there.

"You're nervous," he said. "I've upset you."

"I don't know," I said. "I don't know." *The sight of the thing was what upset me,* I thought.

We knew it was time to leave. We said good-bye with an embrace, no kisses. One kiss would have been too much. But while his arms were around me, Cameron said, "You have my heart."

I said, "And you have mine."

As we separated, our words floated between us, gray as lead. Not *grey,* I thought. Cameron said, "Yes," as if he knew the difference, or as if he could see them, too.

The words moved out over the rushing water. *You have my heart. And you have mine.* They slowly drifted downstream.

Four

The afternoon still had me under its spell as I drove home. The spell lifted only when I was twenty miles or so from Homosassa, when I noticed that the dashboard clock read half past six and remembered I was expected to cook supper. What sort of story could I tell Dashay?

When I got home, the truck wasn't there. I took the yellow tag off the Jaguar's rearview mirror and put it in my pocket. Then I ran inside and into the kitchen. I was making a salad when someone knocked at the door.

Yes, I expected it might be Bennett, but even then, when I let him in it was like admitting a stranger. He didn't walk with the buoyancy he had before. He looked thin, and his shoulders were stooped, as if he were recovering from a long illness. Even his head looked smaller, but that might be because he wasn't wearing the black cowboy hat that Dashay had often teased him about.

I gave him a quick hug, trying not to notice how bony he felt. "Dashay's not here," I said.

"I know. She phoned me. Said she tried to call you, but her call went straight to voice mail." He didn't even talk the same way. The old Bennett had spoken quickly, with laughter in his voice.

I'd shut off my phone when I met Cameron, of course.

He sat on a chair, and I tried not to notice how loose his jeans were, how skinny his legs. They warned me that, as a fellow half-breed, I might be at risk as much as he was.

"Is she running late?"

"She is." He was looking around the room. "Nice to be here again. I've been invited to supper."

"Come and help me get things ready." I couldn't leave him sitting there alone, sunk into himself. Besides, I wanted to find him—somewhere inside that shell was an old friend.

What *is* it that makes someone who he is? Not appearance, really, although others' eyes and mouths are what newborns first recognize. Not smell—at least, not among us. Vampires have no odor, which may explain why our sense of smell is so acute. The way someone talks, the way someone moves—these are important aspects, but they don't constitute identity.

I'd say that identity is a composite of intangible, immeasurable qualities. When I thought of Cameron, for instance, I did think of his appearance—the star-sapphire eyes and the fluid movements of his hands, in particular—but he meant so much more than that. The way he cared about the world was an essential part of him, and so was his passion for shaping its future. The empathetic ways he treated others, even strangers. The way he stayed loyal to his beliefs.

But actions and ethics aside, there was something else, some elusive essence that made him Neil Cameron. Something that had captivated me. When he walked into a room, the room changed. Not the same way it changed when my father entered, when all eyes were drawn to him and the air around him took on an almost imperceptible shimmer—no, Cameron consciously *made* people look at him. As much as my father shunned it, Cameron thrived on others' attention.

"Watch out," Bennett said. "You almost cut yourself."

I put my attention back on the carrots, pleased that he'd come out of his self-absorption to notice.

"You look like you're daydreaming," he said. "You know that old saying. 'Be careful what you wish for.'"

"Is that what happened to you?" I said it without thinking.

But he didn't take offense. "No, with me it was different. My bad blood got the better of my good blood."

His face twitched, as if painful memories were returning, so I didn't ask what he meant.

⌒

By the time Dashay arrived the table was set, biscuits were baking, and a pot of vegetarian chili simmered on the stove. I hadn't learned to cook until last year, but Mãe and Dashay had been excellent teachers. They made cooking seem like dancing, each step rhythmically blending with the next.

Bennett sat in his armchair, sipping a glass of wine, and the expression on his face when Dashay walked in held love and shame and hopelessness, all at once.

Dashay, sufficiently distracted by his presence and mortified about being late (something she'd lectured me about more than once), didn't pay much attention to me. And that was a blessing.

"I tried to buy a horse today," she said. "But the seller didn't want to meet my price." She sank into a chair and crossed her arms.

Each of us clearly was more interested in our own thoughts than in making conversation. At the end of the evening, I do recall Bennett thanking me for cooking dinner and Dashay for her "generosity."

"Yes, yes, you're welcome," Dashay said, looking at the floor.

He shifted his weight from foot to foot, then abruptly turned and left.

"So you're being generous?" I asked.

"I'm letting him stay in the guesthouse," she said. "Only until he gets back to being himself again. He can work to earn his keep. And Blue Heaven can surely use every bit of help it gets."

"He said something strange before you came home. He said his bad blood got the better of his good blood."

"That's the way Bennett thinks. About being half-and-half. His vampire half tries to attack his human part."

I'd never heard of such a thing. "Is that possible?"

She shrugged and began clearing the table. Then she glanced back at me. "Nice shirt."

"Thank you. I didn't spill anything this time, but I'll be sure to wash it tomorrow," I said. Last time I borrowed a shirt of hers, lunch had involved chili sauce and mustard.

Alone in my room, I hid the yellow tag from the park in my journal. Every way that I could, I wanted to remember today.

～

August came, bringing high temperatures, high humidity, and fierce thunderstorms almost every afternoon. Squalls pulsed in from the Gulf, smelling of seaweed and ozone and algae. Some days the sun felt so intense that I swore I could feel it baking my brain.

Rain or shine, Dashay and I went kayaking and horseback riding, slathered with sunblock, wearing hats and shirts designed to shield us from ultraviolet rays. We devoted the remainder of the days to tending the horses, gardens, and beehives. I wanted to keep busy. I didn't want to feel or think. But sometimes, for no reason at all, I remembered the last time Cameron kissed me, and my lips burned.

Bennett had become a regular at our supper table now, and he seemed a little better to me, a little more himself. His sense of humor hadn't fully returned, but one night as we played a board game he laughed at something I said, and I got up and threw my arms around him, thinking, *Welcome back.*

Over his shoulder I saw Dashay, watching us, her face impossible to read. I heard her think, *You can't erase the bad things, even if you want to.*

Evenings I spent writing in my journal, reading, amusing Grace—or sorting through my clothes, trying to decide what to take back to school. I had nearly as much stuff on Tybee, and in a few weeks I'd have to pack it all up. A new semester felt like a chance to become a new person, in a way. But it was hard to revise my image when I couldn't clearly see the one I already had.

The limbo feeling came back, stronger than ever, as if I were suspended between two acts of a play—or waiting offstage, watching the drama build around the other actors. Dashay and Bennett, Mãe and my father, Cameron: they stood center stage, while I waited in the wings. Or had I been written out?

When Dashay said we should think about returning to Tybee, I didn't protest. My feelings all were on hold.

"I talked with your mother on the phone last night," she said. "A little mother-daughter time is what you both need."

So I said my good-byes to the house, the horses, the bees, the gardens, and Grace. "See you at Christmas," I promised them. What sort of Christmas would it be, with my parents in Ireland and Cameron who knew where?

❧

When we arrived at the cottage on Tybee, my parents were sitting in its backyard, talking. It felt as if I'd never left.

Dashay and I sat down and told them about our time at Blue Heaven, but I sensed some reservations in the way they listened to me.

"That's very good," Mãe said after I'd described my work on her moon garden. "I've been reading up on Ireland."

"It must be interesting." I smoothed the cushion of the wicker chair.

They looked thoughtful, as if they were trying to figure out who I was these days. Well, so was I. And it occurred to me that knowing Cameron and keeping him a secret had changed the way I acted, created a space between my parents and me that hadn't been there before.

So we treated each other politely, respecting our mutual need for distance.

Dashay excused herself and said she needed to get back to Florida.

"Aren't you going to spend the night?" my mother asked. "That's a lot of driving for one day."

"I have things on my mind," Dashay said.

Bennett, I supposed.

I think the stiff conversation made her uncomfortable, because she didn't hug us good-bye. "I'll see you all in a while," she said. She paused to blow us a kiss over her shoulder, then shut the front door behind her as she left.

~~

If I had vague doubts about who I was, Mãe had specific reservations.

"Did we really buy these only a year ago?" We were in my room, the next morning. She held up a pair of jeans whose knees had worn through.

"I like them that way." I sat on my bed, watching her sort through my bureau. She was trying to be motherly, I realized. But I'd grown up without all that, and it felt too unfamiliar to be pleasant.

She folded the jeans and set them on the pile of clothes to pack. "You need new clothes."

I might have disagreed. Then the image of Tamryn Gordon returned to me: red lipstick and a form-fitting red dress. I considered the stack of jeans and T-shirts on my bed. "Maybe you're right," I said.

So Mãe and I spent the rest of that day in Savannah, shopping.

Shopping for clothes with my mother had happened only twice before. She had an exceptional eye for color and design, and she urged me to try on outfits I would never have selected on my own.

But I did assert my own tastes in some decisions. And to her credit, she didn't object when I selected a red lace bra and panties instead of more serviceable neutral-colored ones. After only a second's hesitation, she said diplomatically, "Let's get two sets of each."

I didn't buy a red dress—I was too proud to be a copycat— but I found a knit sheath that came from Peru, made of pima cotton woven in muted blue, green, and grey that evoked a seaside landscape. The dress cost so much that I nearly put it back, but Mãe said, "Oh, you must have that. It suits you perfectly."

Money never had been an issue for my family. My father's research contracts and drug patents brought in considerable income. I took our good fortune for granted by and large, but I also was aware of the needs of people all around us. My father's large donations to charities didn't make me feel any more comfortable with our wealth.

So, as Mãe paid for the clothes, I promised myself that one day I'd pay my own way.

We had lunch at a café near the river—very close, my mother said, to the place she and my father first met as adults. (They'd met earlier as children, on Tybee, but she had only dim recollections of their meeting. He claimed to remember it in every detail: the exact spot on the beach where she first spoke to him, the words they'd exchanged, even the color of their bathing suits.)

My mood brightened as we sat on the balcony, cooled by overhead fans, watching a mammoth freighter crawl along the river. When the server delivered the two dozen oysters we'd ordered, he said, "Are you sisters?"

Looking across at my mother's long auburn hair and radiant skin, I felt flattered. She didn't reply.

After he left, she said, "Just once, I'd like to look like your mother."

And I remembered my college interview at Hillhouse more than a year before, when the admissions officer also said we looked like sisters. I'd been too intent on framing my answers to notice her reaction then.

"It bothers you that you look young?" In mortal terms, she looked no more than thirty.

"Of course it does." She picked up her oyster fork, then set it down again. "It embarrasses me, seeing other parents. Their faces have lines in them, lines that tell stories." She looked away from me, out at the river. "My face is like a blank page."

That wasn't strictly true, I thought. She'd crossed over when she was in her late twenties, and her face did have a few tiny lines, like seedlings of wrinkles to come.

I helped myself to oysters, hoping to distract her into doing the same.

"I've thought about having the injections," she said. "You know. Epiform."

Epiform was one of several "cosmetic dehancers" used by vampires to simulate the appearance of normal human aging. Other forms of aging-enablers used lasers and lights that pulsed concentrated UV rays. Along with plastic surgery, they were popular among those *others* who had grown tired of the nomadic lifestyle most vampires lead, moving periodically and adopting new identities to conceal their lack of aging from the mortal community.

"I don't think it's a good idea," I said. "Epiform is so unnatural."

Mãe said, "More unnatural than being a vampire?"

I hadn't realized she considered us unnatural. "What does my father think?"

She sighed. "Oh, he agrees with you. He says the injections aren't necessary. But Raphael is nearly indifferent to the appearances of others. He was like that even before he crossed over."

My mother still hadn't had one bite of lunch. "I've noticed the same attitude in other men who are exceptionally good-looking; they take their own beauty for granted, and somehow it's enough to keep them from seeking beauty in others."

"But *you're* beautiful." More striking now than when she'd been mortal, I thought. I'd seen photos of her early days, in an old album.

She ignored my compliment. "Why should we stay the same when everything around us is changing?"

I thought of Bennett. "Sometimes change hurts."

"I'd rather risk the pains of aging than feel—oh, I don't know. Feel as if I'm a mummy in a tomb."

At this point I couldn't think of anything to say to satisfy or soothe her.

Her face softened. "Oh, Ari. Forgive me. You must think I'm one mess of contradictions. I just *had* to become a vampire, like your father, and now I feel I just *have* to look like a normal mother. I'm sorry."

I remembered something she'd said once, and I repeated it now: "You need never apologize to me." But the words sounded stiff, stagy.

I tried to change the subject. "How are things with you and my father?" Those words sounded off-key, too.

She looked surprised. Then her face and her posture relaxed. She picked up a slice of lemon and squeezed it over her plate. "Things are okay," she said. "Better than I might have expected. Sometimes a woman has to take the initiative."

I wanted to ask her for details, but I couldn't find the right words. Dashay had been right. We needed to spend more time together, to learn a language of our own.

She lifted an oyster shell to her mouth and drained it. Then she turned her head to one side, her eyes quizzical. She removed something from her mouth and set it on the side of the plate: a small ivory-colored orb.

"I found a pearl," she said.

It didn't look like the pearls in her favorite necklace, which were perfectly round and lustrous. This one's shape was slightly irregular and its surface opaque, tinged with gray.

Mãe handed it to me. "You keep it," she said.

When we returned to the cottage, I set the pearl inside an oyster shell I kept on a bookshelf—a souvenir of my first encounter with oysters two years previously. I felt it would be safe there. If I carried it around with me, I thought, I might lose it.

~

And then there was no more time. We had to pack up our things and close down the cottage. I wrapped the oyster shell and the pearl in tissue paper and set them in my suitcase.

On the day before we left, my father and I took a walk along the beach. We didn't talk much; we simply savored the day. He slowed his pace to match mine and as we moved along the beach, people in bathing suits gawked at us, as if we were movie stars. The way he moved was so graceful that when I walked with him I felt graceful, too.

When we returned to the cottage, he said, "I have a birthday gift for you."

My birthday was July 15. He'd already given me a present, a book called *Pale Fire*—an enigmatic novel that described a father's awkward relationship with his difficult daughter.

"This gift arrived late."

He left the room and returned carrying a long box that he set on the kitchen table. I recognized the label: Gieves & Hawkes, my father's London tailors.

I rushed over to hug him, and he laughed at my pleasure. My father's laughter is one of the gentlest, most genuine sounds I've ever heard, and it pleased me as much as the present.

And this was a gift to treasure. Inside the box, I knew, were clothes and accessories made of metamaterials. When I chose to activate them, they'd bend light rays. I'd received a similar set nearly two years ago, and the clothes were beginning to fray.

"Thank you, thank you." I opened the box. This new trouser suit was dark gray, with a fashionably longer jacket and narrow pants. And there were shirts, underwear, socks, shoes, and a backpack, all in the same shade.

"The tailors keep your measurements on file, so any time you need new ones, they can get them to you in about two weeks," he said. "I know I don't need to say this, but I want you to remember it well: use invisibility wisely, if at all. Only when it's absolutely necessary."

I sensed someone watching, and I turned. But it was only my mother, leaning against a door frame, her eyes impossible to read.

That night we sat together in the living room. My father and I read, while my mother worked at the kitchen table, assembling a package of seashells and herbs; she asked me to mail it to Dashay, in hopes it would ease her heartache. From time to time I looked from my book to their faces, then around the room. It seems to me that places change when you're about to leave them; windows and doors that beckoned seem incidental, and nooks and corners that promised mystery have been explored and become mundane.

"The possibilities have shut down," I said.

My parents seemed to know what I meant. "It's not the place that has changed, it's your perception of it," my father said.

But my mother agreed with me. "The season is changing, and the cottage knows we're about to leave it."

Everything *is changing*, I thought. *Nothing will ever be the same again.*

If time is as fluid as some physicists claim, it's possible that somewhere we are still sitting in that cottage: a mother, a father, and a daughter intact and united, safe from whatever the future might bring.

❦

We'd decided to say our good-byes privately, at the cottage. A van would take them to the airport. I'd drive the Jaguar to school, about a hundred forty miles south.

My mother wasn't good when it came to separations, and she struggled to hide her tears. My father and I wore more stoic masks, but the pain ran every bit as deep, I suspected.

Mãe embraced me, then pulled back to check that I wore the amulet she'd given me a year ago. It was in the shape of an Egyptian cat, and, although she didn't know it, the amulet had ruined one of my invisibility attempts last spring. Unlike the special clothes, the cat didn't react to changes in my body temperature.

My mother touched the cat with two fingers and whispered something to it in a language I couldn't understand. Then she kissed me, looked deep into my eyes, and let me go.

"Don't forget to keep your appointment with Dr. Cho," she said. "And to give her my regards."

My annual physical exam had been scheduled for the next day, and I would never have forgotten it. I had important questions for Dr. Cho. As for *regards,* my mother's feelings about the doctor were decidedly mixed. She'd found out that, years before her marriage, Dr. Cho had had a crush on Raphael.

My father and I patted each other's shoulders awkwardly, but at the last minute, when the van pulled in to the driveway, I threw my arms around him.

"Boa viagem, minha filha," he said. He kissed my forehead. *Safe journey, my daughter.*

Then they were gone. I went inside, not wanting to see the landscape diminished by their absence.

Alone in the cottage, I made myself focus on packing the last of my clothes and clearing my room. Another family would live here next month.

When I finished, I walked down the beach, saying good-bye to the day and to summer. The sun was setting, and far from the shoreline, freighters crawled along the coast, their smokestacks gleaming in the dying light.

I thought of lines from my favorite Longfellow poem: *Ships that pass in the night, and speak each other in passing, / Only a signal shown and a distant voice in the darkness; / So on the ocean of life we pass and speak one another, / Only a look and a voice, then darkness again and a silence.*

The curse of my education: I knew a poem for every depressing occasion, and they came back to me whether I wanted them to or not.

Five

The sky looked unusually dark when I awoke the next morning, and light rain fell as I loaded my last bags into the car. The air felt swollen with moisture, almost sticky, and shreds of fog clung to the road that led to the mainland.

My destination was Dr. Sandra Cho's office on Bull Street, in Savannah's Historic District—a moody neighborhood popular with vampires. I found a place to park the Jaguar on a side street and locked the car, since it was packed with all my worldly goods.

As I walked back to Bull Street, I had qualms about my appointment with Dr. Cho. She was the kind of smart and competent person I wanted to be when I grew up. But would I be able to grow up? That was my primary question for her.

She'd been our family doctor for most of the past year, but I'd never visited her new office. The address led me to a modern, nondescript building made of brick. When I'd climbed the stairs and opened the correct door, I felt I'd entered another world: a dark green garden room with sky-lights, plants, a gurgling brass fountain, and long, surprisingly comfortable wooden benches. I sat only for a minute or so before she came out, gave me a hug, and led me into another room, all white, with overhead lights too bright for my liking.

"So, Ari." She beckoned for me to sit on a white-paper-covered table. "We'll do the blood work, all the usual tests. But first I want to know how you're feeling."

Dr. Cho had tiny bones, a serene, oval-shaped face, and long, glossy black hair held back by a clip. Her dark eyes, always alert, seemed almost too perceptive.

"I feel fine." My voice sounded prim, childishly polite. I took a deep breath and tried to make it lower, more sophisticated. "I do have some questions."

She waited, and I began. "I know that appearances are fixed, once someone becomes *other*."

"When we become vampires, yes."

"And I'm assuming that inside, all *that* stays the same as well?"

"Yes."

I made sure my thoughts were blocked. "So does that mean we never mature? Since I was thirteen when I became a vampire, will I always think like a thirteen-year-old?"

The questions rolled out into the white room, the words dark red against its walls.

Dr. Cho smiled at me. "Ari, did you *ever* think like a thirteen-year-old? And, really, what does it mean, to link age with thought patterns?"

"But you must see what I'm getting at." I forgot about trying to make my voice deeper. "Will I ever mature? Do vampires' brains change? Are we all stagnant?"

These questions, so dark they were almost black, joined the others in a shimmering block of words.

Dr. Cho put her hand on my shoulder. "Not necessarily."

"Not necessarily what?"

" 'Not necessarily' is the answer to all three questions." She removed her hand and perched on a tall stool near the table. "You're *half*-vampire, remember? You're a rare case. I don't know if your body or brain will age because of your human components. No one has studied hybrids, as far as I know."

I thought of Malcolm and his tests. "Have you heard of Malcolm Lynch?"

"The name is familiar," she said. "Yes, I heard a presentation he made at a conference. Four or five years ago, I think."

"He's studying hybrids."

"His work must be in its early stages, then. I haven't heard about it."

"Do you think I should take part in his research?"

She sighed. "That's something to ask your parents. I don't know what he's testing or how risky the procedures might be. In any case, to get back to your questions: vampire brains don't grow or atrophy, physiologically, but that doesn't mean vampires are incapable of acquiring experience and knowledge, or new feelings. Far from it. I can't quote any research, but I suspect that we're quicker to gain intellectual and emotional maturity than most humans."

She paused a moment before she went on. "But your questions surprise me, for two reasons. First, because of the emotions that lie behind them. Second, the fact that you're posing them at all. Because I'm sure you could have answered them yourself."

This comment reminded me of my father, who frequently had told me I already knew the answers to the questions I asked—I simply needed to think them out. But he and my mother were gone. I was on my own now.

Dr. Cho stood and put her hand on my shoulder. "We can do the standard tests. See how your heart and blood look. And then I'll tell you about some of the research I do now, some of the therapies that are being developed. The good news is, whatever change you're seeking, you may have alternatives."

I'd always felt alienated from the human world, but suddenly I felt sunk by the fact that I didn't belong in the vampire world, either. I didn't know vampire history or folktales, and I couldn't even use the secret language. "And the bad news is, I'm not one or the other."

"All the more reason for us to say you may have options." Dr. Cho turned away from me and picked up a sealed package containing a needle. "If you think you must have them."

I closed my eyes and imagined myself back at Blue Heaven, with a Russian Blue cat curled in my lap. Still, I felt the needle's sting.

⁓

While I was being tested and monitored and prodded, I remembered what one of Dr. Cho's options might be: a drug called Revité, a drug claimed to make vampires mortal again. Whether it would work for someone who wasn't entirely vampire raised yet another question.

And by the time the tests were complete, I finally realized that all my questions boiled down to one: how much of me was mortal?

When she returned from her laboratory in an adjoining room, Dr. Cho declined to answer that question. She called it "a wrong question."

"You're a complex being, Ari. I could lie and tell you your blood and organs indicate that you're forty percent human, or sixty percent. But I can't measure that distinction. And even if I could, what difference would it make?"

It might make a difference to Bennett, I thought. We were back in the green outer room now, sitting side by side on a bench.

I folded my arms. "It might affect those options you mentioned."

"You don't *need* options, in my opinion." She held up a

hand as I began to reply. "Remember that all your vital signs are good. You're healthy. I'm going to adjust your tonic slightly, but that's in response to your hormone levels."

"I still want to know about the options."

She sighed. "There are new protocols involving synthetic growth hormones that can modify a person's chronological age. Have you heard about them?"

I told her I'd heard about dehancement, about injections like Epiform.

"Those are cosmetic," she said. "These are internal. Growth hormones produced by pituitary glands make organs and tissues reach adulthood, if you will. They affect height, skin, and bone density. And some recent research has shown that new synthetic hormones can be used to make vampires age, but they're still in the experimental stage, and the studies so far have been small and inconclusive. No one has made a long-term study of the possible side effects or risks associated with these therapies."

"So you don't know if they work for *half-breeds* like me?" I hated that expression.

Dr. Cho's eyes met mine. "No, Ari. I don't know if they would work for you. And when I told you about Revité last spring, I didn't know you were half-mortal. That drug might not work for you, either. As I said, the research isn't conclusive. There are relatively few hybrids like you, and fewer still who take part in the clinical trials."

"So I can't become human." I rubbed my hands against the knees of my jeans. "And I can't be all vampire. That means I'm stuck."

"You're complex, with an active brain and plenty of attitude. I don't think you have any reason to feel sorry for yourself." Dr. Cho sounded impatient. "I have dozens of patients with serious health problems who'd change places with you in an instant." She glanced at the clock on the wall and handed me a bottle. "Try the new tonic for a month. Let me know if it works for you or if we need to adjust the formula."

I felt dismissed. I put the bottle in my backpack.

"Don't be disappointed." Her right hand made a funny gesture: the forefinger and little finger spread out wide; the two middle fingers touched in a straight upward line. It looked like twin *V*s.

"I don't know what that means," I said.

She seemed surprised. "It means 'celebrate your true nature.'"

My right hand made the gesture back at her.

"That's it. It's Mentori," she said. "Most humans can't move their fingers quite that way."

⌁

On my drive back to school, I took the back roads, and by the time I finally reached the long driveway that led onto campus, I'd had enough of driving. Luckily I wouldn't need the car for a while.

Hillhouse is called an alternative, eco-conscious school. It's a working farm, and every student has a job besides studying. Classes are interdisciplinary and rigorous but ungraded; instead, students receive detailed written evaluations. I'd chosen it because of its educational philosophy, and because of the place itself. The campus, students, teachers—all had glowed with promise the first time I visited, on a golden autumn afternoon.

Now, after only one semester, the old wooden buildings looked darker, not so much full of potential as haunted by memories. My friend Autumn had been murdered here. The FBI had been called in to investigate, but who did it, and why, had not been discovered.

I parked the car near Seward Hall and sat for a few minutes. All around me, people unloaded cars and carried suitcases, trash bags, and armloads of possessions into the building. *Why do we have so much stuff? Do we need things in order to feel secure?*

My own piles of possessions made me uneasy. Instead of unpacking, I went for a walk.

Away from the dormitories, across the green lawns bordering the dining hall, paths led down to the barn and the recycling plant. I walked slowly, not meeting anyone I knew, getting farther and farther from the dorms. A stream ran alongside the path, and the sound of water moving over stones took me back to that last afternoon with Cameron in the forest.

Then the hairs at the nape of my neck bristled, and the familiar tingle ran down my spine. I turned sharply to look behind me and saw no one. But I heard a cough.

On the slope above me, perched on a rock, someone with long, dark hair sat with a sketchbook braced against his knees. He looked down—a pale face with a pointed chin—and coughed again. "Hiya."

"Hello." I'd never seen him before, and his voice had an unfamiliar accent.

We stared at each other for a few seconds. Then he returned to his sketching, and I went on my way.

⁓

"Who's the new boy?" I asked Jacey. "The interesting-looking one?"

Jacey was my roommate and my closest friend at school. We sat side by side in the old theater building, which also served as the Hillhouse auditorium, waiting to be officially welcomed to the new semester. We'd spent the afternoon unpacking and talking about how boring our summers had been, although in truth mine hadn't been boring at all.

"Someone said he's a transfer student. An art major. From Ireland." She pushed back her braids. When let loose, her thick, long blond hair was a presence all by itself. Her freckled skin made me think of milk dusted with cinnamon.

The new boy sat by himself at the end of a row near the exit doors. He was tall and thin. His dark hair hid most of his profile, and he wore a black suit, which stood out among the jeans and T-shirts worn by the rest of us. He must have sensed my stare, and he glanced over at me. I quickly turned to face the stage.

We spent the next twenty minutes hearing variations on the theme that this would be the best year of our lives. I hoped it might be true.

At the end of the speech, the school president read the names of the entering freshmen and transfer students. The dark boy's name was Sloan Flynn. He was an art major from Dublin. I wondered why someone would travel so far to study art at a small college like Hillhouse.

Then I wondered why I was even that curious about Sloan Flynn.

～

After the official welcoming ended, the socializing began. A bonfire burned in a clearing near the parking lot. Picnic tables had been loaded with food and drinks, and two kegs of beer bought by students were in plain sight, even though Hillhouse was officially a dry campus.

"What's the story?" The voice from behind me belonged to Sloan Flynn, I knew without looking. Nobody else around here had an accent like that.

"Story?" I turned around and saw his full face for the first time, and I wondered how it could be simultaneously strong and delicate. His eyes were dark and deep and had the expression of someone who'd been hurt and had survived, who was determined to never be hurt again. His chin thrust out like a challenge.

Dumb as it may sound, we stared at each other for—I can't tell how long. It wasn't leering or ogling so much as taking in the details.

Jacey came over, carrying a plateful of food. "You must be the new guy," she said, her voice breaking the spell. She smiled.

It was impossible not to like Jacey, and Sloan smiled back, a grin that changed his face completely, made him look less defensive.

I told myself I felt glad that she'd interrupted us. My first day back at school had been unsettling enough already. But it wasn't over yet.

❧

After lighting a sandalwood incense stick, Jacey began to unplait her hair.

We were back in the dorm room, and I was already in bed. She'd asked what was bothering me.

"I was thinking about Autumn," I said.

Autumn had stayed in our dorm when she came to visit me last semester. The following day, Jacey was the first one who saw her body. Now her hands dropped to her lap. "I was hoping you wouldn't mention her."

"I try not to think about her," I said. "But coming back to school brought back memories."

Autumn had been a surly girl most of the time. Not someone I'd have chosen as a friend. For some reason, she'd chosen me.

Jacey's hands returned to her hair. "They never caught the guy who killed her, did they?" Her hair seemed to expand, double its width, as it was released.

"No." I wedged a pillow under my back. "But at least they found her body."

Jacey hugged herself. "Don't talk about that."

"I'm sorry." I'd forgotten how easily she frightened. She'd have been terrified if she knew her roommate was a vampire.

"You're so much braver than I am," she said.

"Not brave, exactly. I'm"—I paused to find the right word—"different."

"Yes," she said. "Yes, you are. I've never met anyone like you."

Six

When I'd been packing my things for the new semester, envisioning myself back on campus, I'd anticipated some awkwardness from my classmates. After all, the murdered girl had come to campus specifically to visit me.

But no one said a word about Autumn. Some might have forgotten her. Even if others remembered, they were wrapped up in themselves and living in the moment, constantly checking their cell phones for updates and text messages from Facebook, NetFriend, Twitter, or Trend. Most were so busy communicating with absent friends that they had little time to spend with anyone in person.

I'd ignored a few invitations to become a "friend" or a "follower." Jacey confided that she'd thought I didn't like her anymore when I didn't respond to her e-mail from NetFriend, asking if she could "friend" me. I'd had to reassure her that it had nothing to do with affection. I simply preferred face-to-face relationships.

Jacey tried to explain its virtues over lunch in the dining hall. "It's an easy way to stay in touch with old friends," she said.

We were eating lentil burgers with cheese. Jacey drank tea, and I had a glass of juice mixed with tonic. I carried the bottle with me everywhere. Jacey thought it was lupus medication.

"And it's great for letting your family know what you're doing."

I didn't have any relatives on NetFriend or Facebook or Twitter. I imagined inviting my father to be my "friend." The idea was ludicrous. "I'm not sure I'd want them to know," I said.

She laughed. "You don't have to tell them the truth."

"Isn't it dangerous, letting the world know where you are and what you're doing?"

Jacey looked thoughtful. "It can be, I guess. There are stories about lurkers who steal your identity, and stalkers who prey on girls."

Her eyes took on the fearful look that was all too familiar, so I changed the subject. "Dinner's not bad tonight."

She was easy to distract. "I love the food here. At home my parents eat meat, and the smell makes me sick."

The dining hall food, most of it organically grown on the campus farm, was very good, I agreed. But it wasn't anything like what Mãe and Dashay cooked. I was about to tell Jacey about the way they worked together in the kitchen, but she was intent on her cell phone, thumbs tapping its keys, communicating with another friend.

My two favorite classes that semester were Special Topics in Japanese Culture and Creative Writing. The other classes—Communications Studies and Web Design—were worthwhile but never so memorable. Hillhouse allowed students to design individual courses of study, and mine focused on communications.

Special Topics began with a discussion of the concept of

wabi-sabi. It's a central tenet of Zen Buddhism, difficult to define since essential Zen knowledge can't be communicated with words—instead, it's transferred from mind to mind. That's why so many vampires are Buddhists, I suspect; being able to hear thoughts gives them an advantage.

Professor Itou was a new assistant professor, not yet comfortable as a teacher. He didn't hand out a syllabus, and he didn't spend the first class introducing himself or the course. Instead he paced the classroom, throwing out words in small bursts. Curiously, his unease probably kept the students more rapt than eloquence would have.

"Wabi-sabi. To you. It may be an aesthetic," he said. He kept his eyes on the floor as he walked. "Easier to say. What it is not." He stopped moving for a minute to gaze out the classroom window. "Not the Greek ideal. Not perfection. Not complete. Not eternal. Wabi-sabi is simple. Wabi-sabi is not pure. It won't stay the same. You may call it ugly."

All around me I heard confusion in the reactions of my fellow students. *I don't get this,* Jacey thought. *Too weird,* somebody in the front row was thinking. Then I heard one thought, clear and light as the sound of a bell: *the broken bowl is glued together. Light passes through its cracks.*

Suddenly I understood. *How beautiful,* I told myself as I turned to see where the thought had come from.

Sloan Flynn sat in the last row, in the chair nearest the door. His back was straight, and his hands lay palms-up on his knees. His eyes met mine. He answered, *Yes, beautiful.*

As a reflexive instinct, I blocked my thoughts, but I knew he had already heard them.

Professor Itou said the word *wabi* originally meant "sad" or "lonely" but also meant "balanced" or "peaceful." *Sabi* meant "the bloom of time."

He presented a slide show next. An image of a tree with a

broken branch came onto the projection screen. "How does it feel?" the professor asked.

Next, an empty wooden bucket lay on its side, splinters catching the light of a dying sun. "Freedom comes with sadness," he said. "The wisdom of rocks."

Some of the images weren't recognizable. Some were half hidden by fog. Others looked as if they'd been captured with a microscope, too small to be seen by the human eye.

Absolute silence fell on the room.

"Can you see the invisible?" Professor Itou asked.

As it happened, I was wearing my metamaterials suit, and I had a sudden whim to turn invisible right there in the classroom. In the darkened room, the students were focused on the slide show. Would anyone notice?

My neck began to tingle. Sloan was watching me—I knew it without turning around. *Don't do it,* my inner self counseled. *Too risky.* But the urge was irresistible—I had to make sure I could still do it. I took a deep breath and concentrated, willing myself to exist only in the present moment. Then I exhaled and let all sense of being pass through me and out of me, slowing every electron of my being to the point where they deflected light. A sensation of weightlessness spread through me.

It lasted only a few seconds. Then I inhaled myself into visibility. Professor Itou stared at me, blinking rapidly. Suddenly he made a slight bow in my direction. I bowed back. The tingling sensation at the back of my neck continued through the rest of the class.

Sloan also turned up in my Creative Writing class, taught by a visiting writer named June Warner. On our first day, I arrived early and took the seat nearest the door. I wasn't sure I'd like creative writing.

Neither, apparently, was Sloan. He came in and looked

longingly at my chair without making eye contact with me. Then he took a seat at the front.

But when the professor came in—her short blond hair tousled and face red, as if she'd been running—she made us rearrange the seats in a circle. I kept my place near the door, and Sloan moved his chair next to mine.

The professor was a tall, stout woman, wearing the kind of polyester clothes that supposedly never cling or wrinkle and invariably do both. She said that she was a poet and that the titles of her chapbooks were listed on the syllabus as recommended reading. Then she read aloud a list of topics we weren't allowed to write about: drugs, dead grandmothers, drinking, small animals, guns. The list went on and on. Religion, politics, sex, nuclear power, UFOs.

Jacey scribbled a comment on her notebook and pushed it over to me. "This is creative?" it read.

I didn't think Professor Warner would feel much at home at Hillhouse, where professors and students alike favored free expression and nonprescriptive instruction. The buzz of thoughts in the room was largely negative, with one exception: Richard Meek, a student who seemed as out of place at our school as Professor Warner. He was thinking, *That's right! Make them follow the rules.*

Sloan's hands clenched the arms of his seat. *Art has no rules,* he thought.

I turned to face him. *Are you really* other? I thought.

He gave me a sidelong glance. Then his hands came together in the Mentori "open mouth" sign.

"Excuse me." Professor Warner's voice had no air of politeness. She was staring at Sloan. "Would you like to tell all of us what that gesture means?"

Sloan's eyes slid away from mine to look straight at the professor.

"We're waiting." She folded her arms across her chest.

His eyes were so dark they looked black. "It means," he said slowly, "that I'm a vampire."

Sloan, the professor, and I were the only ones in the room who didn't laugh.

⟡

On the way out of class, I nearly collided with Sloan. *Do you have a minute to talk?* he thought.

But Professor Warner said, "I want a word with you, young man."

So I went out into the fresh green air, still marveling at his audacity.

I sat on a stone fence near the classroom building, waiting to talk to him, watching students stream out its doors and head up the hill or down toward the barn, most of them talking on their phones or listening to music through earbuds—so much more connected than I was. But I didn't feel sad about my solitude. Was that because I was under the influence of wabi-sabi? Or because now I knew I wasn't the only vampire on campus?

Then my phone rang, connecting me to an unfamiliar number. The voice was pure Cameron.

"How are you?" he asked, and before I could speak, he said, "How's school? What are you doing? I've missed you."

And as I answered his questions, from the corner of my eye I saw Sloan come out of the classroom building and begin walking in my direction. Then he must have seen the cell phone or heard my thoughts. He quickly turned away, but not before I saw the disappointment in his eyes. I felt disappointed, too, but only for a moment.

Cameron said he was in Savannah to attend two fundraising events: a private dinner with rich donors, followed by a somewhat less expensive reception.

"Savannah?" *So near, and yet so far.*

I sensed he was thinking the same thing. I remembered the last time we'd kissed, and the memory hurt.

"It's not a good idea," he said slowly.

I knew that. He'd made things pretty clear the last time we'd met.

"It's an easy drive," I said. I waited, hoping.

"Oh, what the hell." His voice had a rough edge to it. "You could at least attend the reception."

"We can ignore each other." I was already thinking about what I would wear: the new dress made in Peru.

"We can try," he said. "At least we'll be in the same room, breathing the same air."

Back in my dorm room, I changed quickly into the new dress and put on my fanciest sandals. Luckily, Jacey wasn't there. I played with my hair, twisting it and pinning it high on my head, wondering if it made me look older. The mirror reflection stayed fuzzy; I was too excited to be able to concentrate.

On the drive to Savannah, I wondered what we'd say to each other. Would we even have a chance to talk? I stopped at a drugstore near the exit ramp and bought makeup: lipstick, mascara, eye shadow, and blush. Squinting into the car mirror, I applied them as well as I could. If the dress looked as good as my mother said it did, it deserved a sophisticated face to go with it.

I found the address in the Historic District, parked the car, and watched men in summer suits and women in cocktail dresses strolling along the street toward the house. It was a Queen Anne–style mansion, painted white, with a tower, pitched roof, gables, and a long porch. It reminded me of the Victorian houses in Saratoga Springs, painted as carefully as bakers' iced cakes.

As I climbed the steps to the porch, I felt someone watching me and turned, hoping to see Cameron. Instead, I looked into the face of Malcolm Lynch.

Malcolm's pale gray eyes moved from my head to my feet and back again. He smiled. "Little Ari is growing up," he said. "And maintaining her interest in politics. Well, well."

His smile had considerable charm, and I was determined to be civil. Other people were climbing the stairs, after all. But what I thought was, *How can you be nice to me? How could you kill Marmalade? How could you kill Kathleen?*

His smile gone, he tilted his head toward the porch. "Do me the favor of a small conversation before we go in."

We walked around the corner, out of sight of the door. I didn't know why I followed him. The last time we'd met, he'd done the same thing: made me acquiescent.

"Look," he said, "it's time to put an end to that kind of thinking. You *are* growing up, yes? Time to stop the childish patterns of blaming and hating, wouldn't you say?"

"You think I should forgive you?"

"I think you should listen to reason." He clasped his hands behind the back of his raw-silk jacket, as if he were at a debate. "I think you should work with me. Are you acquainted with the concept of acceptable risks?"

I shook my head.

"Surely your father taught you about utilitarianism?"

"The moral value of an action is determined by the extent to which it contributes to the greater good." I'd learned that years ago.

"Yes. And sometimes we take actions that may harm individual lives, in order to produce greater good in the end." His eyes had a remote expression, as if he were reliving an old memory. "We call those risks acceptable."

His words spun in the air like fog.

"Why are you telling me this?"

"To make you see the point." His voice rose slightly. "Sometimes lives have to be put at risk, or even lost, in order to save a greater number of lives. Think of medical research, about clinical trials of new procedures and medications. Say a man has a blocked artery. If untreated, it will cause a heart attack that may kill him. A physician uses an experimental procedure to unclog the artery. Say the man dies on the operating table. But the physician uses the knowledge gained by the attempt to refine the procedure, which ultimately saves more lives."

He unclasped his hands and held them toward me, as if they were holding a present. "Would you rather the physician didn't try the experiment?"

I stood under a hanging basket of drooping crimson flowers that I recognized from Dashay's garden, appropriately named bleeding hearts—though hers were black. "I wouldn't want to be the man on the table," I said. "Would you?"

"That's an entirely different question. The point is, the risk was worth taking."

I looked into his eyes. Dashay had taught me how to spot internal demons that show up as a kind of flicker on the iris. But Malcolm's eyes were as sharp and cold and deep as a glacial lake. Whatever possessed him, it wasn't a demon.

"But to answer your question"—he sounded as if he was straining to be patient—"I'd be willing to risk my life in order to save others. I already have."

It wasn't the answer I might have expected. Yet somehow I believed him.

Malcolm clasped his hands again. "Imagine that your

father's lungs failed him—don't look that way, Ari. Vampires aren't susceptible to lung failure. This is all hypothetical. But imagine that his best chance to stay alive required a living lung transplant. Would you be willing to donate one of your lungs?"

"Of course." I didn't even have to think about that decision.

"But living lung donors face a range of possible complications. The surgery itself is risky. Afterward, they're susceptible to pulmonary artery thrombosis, empyema, bronchial stricture and fistula . . . I could go on. Would you still be willing?"

"Of course." Again, I didn't hesitate.

"So would I. Those risks would be worth it, to keep him alive. Personal feelings aside, he has the intelligence and scientific talent to produce work that will save many other lives. So, you see, you and I are willing to take acceptable risks."

I thought, *Maybe. But would my father want us to take them?*

Then I saw where this conversation had been leading all along. "You still want me to be part of some kind of clinical study."

"You have a unique chance to contribute to the greater good," Malcolm said. "We've already begun testing others like you, developing physiological profiles. Once our project is complete, the results will help us create risk assessment and prevention plans for everyone—vampires, mortals, and hybrids alike. Shouldn't you take part?" His gray eyes gazed into mine, as if he were willing me to respond. "Won't you?"

I looked away, back at the bleeding hearts. The sounds of the reception drifted out to us: a pianist playing songs written by Johnny Mercer, Savannah's favorite lyricist and composer. Dashay and Bennett had often danced to his music, moving gracefully through the moon garden back in Homosassa. I recognized the song: "Out of This World." Then it hit me: Malcolm's research might help Bennett, in particular.

An intense urge to see Cameron swept through me. I'd had more than enough of Malcolm and his ethical bargaining for one day. But as I turned my back on him, I heard myself say, "I'll think about it."

～

The woman at the desk inside the front door looked from my fake ID to my face and back again. "You look older than nineteen," she said.

"Thank you." I replaced the ID in my wallet. She didn't know what a compliment she'd paid me.

The reception was under way in a large, softly lit room, probably once used as a ballroom. The glow of its apricot-colored walls made everyone look interesting: a mustached man wearing a pinstriped suit, a woman in a distinctive print dress by a designer whose clothes I'd seen only in magazines— they looked as if they led fascinating, complicated lives.

What was one supposed to do at a reception? Mingle and talk, I supposed. But what could I say? What could I possibly have in common with any of them?

So I stood near the door, feeling nervous. Then I saw Cameron, far across the room, surrounded by yet more beautiful people. Our eyes met only for a second, but in that second it was as if my blood caught fire—an intensity of feeling that shocked me.

Around me people swirled, pressing ever closer to the circle around Cameron. Even those deep in conversation glanced at him every few minutes, as if his presence gave them definition.

And Cameron basked in their adoration. He seemed to

drink it in with each breath. His eyes moved from face to face, and I was impatient for them to reach mine again, to let me know that I was more special to him than anyone.

Suddenly I realized that a man in a blue suit was talking to me, asking what I did. When I said I was a student, he moved away quickly. I guess he thought students were too young to talk with.

Then I noticed Malcolm standing close by, watching. His face showed understanding, even sympathy.

~

Next to Cameron stood his aide Tamryn, wearing a knee-length silver dress so simple, yet so perfectly cut, that she was easily the most striking woman in the room. Her hair fell in glossy waves that curved around her face, whose profile was as sharply etched as a cameo's. She was talking to an older, white-haired man: Joel Hartman, rumored to be Cameron's likely running mate. When she noticed me, she broke off her conversation with Hartman and strode across the room.

"Malcolm," she said, extending her hand.

He shook it once, languidly. "Hello, Tamryn. You're looking well."

"Ms. Montero." Her voice sounded cold.

"Ms. Gordon." We shook hands. Hers felt frigid. I sensed her hostility, but the lingering power of having met Cameron's eyes kept me calm.

"Could I have a word with you?" It wasn't a question. She put her hand on my arm and swiftly steered me out of the room, back onto the porch. Her fingernails, long and sharp, pressed into my skin.

She didn't waste time. "Why are you here?"

"I was invited," I said. "Cameron invited me."

She looked skeptical. Yet I could tell she wasn't sure I was lying, even though I couldn't read her thoughts. *She must be a vampire.*

She was saying something in her raspy voice, and I tuned in to the middle of it: "—so if you really believe that you *care* about him, you'll leave him alone."

"I do care," I said. "But I'm not leaving him alone." The confidence in my voice surprised me.

I went on, making my words as cold and hard as her handshake. "You needn't worry. We won't do or say anything that might hurt his campaign."

Later I would remember those words and wonder how I could have been so naïve.

As I left the porch, I heard her think, *Oh well, it won't last, anyway. He knows she's much too immature for a man of his stature.* I realized that she'd sent me her thought deliberately, but that didn't lessen the sting of the words.

The apricot-colored room didn't seem so charming now. I saw no sign of Cameron. The good-looking people's mouths looked smug or sinister, and the heat from the candles on the buffet table made the room uncomfortably warm. I told myself to calm down, but Tamryn's words kept echoing in my head. *Too immature.*

"Here." Malcolm handed me a glass of ice water.

Wary, I handed it back. He shrugged and drank it himself. He thought, *I could help you. I can make you older.*

～

When I left the house I almost ran until I saw the Jaguar parked up ahead, under a streetlight. Then I slowed my pace and made my breathing deeper, more regular.

The ringing of my cell phone sounded much too loud in the quiet street. Another unfamiliar number calling.

"Ari?" Cameron said as soon I as answered it. "Where are you?"

"Outside," I said, keeping my voice low. "Heading home."

Background voices and static came through the receiver. Then he said, "I'm sorry. Your coming here. I guess it wasn't a good idea."

"I guess it wasn't." I took another deep breath and kept walking. The street smelled of night-blooming jasmine. "I had an interesting chat with Tamryn Gordon. She let me know that you think I'm immature."

My words hadn't been planned, and they surprised me.

"What did she say?" He sounded concerned.

"She didn't say it, she thought it. She's a vampire, isn't she?"

"I couldn't say." His voice sounded guarded.

"Did you tell her I'm immature?" I realized as I spoke that I simply wanted him to deny it.

Instead, he said, "I may have told her you were young, that you have some growing up to do." More background noise. "But I never said *immature*."

The car was in view now. But it wasn't empty. Two people sat in the front seat.

"I have to go," I said, and disconnected the call.

How did they get into my car? I must have forgotten to lock it.

I couldn't see their faces. The light was too dim even to tell if they were men or women. All I saw were two grey shapes, torsos and heads roughly the same size as mine. One of them raised its arm, as if in greeting.

Fear, alarm, panic, whatever name you give to the anxieties that seem to gather in your chest, encircle your heart—I felt them surge, grip me tight. More than anything I wanted to run away. I made my legs keep moving toward the car.

But with each step I took, the filmy shapes grew less distinct. By the time I reached the car, they simply weren't there.

Perhaps they were tricks of light, or the silhouettes of the head-rests. I stood outside the car for a minute, looking through its windows. All I saw was the plastic drugstore bag that held the makeup I'd bought. It made me recall how much I'd looked forward to this evening, how excited I was.

What a fool I'd been.

Then I reached for the door. Yes, it was locked.

Even so, I scanned the back seat and car floor, and got out again to check the trunk, before I started the engine and drove away. I kept glancing at the rearview mirror. No one followed me and no one sat behind me, but my neck never stopped tingling on the drive back to school.

Seven

For the next few months, reading and writing and attending class took up most of my time, along with the sorting work I did at the campus recycling center. The busier I stayed, the less time I spent brooding about Cameron. He hadn't called since the night of the reception. And we'd agreed that I shouldn't call him unless it was an emergency. It was part of what he called keeping our relationship "low profile."

The prickling sensation became almost constant. Some days it felt stronger than others, but it rarely went away entirely. It felt as irritating as living with a perpetual dull headache.

I mentioned the sensation to Dr. Cho when I e-mailed her my review of the new tonic; I asked her if maybe my hormones weren't a little *too* intense. She wrote back that teenage girls and raging hormones went together like oysters and pearls—a comment I found vaguely Zen-like and not especially helpful. But she did adjust the tonic formula, and later she mailed me a case of the stuff.

When I wrote again, to thank her, I asked if vampires might be more prone to depression than humans—a question I doubt I'd have asked had we met in person.

She wrote back almost immediately: "This is another area in

which insufficient research has been conducted. But speaking from my own professional practice and personal experience, I think it likely that we are more susceptible to depression, and to elation as well. Our senses are keener, and we experience life with greater intensity than the majority of mortals do."

≈

Something Jacey said helped me come to terms with my feelings. Her parents had given her a subscription to the *New York Times,* and one day at lunch she read me portions of an article about an experimental drug called ZIP. When injected into the brains of rats, the drug caused immediate loss of long-term memory.

Jacey read, "'This possibility of memory editing has enormous possibilities and raises huge ethical issues,' said Dr. Steven E. Hyman, a neurobiologist at Harvard.'"

The article said the drug didn't affect short-term memory and that its effects were reversible; you had to keep taking it to block the long-term memories, and if you stopped, they flooded back.

"Imagine that," she said. "You could give your brain a makeover. Take away all the memories that cause you pain."

"Would that be a good thing?" I was trying to imagine living without remembering the deaths of Kathleen and Autumn. Yes, I'd be a happier person, but I wouldn't be *me*. "Aren't we defined by our bad experiences as much as by our good ones?"

"I don't know." Jacey dragged a fork through her plate of macaroni and cheese. "There are some things I'd prefer not to remember."

Aside from Autumn's death, I had no idea what "some things" might be, and I wasn't about to ask. How little I knew her, this person I considered my close friend.

Then I thought of Cameron. Given the pain of separation, would I prefer to forget him completely?

No. I wanted to keep my memories of him, even if they hurt. I thought, *Yes, you can give your brain a makeover. But what about your heart?*

In the journals I've kept since I was twelve, negative entries take up more space than positive ones. I suspect it's because we remember painful moments in greater detail than pleasant ones; our memory networks function best when we're having strong emotional reactions. Sad to say, twenty years from now I'll probably remember the night of the reception more clearly than the day Cameron first kissed me.

❧

Not everything that year was depressing. There were fall days that began with crisp blue mornings, led to golden afternoons, and ended in starlit nights perfumed by the incense of burning leaves. We rode horses, read books, and stayed up late talking about trivia or debating weighty questions that we were all too young to fully understand.

Except, perhaps, for Sloan. I didn't know how old he was, but his depth of understanding and grasp of issues clearly exceeded everyone else's. He also had a healthy appreciation for absurdity.

Our creative writing classes were dedicated to fiction workshops in October; the professor said she wanted to get the fiction over with first, so that we'd have more time to focus later on poetry. And one of the first stories we workshopped was written by Sloan.

The writer had to distribute copies of the manuscript during the class before the one in which we discussed it. So far, most of the stories had been written in the present tense and sounded as if the writer had thrown them together at the last minute. Professor Warner had a list of things we couldn't say in the workshop discussion. We could suggest that a character was so intriguing he deserved more development, but we couldn't say that the character was stereotypical or badly drawn or boring. Every comment had to be phrased as a positive suggestion.

The night after Sloan passed out his story, I came back to the dorm to find Jacey lying flat on the floor of our room, her face streaked with tears.

Immediately I knelt next to her. "What's wrong?"

She shook her head silently, then burst out laughing. More tears ran down her face. When she finally could talk, she said, "Sloan's story. You *have* to read it."

I did.

The story featured a grandmother who, although quite dead, was addicted to heroin and whiskey and spent her quality time shooting small animals. She had a passionate romance with a politician she'd met at an anti-nuclear-power rally, but their affair was doomed since he was Catholic and she was Protestant. The story ended when the two of them crashed their UFO. "As their craft plummeted toward Earth, Emily Newgate knew they were going to go to hell," the ending read, "but she didn't mind, so long as they both ended up in the same hell."

In the space of five pages, Sloan managed to break every single one of Professor Warner's taboos. And, despite the inane material, his writing style was flawless.

My reaction to the story was more subdued than Jacey's. Yes, it *was* funny. But it also seemed more than a little juvenile to break all the rules simply because you could.

Professor Warner began the next class with a lecture. "Writing is a serious art, not a game," it began. Although she never mentioned his name, we all knew whom she was talking about.

Sloan sat very straight in the chair next to mine. *Art is a game,* he thought.

"And a writing workshop is an opportunity to learn, not to play." Professor Warner's face was crimson as she paced the front of the classroom.

Suddenly Sloan stood up. "I apologize," he said. "I wasted everyone's time, and I'm sorry. I usually overreact to rules and regulations. It's a childish habit of mine, and one of these days I hope to outgrow it."

Professor Warner looked confused, but not angry. She told Sloan to sit down. Then she gave us a writing assignment—describe the room you remember best from your childhood—that took up the rest of the class. I had no problem describing my bedroom in Saratoga Springs, from its dark blue drapes to the old oak bed to the lithophane lamp on the bedside table.

When I finished, I looked up. Everyone else was still writing. Professor Warner watched Sloan, her face still puzzled. She was thinking, *Am I a bad teacher?* I felt sorry for her.

Once again, I waited outside the classroom building to talk to Sloan. When he came out, I said, "That was a brave thing to do."

He shook his head. "Sometimes I act like a five-year-old."

We walked along the path, away from the buildings. A breeze came up, making me hug my sweater to my skin. "How old *are* you?" I asked.

"Oh, that's a good question." He bent to pick up a rock, examined it, let it fall to the ground again. He looked behind us before he spoke. "I was fifteen when I was taken."

I hadn't heard that expression before. "You mean, when you became *other?*"

"Yes. But now I'm twenty-two."

"How can that be?"

"I had the injection, you know. In Ireland they call it Septimal. Don't they have it here?"

I didn't know. "It's an aging drug?"

"Yeah," he said. "Septimal. One shot takes you along seven years. More than that, if the dose is adjusted. You can be any age you want. I figured twenty-two was good. Peak strength and mental ability, you know?" He kicked another stone out of the way. "Only sometimes, it's like I revert. Act like a kid again."

"How does the drug work?"

"It accelerates your cell growth, so you get taller, your bones get stronger, that sort of thing. Your face changes, looks more adult. Your brain ages, too." He looked at me. "How old are you?"

"I crossed when I was thirteen. That was two years ago."

"And thirteen feels too young." He didn't phrase it as a question. "Yeah, I get that. Although you don't look your age, really. Actually, I've been studying you."

"Me?" We'd come to the second barn, where the art students had studios.

"I did a sketch of you in class one day. Want to see it?" He gestured toward the barn's upper story.

I'd been in that barn only once. It smelled pleasantly of turpentine used by the artists and faintly of horses, who'd been kept there until they were moved to a more modern stable down the road.

We climbed a ladder to the loft, which had been partitioned into studios. Skylights had been built into the roof. Sloan's studio had a threadbare carpet on its floor, an easel, and a table, smeared with generations of paint, that held brushes, a palette, and tubes of color. Two chairs with cane seats stood against the wall, which also was smeared with paint. A card table stacked with paper and sketchbooks had been set in the corner.

"Do you draw?" Sloan asked, watching me take it all in.

"Not well." My father had taught me simple sketching techniques, but we both agreed that I showed no special aptitude for art.

Sloan took a sketchbook from the table, opened it, and set it on the easel. "This is the drawing I made the day I met you."

It was a landscape, almost scientific in the precision of its details. At first glance it resembled a black and white photograph of a hillside with a stream meandering through the background.

But when you looked twice—and you had to look twice, because the drawing pulled you back into it—each trunk, each twig, each blade of grass had been subtly altered, made unnatural. Real trunks didn't have quite that texture. Actual twigs didn't form those patterns. And the grasses, naturally graceful, were so bent and twisted that they looked arthritic, menacing.

The aberrations were subtle enough to barely register at first. As I looked deeper, they contrived to produce a sense of unease, even nausea. I tried to look away, but my eyes stayed with the drawing, fascinated by the force of its repulsiveness. The strange landscape, each detail precise but somehow *wrong*, pulled me into it. The tall grasses seemed to beckon and threaten, all at once. A wave of vertigo came over me, and I had to step back, touch the wall for support.

Sloan was watching me intently. "I wanted to make something unsettling," he said.

The dizziness passed. "Why did you want to do that?"

"It's how I see the natural world," he said. "Every living thing embodies its own death."

"Very wabi-sabi." I sat on the floor, my eyes still on the sketch. Even from this angle, it arrested my eyes. I braced my hands on the carpet and willed myself to turn my head and look away.

Sloan picked up the sketchbook and leafed through its pages. Then he folded the book and set it on the easel again.

This sketch seemed to have nothing in common with the other one. My first reaction, had I seen both works in a gallery, would have been that they weren't made by the same artist. The sketch was me.

The face I tried so hard to glimpse in the mirror gazed back at me, recognizable despite a lack of detail. With a few pencil strokes he had made a realistic, complex portrait. Sloan was a talented artist indeed.

I stood up and walked to the easel. My eyes, very like my mother's, gazed back at me. I had her chin, too. My nose was a blend—not as small as hers or as long as my father's. But I had his mouth. Ears like hers.

"What do you think?" Sloan crossed his arms.

"Oh, I like it. Very much." I couldn't take my eyes off myself. For the first time I knew how others saw me.

The impression the sketch gave me was of someone who was curious, sensitive, vulnerable. I decided that I liked her. "It doesn't make me uneasy at all. Why is it so different from the other one?"

"Because you're not going to die." He sat on the floor, looking up at me, and the words, translucent crimson, wafted like dust motes.

And for the first time in a long while, I felt glad I was a vampire.

"I'd like to do a real portrait of you, if you're willing to sit for it," Sloan said.

Yes, I was willing. I wanted to see more.

Eight

As October lurched toward November, we heard about our spring internship assignments. Sophomores at Hillhouse traditionally spent the first half of the spring semester working in the "real world," in locations far from both campus and home, at jobs related to their programs of study.

Since my major was interdisciplinary studies, with a concentration in communications, the internship office sent my student profile to newspapers, magazines, online publications, and similar companies. My fantasy had been to work for a newspaper in DC, covering Cameron's campaign. Even if we couldn't technically be together, I could at least be in the crowds watching him, then writing about him.

Instead, I learned, I'd be spending spring in New York, interning at NetFriend, the social networking website company. Exactly what I'd be doing there wasn't described, except that I had a start date, an address, and a job title: "intern."

I guess my disappointment showed, because Jacey tried to make me feel better. "You'll have a ball in New York," she said.

Her assignment was working at a day care center in Pittsburgh, observing how the theories she'd learned in her education classes worked in the real world. "Pittsburgh!" she said, her eyes shining. "I've always wanted to go to Pittsburgh."

Sloan would remain on campus, finishing his junior year. It would be odd not to have him around to talk to, I thought.

I wanted to call Cameron, to tell him about my assignment. But this was no emergency.

When I called Dashay, she said, "New York? Not bad. Maybe we'll come up and visit you. See a show."

"How's Bennett?" I asked.

"He's making some improvements to the stables," she said. Then she changed the subject to horses.

❧

Meanwhile, the only news I had of Cameron came from a newspaper.

Jacey and I were among a very few Hillhouse students who cared about politics.

Her subscription to the *New York Times* meant that I saw photographs of Cameron nearly every week.

"He's pretty cool," she said one morning, holding up an article headlined, CAMERON CAMPAIGN DONATIONS TOP $5 MILLION. Next to it, the photo showed him smiling, but his eyes looked tired.

"Remember when we heard him in Savannah?" Jacey said. She didn't know that I'd seen him several times since our class field trip. "I thought back then that he might be our next president, and now I'm sure of it."

I wondered if she'd be so positive if she knew he was a vampire. In any case, Cameron wouldn't even be officially nominated until his party's convention next summer. And anything could happen before that.

"It's too soon to tell," I said, but I was thinking, *Why doesn't he call me?*

❧

I began doing most of my schoolwork in Sloan's studio, sitting on the floor with my laptop, books spread around me. As I studied, he worked on my portrait. We didn't talk much. We felt comfortable sharing silence.

My third time there, I made a point of looking at the canvas as I was leaving. All it contained was a partial sketch of the wall behind my chair.

Sloan leaned against the wall, his hands in his pockets. "I begin with the not-Ari in order to see the Ari."

He sounded more cryptic than Professor Itou. But I'd heard of the concept of negative space, and so I did the polite thing: I nodded as if I completely understood. In order to see what *is,* you must consider what is not, I told myself.

Professor Itou's influence marked every one of his students. Several began to talk as he talked, in abbreviated bursts of words, and walk as he walked, eyes directed toward the floor or on the fields beyond the windows. He made us want to see beyond the real. I imagined his life as always artful.

And, during the third week of October, he taught us what it was like to be dead.

"Now we come to Butoh." Professor Itou gestured toward the classroom window. A few leaves clung to the trees outside, but the branches were mostly bare. "The dance of darkness."

As he defined it, Butoh wasn't so much a style of dance as the antithesis of style, a reaction to classical dance forms. It had developed in Japan after World War II, during a period of unrest and rebellion.

"A celebration. Grotesque. You might say. It subverts. What you think. Is dance," he said. "Pranks and chaos. They make Butoh."

I'd finally got to the point where I thought I understood wabi-sabi, but Butoh completely eluded me—until the professor played us a videotape of a performance.

A naked man, his thin body painted black as if horribly burned, moved across a field of snow. His body twisted and contorted and spasmed into positions I'd never imagined a human could assume. The stark contrast between the dancer and his environment frightened me; it spoke of decay and death, and yet managed to be beautiful, graceful, powerful. Its unnaturalness seemed natural. Finally the dancer spiraled and fell facedown into the snow. We knew he was dead.

No one said a word for a long time after the video ended. Then the professor made a raspy sound deep in his throat to get our attention. He beckoned for us to leave our seats and come to the front of the classroom. Only Sloan remained in his chair. I couldn't hear what he was thinking.

As we stood there, Professor Itou came to us, one by one, and tapped our shoulders. One by one, we began to dance.

It was a dreadful dance, a rite of recognition that we, too, were going to die. I barely saw the others. I forgot who I was as my body twisted and contracted, simulating death. No one had taught me how to do this, but somehow my body knew.

I don't know how long the dance went on. When I stopped, I felt utterly empty. Sloan wasn't in the room. The rest of us left the class without speaking.

Later that night Dashay called me. "So what are you learning, child?" she asked.

"Learning how to die," I said. It took me half an hour to explain it to her, and when she'd stopped asking questions, she said, "Well, I didn't learn anything like that in *my* liberal arts education."

"Too bad," I said.

"Uh-huh. I guess." She sounded skeptical. "Listen, Ari, your mother called me. She doesn't want to call you because I guess your voice would make her cry, but me she can talk to. She wants to know why you never answered her letters."

I hadn't received any letters, I told Dashay. Yes, I faithfully checked my mailbox. Our boxes were open receptacles mounted in rows on the walls of the dining hall basement. Mine was almost always empty.

"She sent you three of them. You think someone is stealing your mail?"

It was entirely possible, although I couldn't imagine why anyone would want my mail. "Tell Mãe not to worry," I said. "Tell her I'll write to her, and she can send me her thoughts in my dreams."

"I will do that," Dashay said. "But I won't be telling her about your dance of darkness, and I hope you won't tell her, either. That's the sort of thing to make a mother worry."

After the experience of Butoh, Halloween didn't seem at all scary. But then it never did, to me.

Many students considered it their favorite holiday—a chance to wear costumes and makeup more extreme than what they wore every day. Most came to class in disguise. Sloan and I stood out by looking comparatively normal.

When classes were over for the day, Sloan and I were heading for the artists' barn when Richard Meek swooped down from the hillside. He wore a black cape and artificial fangs, and he lunged at us. "I'm here to bite you!" he shouted.

We sidestepped him without pausing, leaving him to attack the students behind us.

"It's a shame, really," Sloan said. "People like him will never get beyond the stereotypes, will they?"

Richard had other stereotypes that bothered me more than that one. "For him," I said, "being a vampire is only a Halloween game."

Sloan stopped walking and looked around to make sure no

one else was listening. "Don't you want to show them who we are?" His skin looked unnaturally pale in the faint light, and his eyes had a strange gleam to them.

I shrugged. Of course I did, but I'd been taught not to do that.

"Well, I'd like to show them." We began to walk again. He imitated Richard: "I'm here to bite you!"

"Maybe you need a stronger tonic," I said. To my relief, he laughed. I glanced at his lips and found myself wondering, guiltily, what it might be like to kiss them. I hadn't heard from Cameron since the party in Savannah more than a month ago.

Once in Sloan's studio, I usually went to my spot on the frayed carpet and he to the easel. But we couldn't settle down that day. I fidgeted, picking up silver tubes of paint from the table and setting them down again. Viridian. Cadmium yellow. Burnt umber. Alizarin crimson. The names had a kind of poetry for me.

Sloan watched me for a while. Then I heard him say, "I'm not going to fall in love with you." His voice was so low he might have been talking to himself.

Should I have pretended not to have heard?

Instead, I said, "Why not?" I looked over at him. His face looked even paler than before as he hunched against the wall.

"My heart's broken," he said. "It can't be mended."

"Tell me how it happened." My voice had an urgency that surprised me.

Feeling weak, I sat on the floor, and he told me.

～

Sloan had grown up in the Falls Road area of Belfast—"an ugly part of the ugliest city I know," he said—a neighborhood known as a frequent location for the Troubles, the Irish phrase for the persistent outbreaks of hostility between Protestants and Catholics. His family was Catholic.

"Dad was on the dole," he said. "Ma had her hands full: five girls and two boys to mind. I was the baby of the family."

He said that from an early age he'd felt like an outsider at home and at school. "My brother is a skanger. You don't know that word? He shaves his head, wears gold chains and trainers, goes crazy over football, drinks too much, sleeps with every woman he can get. There are thousands exactly like him. But see, Ma loves that. She understands him, talks to him in ways she never could with me."

I wondered if his parents might be vampires, but I didn't interrupt.

"I'm the artist in the family." He said it with scorn. "From the time I was a wee lad, I always had a pencil and paper in my hand. For a while they thought I was gay. Then, when I fell in love with Delia, that was even worse, because she's Protestant." His eyes moved rapidly around the room, as if searching for something. Finally he said, "She's a quiet sort. Never has much to say."

How can religion obsess people so? "Couldn't you have kept her a secret?"

He laughed, a bitter sound. "We tried. We needn't have bothered. Belfast is more like a small town than a city, and everybody keeps an eye on everybody else. Try keeping secrets when you live in a house where nine people sleep in three bedrooms.

"And then, what takes the biscuit: I was bit by a vampire." His words turned that translucent crimson color. "Strange to say, it happened on Halloween, when I was fifteen. Seeing Richard in his clown suit brought it back to me just now. There aren't many vampires in the north; they congregate in the south, where people tend to be more tolerant. And besides, the Vunderworld has a strong network, based in Cork, that helps out with relocating newcomers—places to stay, where to find tonic, how to sign up for the dole, if necessary. That's not on over here?"

I couldn't say. "I know it exists," I said. "I just don't know how active it is."

"Anyway, this bloke grabs me at a bonfire. I thought he wanted to fight, and I was more than willing. The best fighters in my neighborhood were the skinny lads like me, not the burly skangers. But instead he bites me, and next thing I know I'm biting him back." Sloan spread out his hands in what I thought must have been another Mentori sign. "You know what comes next."

I remembered my own early days, after I first bit someone: the physical discomfort, the mood swings, the overpowering thirst for blood.

"After that, things got even worse at home. They sensed I'd changed, gone from oddball to some kind of freak, and they didn't like it. My dad said if I didn't shape up, they'd disown me. That was his idea of a joke. So I left."

I tried to imagine leaving my parents, never wanting to see them again. "Don't you miss your family?"

"Only one of my sisters. But once I'd crossed over, she became frightened of me. I could tell by the look in her eyes. It was something of a relief to get away." He stared at the floor, his hair hiding most of his face.

He told me he'd traveled south, to Dublin, changed his name, worked as a dishwasher in a pub. In time he became a barman, and thanks to chatty customers he learned about Hillhouse and about Septimal. "I'd won a few art competitions, and I liked the idea of a school without grades," he said. "So I wrote to them asking about scholarships, and they sent me the forms."

"What happened to Delia?"

He winced. "She stopped loving me, once I became what I am. She told me she couldn't love someone who wasn't human. She wants to have a family one day, and you know how it is for us."

How it might be. He didn't realize I was the product of a union between a vampire and a mortal, and I didn't think this was the time to tell him. But one day, I thought, I might try to have children myself.

"When I looked over the application forms, I decided I might as well take the Septimal. I thought being older would help me bear up. And it has. It's a lot easier, being twenty-two." He sighed. "Listen to me, nattering on."

"Did it hurt?"

"The Septimal? No, not really. It's like any other injection, you know. Stings a bit. And after, when it takes effect, you feel out of sorts from time to time. Growing pains, you might say."

"Did you know that when you talk about vampires, your words are the same color as"—I reached for the tube of paint on the table—"alizarin crimson?"

"I hadn't noticed. You're right." He took his hands out of his pockets and straightened his shoulders. "I want to hear your story. I want to know why it's so important for you to get older. But not tonight. At the moment, I'm keen to get on with the portrait, if that's all right with you."

I opened a textbook, but the words I read didn't register. After I thought about all Sloan had been through, I decided it was a good thing that he couldn't fall in love with me. He seemed even more complicated than I was. And besides, Cameron was still on my mind—and somewhere in my heart.

⸻

And that night, he was on my phone. When I answered it, I was walking back from dinner with Jacey. I held up a hand of apology to her and she walked on, already pulling her own phone from her jacket pocket.

The sound of his voice made me wish he was standing next to me, breathing in the dampness, watching the students in their silly costumes, and hearing eerie music coming from the theater building. I absorbed his voice as if *it* were music, barely paying attention to the words, until he said, "Ari? Are you still there?"

"I'm here."

"So that's okay with you, then?"

"What did you say?" That voice of his, it soothed me so that I heard rhythm and melody more than words.

He said a security company was running background checks on everyone associated with him: friends, employees, his advisors, and his probable running mate. And me.

"Basically everyone who's part of my life," he said.

So I *was* part of his life? The words warmed me. "What's a background check?" I asked.

"They look at public records relating to your credit history, educational background—that sort of thing. This is only a precaution. If the campaign goes ahead, the media will be scrutinizing everyone around me, looking for scandals."

I took a deep breath. "But I'm not around you. I haven't heard from you in weeks. I don't know why you'd bother to have someone examine *my* past."

Two noisy students costumed as a skeleton and a devil swept toward me, and I stepped off the path.

His next words came out in a rush. "But don't you remember the talk we had about needing to be patient? Just because we can't be together now doesn't mean we won't be, someday."

"When?"

He sighed. "When you're older."

"How much older?"

"Well, I've been thinking about that," he said. "Your records have you listed at age nineteen, right?"

"This isn't going to work," I said. "I have a fake ID saying I'm nineteen, yes. And I have a forged birth certificate I used to get a driver's license. But Hillhouse records list my real age." They'd admitted me as a prodigy, based on my test scores and admission essays.

He didn't speak for a moment. I watched two students dressed as ghosts come down the path.

"Let me think about this," he said. "Maybe there's a way those records can be altered."

I wanted to ask how, then realized I was better off not knowing. Doing such a thing sounded risky, even criminal, to me. "Okay, say that happens," I said. "What's the magic age that lets us be together?"

"Twenty-one, twenty-two. Somewhere in that range. That's what my aides say. So we'd only have to wait two or three years."

Two years sounded like an eternity. "Why do we have to wait? Can't we at least spend a weekend together?"

There, I'd done it. As my mother said, sometimes a woman has to take the initiative.

"You know I'd love to spend a weekend with you." His voice was softer and lower now. "But we can't risk it. So much is at stake. And the timing isn't right. When it is, we'll be together."

I tried to see it as he did: we could be together for a *real* eternity. But when I tried to imagine life with Cameron, I couldn't see beyond the present: the distance, the "age problem," the need to keep everything secret.

"I know it's hard," he said, his voice nearly a whisper. "I've been waiting for you for centuries."

The two ghosts came closer. They seemed to shimmer and float through the air. Their forms looked vaguely human, not like sheets with eyeholes cut out. Good costumes, I decided.

Then, as they neared me, what had been two distinct forms moving along the path dissolved into nothingness. It was as if the damp October night had consumed them, absorbed their essences, spirited them away.

"Ari? Are you there?"

I shivered.

Nine

Every few years, someone commissions a poll to find out how many Americans believe in ghosts. The results vary widely, typically from roughly 30 to 50 percent.

How many vampires believe in ghosts? Virtually all of us, although some prefer not to say so. It may be easier for us to see them, since our vision is keener than that of mortals.

Cameron told me that night to be careful. "You can never be sure why a spirit appears, but there's usually a reason," he said. "They don't often make random visits."

We said good night. I saw no more ghosts as I walked back to the dorm. Back in our room, I wanted to tell Jacey about what I'd seen, but I knew it would frighten her as much as thrill her. So I kept my spirits to myself. Next time I saw Dashay, I'd ask her what they might mean.

⁂

The following night, someone set a fire in the registrar's office. All the application and admission records were destroyed. Someone also hacked into the computer system and deleted all of the student files.

This was the biggest sensation on campus since Autumn's murder the spring before. Students were summoned to an assembly with the faculty and administrators. Anyone who had information about the thefts was urged to come forward, but no one did.

I sat near the back of the auditorium, too shocked to feel much, wondering what Cameron might have done. I didn't have any real information. All I had was a strong hunch.

～

The next day students had to fill out a new set of Hillhouse forms. I listed my age as twenty-two. I told myself that this was simply one more of the necessary lies vampires tell in order to live among mortals. Then I tried to put the age issue out of my mind. My first poem for our creative writing class was due in two days, and I hadn't begun writing it yet.

Earlier I'd submitted a short story about learning to drive—a subject that seemed safe enough, given Professor Warner's many prohibitions. I'd told it from the point of view of a teenage girl taught by two women who gave her conflicting instructions and advice. It was loosely based on my own driving lessons. Of course, I changed the characters in the story and made sure the girl wasn't anything like me.

Professor Warner had said the story was a strong one. Her only suggestion was that I might consider telling the story from a different viewpoint. "Let one of the older characters tell the story," she said. "I think it will gain much more dramatic depth that way."

Her comments made me nervous about attempting a poem.

My father had taught me Shakespeare's sonnets, Keats's and Wordsworth's odes, and a range of more modern poems. Thinking of them intimidated me further.

Jacey had already turned in her poem, one of the best ones

so far, about a child afraid of the dark. "Write about something simple," she said. "Something you know a lot about. Start with an image."

I ended up writing about the Victorian oval shadow box that had hung on a wall in our house in Saratoga Springs. What became of it when the house was sold, I didn't know. Under its convex glass cover lay an arrangement of wheat sheaves, a monarch butterfly, and three brown wrens. When I was a child, I'd imagined the birds were my parents and me, trapped and longing to free ourselves to fly away.

The poem I wrote was from the viewpoint of an observer noticing the shadow box and describing its contents. I was careful not to write anything objectionable or biased; I wanted readers to see the box without the poem dictating an emotional response. I don't think it was a particularly good poem; in any case, I threw it away when the semester ended, and I'm not going to try to re-create it here.

In Professor Warner's workshops the author wasn't allowed to speak on the day her writing was reviewed. Each of the other students was called upon to make a comment, and then the professor would weigh in.

My poem received comments like: "Shadow boxes sound cute!" "I think my grandma had one of those." "Why would someone want to frame dead things?" (The last one came from Richard.)

"Think positively!" Professor Warner said.

When it was Sloan's turn, he said, "The images aren't enough to convey the claustrophobia. Something's missing. You might try writing it from the viewpoints of the birds."

After the writing class ended, it was the custom for most of us to walk into the small town near campus. At a distressed-

III — *The Season of Risks*

looking bowling alley called Leo's Bowl, we'd drink beer and
eat greasy French fries and talk. A few of us might even
bowl.

No one ever checked our IDs at Leo's. Its owner, whose
name wasn't Leo, had some sort of arrangement with the local
police. They never bothered him or us. I think that if we'd
been driving instead of walking, things might have been different.

As we walked into the alley, I was still smarting from some
of the more sharp-edged comments about my poem, most of
them made by Richard. Even though I told myself that the
criticisms were directed at the poem, not at me, I felt as if
I'd been personally attacked. Many artists feel this way, I've
found out since, but with vampires the hurt cuts deeper, just
as praise lifts us higher.

My cell phone rang before I had a chance to sit down. I
turned and walked back outside again. Another unfamiliar
number.

It was Cameron calling. He used a different phone every
time, and by the time the call ended I knew why.

He didn't even say hello. "Ari, you've got an FBI record.
Why didn't you tell me?"

"I didn't know—"

"You didn't know they kept records?"

I cringed at the tone of his voice—not loud, but brusque
and dismayed. It made me wish I could disappear—but I
wasn't wearing the suit. I leaned against the wall of the building, making myself small.

"You must remember agents interrogating you after your
friends died." His voice sounded furious. I hadn't met this
particular Cameron before.

"Yes, they did."

"Why didn't you tell me?"

I took a deep breath. "I should have told you about that, but—"

"You knew how high the stakes are."

"I didn't. I didn't tell you because I was afraid you'd—"

"Afraid I'd what?"

I looked up at the live oak tree at the edge of the parking lot. From one of its branches, a mockingbird stared down at me. I couldn't think of the right words. *Stop caring? Abandon me? Banish me?*

"I don't know," I said. "I can't think."

"Are you too young to understand how serious this could be? You wouldn't believe the trouble my staff is going to, trying to protect you."

Wouldn't. Too young. Words I didn't like then and hate now. I ran one hand across the bricks of the building's wall, feeling their rough edges scrape my knuckles.

"Your staff needn't bother," I said. "I'll give you up."

"Oh, Ari." His voice sounded less angry now. "I shouldn't have spoken to you that way. But—"

I cut him off. "You said it yourself: the timing is all wrong."

I broke the connection and turned off the phone. Then I walked back into the bowling alley.

My friends sat on plastic benches bordering a table holding two pitchers of beer and a bowl of corn chips. Jacey looked up as I came in. She nudged the person next to her, who happened to be Richard.

He stared at me, looked from my face to my hands. His cheeks flushed. Coughing, he stood up, beckoned for me to take his seat. Then he leaned over to whisper in my ear. "I feel bad. I didn't think what I said would upset you so much."

Jacey said, "What happened to your hand?"

Apparently it was bleeding. Now it began to hurt. I let them fetch antiseptic and a bandage, pour me a glass of beer, and say soothing things, but inside I felt as if my lungs were collapsing.

What have I done? I thought. *What should I have done?*

From the end of the table, Sloan kept his dark eyes on mine. He knew I wasn't reacting to criticism of my poem. He knew how to recognize heartbreak.

～

November was never my favorite month. It has a mottled brown cast, like the color of petrified wood.

At Hillhouse, classes ended the first week of December. Final papers and studying for exams made days become nights become days again. We drank coffee and energy drinks that tasted like fluids designed to make machines run more efficiently.

Sloan stopped working on my portrait in order to write stories, essays, and a research paper. He didn't take any science or math classes, so he faced no exams. Once his papers were done, he and his sketchbook could be seen around campus, making quick studies. We were either too busy or too exhausted to continue the portrait.

One afternoon I took time out to write my parents a letter—a fine piece of fiction, better than anything I wrote for creative writing class—meant to assure them that all was well with me. The Ari I created for them was a busy, happy student, breezing through her semester. The only true line in it was this: "I am learning a great deal."

When I walked back into the dorm after mailing the letter, I saw Jacey with Richard, sitting in the lounge. They stopped talking when I came in, and I knew they'd been discussing me. Jacey was thinking, *No matter what anybody says about her, Ari is my friend.*

I didn't even say hello. I walked past them and went

straight to our room. It wasn't locked, and when I threw open the door, the room wasn't empty. Someone was trying on my clothes.

She wore the Peruvian dress—or rather, the dress was worn by someone, female in form, made out of smoke. Her skin was translucent, as was her hair, and though she kept her face averted she looked familiar.

And then I saw a second form, sitting on my bed, watching.

In seconds they were gone. Not a trace of smoke lingered. The dress fell to the floor. I picked it up, shook it hard, sniffed it. The fabric smelled faintly bitter, like mold or dead leaves.

Ten

D ashay drove up on Thanksgiving weekend. Seeing her step out of the familiar battered truck, wearing a pumpkin-colored jacket and a cranberry-colored scarf, made my heart ache—with happiness that she was here and with sadness that she soon would be leaving again.

I flung myself into her arms.

"You want to knock me over?" she said, but her hands stroked my face gently. She shook her head. "My, my. Don't you ever have any fun? What happened to the Ari I saw last summer?"

"Too much happened to her," I said. "Or maybe not enough."

Her eyes were full of concern. She sent me the thought: *I want to hear it all. But first we eat.*

Dashay had brought two large wicker hampers filled with food, plates, and glasses. We set up a feast in the lounge. Jacey came, and Sloan.

We ate roasted oysters, stuffed squash, mashed potatoes with vegan gravy, green beans, pureed cranberries, and biscuits. Dashay had brought Scotch bonnet sauce made from her secret recipe. I knew it included peppers and vinegar, but I could never quite figure out the other ingredients. The sauce wasn't as fiery as the hot sauce I'd first tasted in Georgia, when

I'd been introduced to oysters. No, Dashay's Scotch Bonnet made a first impression of being mellow, fruity. Then it spread across your tongue, waking up each taste bud. It began to warm and sustain you—your mouth, your throat, your stomach. Its heat made every part of you feel alive.

"What's in this stuff?" After one taste, Sloan poured it on everything, including the cranberries. He ate as if he'd been starved.

"Secrets," Dashay said, watching him drain the bottle. "I have more, if you want it."

"Would a duck swim?" Sloan said.

Finally came pecan and pumpkin and sweet potato pies, whose tops featured whimsical crust forms: pumpkins and nuts and squirrels. I wondered if Bennett had helped make the crusts.

Between mouthfuls, Dashay made light conversation with everyone, but she sent me a look that meant the real talking with me would take place later on.

After we'd finished the meal and cleared the table, the others said they'd wash the dishes. Sloan said, "Thanks for the lovely grub."

Dashay smiled at him, as if those were exactly the right words.

～

The air outside felt cool and crisp. Dashay and I had decided to hike through the woods that bordered the campus's western boundary. As we walked, she said, "I like that boy Sloan. What a nice young man. And nice that you're not the only *other* at Hillhouse."

I buttoned my sweater. "I like him, too."

She glanced at me. "So he's not the *one,* then."

I didn't have to ask what she meant. "No, he's not the *one.*"

I tried to keep my thoughts on the pine trees around us, on the differences between manmade forests and natural ones. *Think trees,* I told myself.

"It has to be *that* one, then. The politician man, yes?" Her words spun out, green and pink in the afternoon air.

I gave up. "How did you know?"

Dashay smiled. "How could I not know? Every time his name came up in conversation or he was on the television, your face was such a sight." She made her eyes huge and moony, her mouth pursed as if to kiss.

"I never looked like that."

"You did!" She made the moony face again, and I laughed.

She laughed, too. "Welcome back," she said. "So now. What did that man do to you?"

We came out of the forest, into a clearing bordered by two river birch trees. Some of their leaves had turned yellow, but most remained stubbornly green. We sat on a stone wall, our sweaters a buffer, and I told Dashay the story of the relationship that ended before it had barely begun. As I talked, I basked in the sympathy of her eyes. They made me think of liquid amber.

"Most of our problems came about because of my age," I said. My fingers trailed across the edges of the stones, feeling their cold irregularities. "What if I were older?"

Her eyes turned wary. "What are you talking about?"

"Sloan told me about a drug called Septimal. Do you know about it?"

She pulled her scarf tight to her neck and looked away, as if she, too, had suddenly realized that the trees were fascinating.

"Sloan took Septimal, and it made him seven years older." I rubbed my hands against my jeans, to warm them. "He says it's no big deal."

She turned toward me, her jaw clenched. "So now you want to be twenty?"

I shook my head. "Twenty-two. Same age as Cameron was when he crossed over. Same age as Sloan. I'm fed up with being younger. Can't you understand?"

"Yes, yes. I can understand that." Her mouth turned into a wry grin. "Once upon a time, I did that same thing myself."

Dashay had come to the United States from Jamaica after her parents and fiancé died in a car accident. She'd been made a vampire in Miami, hours after she got off the plane from Montego Bay. I'd already heard that part of the story.

But the next part took my breath away.

"I was eighteen, only eighteen," she said. "Brought up the way I was, more like twelve in American years. I didn't know much. And once I was vamped, I didn't know how to get by, from day to day. You understand? I scared myself. I had a plan to stay with cousins in Florida, but I would not let them see me that way—the mood swings, the always hungry, the hunting for blood. You know how it is at first."

I knew.

"So, I found me a vampire doctor. There are many, many doctors in Miami; it wasn't hard. I asked him how was I going to *live*. Was there some medicine I could take to stop me, stop the hunting and biting?

"He told me about the blood substitutes. And about a drug that would make me older. Wiser, too. So, I said yes. I wanted the tonic and the Septimal injection. I had savings to pay for them."

"Then how old are you?" I'd never known her age.

She tilted her head, as if to say it wasn't important. "The Septimal, it did make changes in the way I think, in the way

I decide about things. The way we think at twenty-five years is very different, you know, from the way we think at eighteen.

"Ari, you know the treatment is not reversible? I mean to say, I had good reasons to skip ahead seven years. But you, you have your vamp act pretty much together. What would you gain by this? Only that man?"

"It's not only about him." I'd spent considerable time and thought on these questions. "I don't want to go through life always being thirteen. Thirteen is naïve. Thirteen is passive, doing what you're told. Think about it. Would you want to be a juvenile again?"

Dashay shook her head.

"Say you'll help me find a doctor."

The sun, a wan yellow ball, sank behind the tops of the birch trees, and our stone seat seemed to instantly grow colder. Dashay stood up and stretched.

"No, that I will not do," she said. "I don't know any doctors in Miami these days, and besides, I don't want any part in this business. Why don't you ask Dr. Cho?"

I'd considered that already. "I don't want her to know. She'd contact my parents, I'm sure of it. And I think they like keeping me a child." I thought, *I could call Malcolm.* Then I shuddered. There had to be some other way.

She wrapped her sweater around her. "I don't know what to say to you." Her voice sounded forlorn.

I had no more to say, either. I felt she'd failed me somehow.

As we walked past the river birch trees, a sudden wind hit them. Yellow leaves swirled in the air and fell to the ground. If I climbed a tree, might I be able to decipher their pattern, read them like tea leaves?

We walked back to the dormitory, chilled.

⚮

Jacey lay on the beat-up futon in our dorm room, reading the Sunday paper.

I'd said good-bye to Dashay, feeling guilty and disrespectful. She made all that good food and brought it to us, and now, instead of feeling appreciated, she would make the long drive home with my questions her only company. I had stood in the road watching the truck drive away, wanting to shout after her to stop, come back, let me find words that would bring us close again. But I did nothing. The truck disappeared, and I shivered in the cold. I realized that I'd never even told her about the ghosts.

"Check it out." Jacey handed me the magazine section of the newspaper. On its cover, so handsome that it hurt to see him, was Neil Cameron, under a caption: Our Next President?

I didn't say anything, but Jacey wasn't stupid. "Oh, Ari," she said. "You *love* him?"

I tried to think of the best lie, but what was the point? I said nothing.

"Those times when the phone rings, and you walk away— is that him?"

I stared at the wall.

"Wow," she said. "Okay. You don't have to answer me. Your face always gets the same look when he calls."

Stupid thirteen-year-old face, I thought. And then an image came to me: a moat, so deep that no one dared cross it. I would have to dig and fill that moat and keep it around me, for protection, so long as I was thirteen masquerading as nineteen.

"Does he love you, too?"

I had to make her stop. "Jacey, whatever there might have been between us is over. And it wasn't much. A kind of flirtation, I guess." I hated these words. "Please promise you won't tell anyone."

"Don't worry," she said, her voice solemn. "You can trust me, Ari. I won't tell a soul."

I sat down on my bed.

"But you're so lucky." She leaned forward, her face pink with excitement. "Cool men keep falling for you. First Sloan, and now our next president? Ari, that's pretty amazing."

I rubbed my forehead, wishing I were somewhere else. "Sloan hasn't fallen for me," I said. "We're just friends."

"Yeah, sure." Jacey wasn't going to stop talking, I realized. "He gets the same kind of dreamy look when you're around. You haven't noticed that?"

I said I hadn't. Then I said I really needed to study.

Later, while she was in the bathroom getting ready for bed, I began to read the magazine article. Its subheading was THE CAMERON NOBODY KNOWS.

"Watch him run," the article began. "Every morning, rain or shine, Neil Cameron hits the trail. He does five miles, whether in his posh neighborhood on St. Simons Island, Georgia, or in any city on his campaign route. Even on the hottest day, he never seems to break a sweat."

Big deal, I thought. *Vampires don't sweat.*

"Neil Cameron is in the public eye every day of his life," the article continued, "but the thirty-one-year-old senator from Georgia has a private life that he intends to keep very private indeed."

Jacey came in, saw me reading the article, and shook her head. I kept reading. I skimmed through the summary of his political views—very green, very global—in search of the personal stuff. Besides running, his hobbies were sailing and collecting antique maritime equipment. I thought of the brass lamp on *Dulcibella.*

Then the phrase *eligible bachelor* caught my eye.

"Although he's never married, Cameron says he's recently

been in love, but wouldn't comment on the person in question. 'Campaigning for president and having a personal life don't seem compatible for me,' he said."

"Stop reading," Jacey said. "You're going to make yourself depressed. And you should be happy. At least you've had boyfriends."

"Haven't you?"

"Only one."

"Somebody I know?"

Her face turned red. "I don't want to talk about it."

"You sound exactly like *him*." I couldn't say the name *Cameron*. Nonetheless, I returned to reading the article.

"'Of course, someday I want a wife and a family, when the time is right,' Cameron said." *When the time is right.* That's when I made the final decision: no matter what else happened that year, I *was* going to grow older.

The article ended with a list of questions and Cameron's responses. One was "Who are your favorite real-life heroes?" Cameron answered, "Women and men of genius leading ordinary lives."

But the one that stood out for me was the banal question: "What's your favorite color?" Cameron said, "Grey, with an *E*. Not g-r-a-y, which, as a dear friend once taught me, is a different color entirely."

I handed the magazine back to Jacey, who set it on her desk. "Okay," she said. "If you must know, it was Richard."

"Richard!" I couldn't imagine them as a couple. As long as I'd known him, Richard's girlfriend had been a tiny blond girl called Bunny. She never said much but followed him around, laughing at even his lamest jokes.

"He wasn't so bad, his first semester here." Jacey carefully spread her hair over her pillow and switched off her bedside lamp. "He liked to take me to movies." Her voice sounded sad.

"What happened?"

"Oh, he met Bunny. She's cuter than I am, and richer, too. Her dad's some kind of judge. And that was when Richard began to get all political. She went right along with it. I got left behind."

I switched off my lamp and remembered something Dashay once said: *love is misery*. I wanted to say something to comfort her, but comfort was in short supply that night. "I'm sorry," was all I could manage.

Then I said, "Good night." *Sweet dreams* would have been too much of a stretch.

~

I spent the next afternoon in the library, researching how the human body ages.

The books I consulted agreed: mortals may mature at different paces, but there are distinctive phases.

A human stops growing and is physically mature by age eighteen, and after that, the human brain may lose more than a thousand cells each day. Since the brain has more than a hundred billion cells, the loss isn't considered significant. Cognitive abilities continue to grow.

Beginning at twenty, skin begins to thin. Wrinkles and gray hairs may appear, and hands and neck lose firmness.

By age thirty, the body's major organs begin to decline.

This was the point where I wanted to stop reading, but I pressed on. Muscle strength, vision, hearing, and bone density may diminish beginning at age forty. After sixty-five, chronic conditions such as cancer, heart disease, arthritis, and osteoporosis often set in.

The life expectancy of the average human is seventy-seven and six-tenths years. *Such a short time.*

I closed the books. Would any of those awful things happen to the human elements in me? Malcolm's research might hold the answers, I thought. But did I really want to know?

Maybe as Septimal worked to advance age, it also maintained it, fixed it in time? None of the library books could answer that question.

But if I could fix my age, twenty-two sounded about right.

～✦

The last week of our Japanese Culture class focused on folktales. Professor Itou read one aloud to us. Its title was "The Woman of the Snow."

We sat, slumped in our chairs, drained as if we'd been dancing Butoh. We wanted nothing more than for the semester to end so that we could go home and revive, recharge ourselves.

But as the professor read, I became uncomfortably alert. The tale concerned two woodcutters, one old, one young, lost in a snowstorm on their way home from work. They take refuge in a hut and fall asleep. When the young man awakens, he sees a beautiful woman dressed in white bent over his companion, breathing on him. Her breath is like white smoke, and it turns the old man to ice.

Then she turns to the young man, bends toward him. He is overwhelmed by her beauty and terrified of her powers. After staring into his eyes, she smiles. She says, "I had planned to treat you as I did the other man. For you I feel pity, because you are so young."

But she warns him that if he reveals her existence to anyone, she'll come back to kill him.

I steeled myself for the story's resolution. Yes, the young man did go on to meet and marry a beautiful woman, but this time they had ten children, not two. Yes, one night he remembered the woman of the snow, and he told his wife the story. And yes, she immediately manifested herself as the snow woman, in all her terrible beauty.

But unlike Cameron's vampire tale, in this one she did not kill him. Instead, she spared his life, this time on condition that he be a good father. If ever he wasn't, she said, she'd come back and he would die. Then the woman, O-Yuki was her name, disappeared in a cloud of snow and ice, never to return.

Once again, the professor had managed to cast a spell over the class. We sat in our seats as if frozen there. Later, when we'd thawed, I began to wonder why Cameron's story had such a different ending.

᪲

Every culture has its monsters, and every ocean and lake of any size in the world is supposedly inhabited by at least one.

That doesn't surprise me. Gazing at a body of moving water, our eyes can play tricks on us, and our imaginations are ready to do the rest. This is not meant to discredit cryptozoology, the study of unseen or hidden animals, in any way; for all I know, lake monsters may be real. Their existence simply hasn't been proven.

But other recurring monsters are harder to explain. Some consider Eve in the Bible a femme fatale, like O-Yuki. Egypt's Cleopatra and Greece's Aphrodite and Helen of Troy are other women who drive men to the point of making irrational, even fatal, decisions. What causes so many different cultures to demonize charming women?

Karl Jung believed that in creating monsters, we're simply projecting shadows, our own inhuman qualities. Do femmes fatales simply personify our own shadows? Do ghosts?

I wrote about these questions in my final Japanese Culture paper, and my head was still spinning with ideas after I finished it. I wanted to write about shadows in my final Creative Writing portfolio, too, but ghosts and monsters were taboo topics in Professor Warner's class. Instead I wrote about a girl who was homeschooled until she ran away, then found out she didn't know how to survive in the world.

⚘

The dining hall called our last meal on campus a pre-holiday feast, featuring all manner of faux meats and real vegetables. Sloan piled his plate high. Jacey called it the last good meal she'd have until January. She would return home to her parents' house in Tennessee for the holidays, then head for her internship in Pittsburgh.

"This is our last supper together until March," she said. "Poor Sloan will be here without his sophomore buddies.

"How are you spending the break, Sloan?" she asked him.

He pretended he hadn't heard the question. After she'd repeated it, I realized that he didn't know the answer.

"Probably going to Savannah at first," he said. "To a hostel there that I think I can afford."

It sounded too bleak to be real, spending Christmas alone in a hostel. Jacey and I looked at each other. She was thinking, *My parents would hate him, and he'd hate them.*

I said, "That's a terrible idea. Why don't you come home with me?"

His face looked so uncertain—his dark eyes startled, then hopeful, then afraid. He was blocking his thoughts.

"Come on," I said. "You met Dashay. She'll be cool with it."

Dashay was more than cool with it. I phoned her after dinner, and she insisted on inviting him herself. When he handed the phone back to me, he said, "That's grand, then." I think it was a version of *thank you.*

⚘

Jacey and I promised to e-mail, and try to visit each other, once we'd settled in our new cities. She would rent a room in Pittsburgh, in a house owned by the day care center's director, while I'd sublet an apartment in New York. She said she'd miss me, and I realized how much I'd miss her, too. It seemed I was always saying good-bye that year.

In the car, driving to Florida, I kept quiet for the first half hour or so, wondering what the next year might hold. Sloan wrote in a battered journal, pausing to stare out the window from time to time. I couldn't tell what he was thinking.

For some reason, being around him wasn't as comfortable as it had been only a few months ago. I kept noticing him: his breathing, his posture, his hands.

When he finally shut the notebook, I said, "Is that your diary?"

"It's a dream journal," he said. "Every night my dreams are full of images. I write them down, and sometimes I try to sketch them. Last night I dreamed about Jacey. But in the dream, her hair was bleeding."

I glanced at him. He didn't seem disturbed.

"That's a horrible image," I said.

"Is it? I don't think dreams are prophetic, if that's what's bothering you."

"I don't want anything to happen to Jacey. Two of my friends already died." I hadn't planned to say it, but there it was.

He didn't act surprised. "Death is part of life."

"They were murdered. I'd hate it if anything happened to Jacey."

"I don't think bleeding hair has anything to do with death," he said. "To me it symbolizes a kind of rebirth."

"Dream interpretation isn't one of my strong suits," I said.

I repeated what my father had told me: dreams inevitably center on birth, death, and/or anxiety. And when I asked him about love dreams, he'd said, "Birth, death, anxiety. Love can be any combination of the three."

Sloan said, "That about covers it. I'd like to meet your father. Will he be with us for Christmas?"

I explained that my parents were in Ireland, and I began to tell him about them but stopped when I sensed his unease. He didn't want to think about Ireland. For him it meant family, and Delia, the girl he'd loved.

So I changed the subject. I told him about Blue Heaven, about the horses and the gardens. He listened politely.

Finally I said what was really on my mind. "I want to be older. Can you help me figure out how to do it?"

"Maybe." I felt his eyes on me. "Why don't you tell me why it matters so much?"

Keeping my eyes on the road, I told him about a few of the disappointments and humiliations I'd known since I met Neil Cameron. I hadn't mentioned him before.

Sloan didn't say a word until I'd finished. "Is this bloke really worth that much to you?" His voice carried no emotion. "This politician? Never mind. I can see that he is."

"He's more than *this politician*," I said. "Besides, I'm not doing it for him. I'm doing it for me."

Sloan gazed out the window. Finally he said he'd e-mail his doctor in Dublin and ask for names of American doctors familiar with Septimal.

I felt relieved. I wouldn't have to turn to Malcolm, after all.

Sloan said, as he had before, that the procedure wasn't painful or all that complicated. And that afterward, the biggest change he'd noticed was that his brain seemed to process experiences differently.

"You don't have the giddy energy that a teenager has," he said. "Which frankly I found distracting. You're a bit more calm, not so ready to fight."

Well, that's how it might be for boys. I'd never felt much urge to fight anyone.

"And you seem to make better decisions, to look at the long-range effects of things instead of going after immediate gratification." As he spoke the last words, he gazed out the window. We were crossing the border into Florida. A sign welcomed us to the Sunshine State. "Is all of Florida like this?"

He waved his hand at the souvenir shop we were passing. An aluminum hut had been painted flamingo pink, and giant signs outside it read FRESH OJ. LIVE GATORS. GATOR JERKY! BOILED P-NUTS HERE! MOON PIES!!

I grinned. I looked forward to introducing him to the more subtle pleasures of Homosassa Springs.

～

Last December Dashay had volunteered to find us a Yule tree. She came home with something called a cryptomeria, a live cedar with foliage like feathers growing in spirals, nothing like a traditional Christmas tree. The cryptomeria now loomed over her garden of gloom.

This year's tree looked about as strange: six feet tall with sparse, twisted branches, scaly triangular spikes, and a few brown seedpods the size and shape of cucumbers. *Does she deliberately choose the ugliest trees?*

Dashay heard that thought. "This, my friends, is a monkey puzzle tree," she said. "A fine specimen of an evergreen. Yule trees *are* traditionally evergreen." She flung out her hands, as if to say, *Case closed.* Then she said, "It is not *ugly.*"

Sloan loved the monkey puzzle. It looked like something he might have drawn, a perversion of an actual tree.

He and Bennett—a sturdier-looking Bennett, though still not as muscular as he'd once been—sprawled in armchairs in the living room, glasses of Picardo in their hands, clearly enjoying watching Dashay and me face off.

"Yule trees are supposed to be decorated." I wasn't giving up yet. "How can you decorate a thing like this?" I touched one of its branches gingerly. "It hurts!"

Dashay handed me a box holding strings of lights and ornaments. "Wear gloves," she said.

Sloan slid off his chair and began to untangle the lights. I unwrapped the newspapers protecting ornaments shaped like pinecones and nuts. Bennett went to the kitchen and came back with a box of rubber gloves. I put them on, but Sloan didn't.

And Dashay went to the phonograph and put on a raspy record featuring sleigh bells—something by Prokofiev, she said.

No carols or sentimental Christmas stuff for us. But I liked our traditions better, monkey puzzle and all.

Twice, as Sloan and I trimmed the tree, our fingers accidentally touched. I felt glad I was wearing gloves. My feelings were as tangled as the lights had been.

And they stayed that way throughout a week of horseback riding and boating and pitching in on the farm. Around the middle of the week, I logged in to the Hillhouse web page and read my professors' evaluative reports. They all sounded positive, except for my mixed evaluation for Creative Writing.

"She is a capable writer whose work needs to go deeper," Professor Warner wrote. "Clearly she has some growing to do."

Sloan checked his next—again, all positive except for the one from Professor Warner. "His work is strangely facile," she'd written.

He fell onto the carpet, laughing.

Sloan seemed enchanted by Blue Heaven. As usual, he didn't say much, but his attitude, his face, and even his posture grew more relaxed, less wary. He'd never ridden a horse before, but he took to it so naturally that both Dashay and Bennett seemed impressed.

Dashay and Bennett—they weren't back together as a romantic couple, as far as I could tell. Instead they'd formed a partnership based on hard work and good food, and maybe, I thought, those things were as good as love. *Maybe.*

At the end of the week, we celebrated the winter solstice with a special dinner, and afterward we burned a Yule log in the fireplace, even though we weren't a bit cold.

Dashay stared into the flames, her eyes opaque. She shook her head, as if clearing her thoughts, and returned my gaze. "I think it's time to open presents," she said.

Dashay had suggested that we exchange only handmade gifts this year. I'd thought that idea stemmed from Bennett, and Sloan's lack of money, but later I realized that Dashay and Blue Heaven also were operating under tighter fiscal constraints. The economy in general was suffering, and few had the kind of wealth that my father enjoyed and I'd taken for granted. Mãe had refused to let him put money into Blue Heaven, wanting the farm and horse business to be self-sufficient, and so far it was, but rebuilding after the hurricane had been expensive.

Ironically, I was the one who had money from my allowance to spend on holiday presents but no talent to make anything worth giving.

Dashay gave everyone a jar of honey, and candles made from honeycomb harvested from Blue Heaven hives. Bennett had whittled whimsical small animals out of dead branches from the basswood trees in our yard; mine was a tiny kingfisher. "My favorite bird," I said.

"I knew that." He grinned.

I'd worried that Sloan wouldn't be able to give presents, but he surprised me. Working late at night, he'd been making sketches of each of us, and the simple drawings managed to capture our essential natures: Dashay's communicated pride, Bennett's hope, and mine . . .

"I look wistful," I said. "Is that how you see me?"

"This week, yes."

"You have a good eye," Bennett said.

"You've got real talent." Dashay couldn't take her eyes off the sketches.

Sloan looked at the floor, trying to hide his pleasure at their praise.

My parents had sent a box to all of us, filled with Irish books and foods—soda bread, chocolates, oatmeal—but what I liked best was a thick envelope addressed to me in my mother's handwriting. I set it aside to read later.

I set down the sketch to pass around my gifts: small loaves of honey cake, made from one of my mother's recipes, wrapped in napkins made of vintage cotton whose hems I'd stitched clumsily by hand. A small stalk of edible lavender flowers was embedded in the top crust of each loaf.

"It's not much," I said.

Bennett and Sloan were already eating theirs.

Dashay lifted the cake and sniffed it as if it were a worthy wine. "You used the lavender honey," she said. "Very nice."

❧

Alone in my room I opened Mãe's letter.

Mãe's handwriting raced across the page, each letter slanted right as if ready to take off. She said she'd been busy gardening and tending the beehives on the new property in Kerry. She listed all the plants in the garden and described their temperaments as if they were people. She'd also supervised painting and redecorating the house, while my father worked in his new lab.

"Raphael has buried himself in work, as usual," she wrote. "He's part of the Vampire Genome Project—have you heard about that? They're trying to identify all the vampire genes. He says the results may help prevent or cure some human diseases, and might even help make vampires more resistant to fire."

It sounded similar to, but on a larger scale than, the project Malcolm had described. I wondered if they knew how similar. I was sure they'd never collaborate—my father wouldn't even consider it.

The letter finished: "We can't wait to show you our corner of Ireland. We'll have our own solstice celebration once you're here."

We can't wait. But they would wait. I would wait.

I folded the letter, kissed it, and put it on my dresser next to my kingfisher amulet and the charcoal sketch of a sad-eyed, vulnerable me.

Late that night Sloan sent me another present. When I checked e-mail on my laptop, I found a message he'd forwarded from his Irish doctor. "U.S. Septimal specialist: Dr. Godfried Roche, Miami, Florida." I whispered the name to myself over and over as I went to sleep.

Maybe an hour later, I awoke. Someone was tapping on my bedroom door.

I opened it grudgingly. Sloan said, "Quick, come on. You've got to see this!"

"See what?" His hair needed combing, I thought.

"Ari," he said, "you've got ghosts!"

Eleven

Yawning, I put on a robe and followed Sloan outside, into the moon garden. The flowers bobbed, their petals snowy against foliage so dark it looked black.

No ghosts.

"They were *here*." He looked so disappointed, and so sweet in a borrowed red flannel bathrobe, that I forgave him for waking me up.

"Haven't you ever seen ghosts before?"

He shook his head. "And there were two of them. Girls, looked like. Playing some kind of game, I think. I asked them who they were, but they wouldn't speak to me."

"You be careful what you say to a ghost." Dashay stood behind us, ghostly herself in a silver caftan. "They might take it the wrong way, and then no telling what kind of harm they bring."

"How can they hurt *us*?" Sloan clearly didn't like the idea that ghosts could overpower vampires.

"Think about it." Dashay crossed her arms. "How can *we* harm *them*? They are *dead*."

I thought, *So are we, technically.*

Sloan's eyes bore down on me. "No, we're not dead. We're the undead, remember?"

I had an urge to untangle his hair with my fingers.

Dashay sighed. "Undead children better come inside. Go back to bed. We can talk about ghosts and such in the morning."

꙳

They sat at the breakfast table. Dashay and Bennett seemed determined to educate Sloan in ghost etiquette. If you speak to a ghost, they said, choose your words *very carefully.*

Bennett added, "Or they may come back to haunt you."

Bennett made a joke? I thought.

Dashay grinned. Sloan looked confused, and Dashay began to explain it to him.

I went back to my room to make a phone call.

We'd slept late, and it was nearly ten when I dialed the number in Miami. A recorded voice said, "You have reached the office of Dr. Godfried Roche, winner of the Xavier Prize for Innovation in Medical Research. Currently we are scheduling appointments for March. Please leave your name and number."

March? I couldn't wait that long. "My name is Ariella Montero," I said. "I need to talk to the doctor. But I'm leaving Florida in a week, and I really need to see him before I go. I'll take any available appointment." I left my telephone number, repeated my name, and said, "Please," instead of good-bye.

After that, the week went quickly. Bennett taught Sloan how to fish, so we had fresh grouper on the barbecue for dinner three nights in a row. I cleaned out my closet, producing four large bags of clothing to donate to the thrift store run by the local no-kill animal shelter. But all the while, I was in a haze of anticipation.

Dashay came in one afternoon while I was sorting through a pile of shirts.

"Why are you giving that one away?" she said as I threw a blue T-shirt into the fourth bag. "It looked nice on you."

I'd decided the shirt was babyish, the kind of thing a twelve-year-old might wear. "It's time to put away childish things," I said.

"Oh my." Dashay shook her head and went away.

Good thing she did, because my cell phone rang seconds later. The same cold, sharp voice I'd heard on Dr. Roche's answering machine informed me that a rare cancellation had occurred. Could I see the doctor at noon on January third?

Only four days away. Excited, nervous, elated, scared, I assured the voice that yes, I would be there on the third.

✦

New Year's Eve came quietly in Homosassa Springs. We watched a fireworks show over the Gulf and came home to eat a stew made with black-eyed peas, rumored to bring good luck.

I spent the first few days of the new year saying good-bye again—to Grace, the bees, the gardens, the horses. The horses' long-lashed eyes spoke of love, loyalty, and patience. Would they recognize me when I returned as a twenty-two-year-old? And what would my family make of me?

A verse from the Bible kept running through my mind: *when I was a child, I spoke as a child, I understood as a child, I reasoned as a child: but when I became a man, I put away childish things.*

I told myself, so could a woman.

Then came the time to say good-bye to Sloan. Bennett had offered to drive him back to Hillhouse, so that I could load my car and drive straight to my internship in New York. I'd be staying at a hotel until I found a sublet or a room to rent.

Sloan said it had been a fine holiday. "You've all made me

welcome," he said, his eyes going from Dashay to Bennett to me. "It's been grand."

I gave Bennett a good-bye hug. He tilted his head toward Dashay, then climbed into the truck. Dashay hugged Sloan, and I did, too. It was a brief embrace, but he hugged back harder than I'd expected, and his body felt a little less skinny and stiff than it looked.

We pulled apart. "Are you going to finish my portrait?" I asked him.

"Nah, I need you around to do that." But he stared at me, as if memorizing my face. "You'll be back in March, isn't it?"

"Yes," I said. "March."

"Well, then." He stowed his backpack on the cab floor and sat squarely in the passenger seat.

As they drove off, I sent him a thought: *next time you see me, I'll be older.*

Sloan didn't look back. I wondered if he would like me more, once we were the same age. I wondered how I'd feel about him.

↬

Dashay probably knew I wasn't driving straight to New York. Even though I blocked my thoughts, she had intuitive powers that went farther and deeper than anyone else's.

She didn't say anything. She helped me pack up the Jaguar, gave me a perfunctory hug, opened her mouth as if she wanted to give me last-minute advice, then didn't say anything. I drove away from Blue Heaven with a lump in my throat.

As I fastened the gate behind me, I looked up the winding driveway, thinking of all I was leaving behind. For a second I thought I saw two figures standing in the grass near the bend, waving good-bye.

But when I looked harder, nothing was there. As I drove on, I checked the rearview mirror every few miles, just in case.

❧

A few miles out, the lump in my throat began to dissolve. I grew giddy thinking about what might be waiting ahead to greet me.

Nearly everything I'd heard about Miami had been negative. Dashay called it a "vicious" place, home to vampire gangs that stole blood from hospitals and blood banks and fed on mortals freely. As I drove off the highway and came into the city, I made sure the car doors were locked—not that a locked door would have been enough to stop a rabid vampire gang.

Dr. Roche's office was in South Miami, in a high-rise office building called the Center for Integrative Neurosciences. I parked in a garage and found the elevator labeled CIN. A hot breeze gusted at me when I stepped out, swirling the skirt of the blue dress Dashay had given me as a New Year's present. The air smelled of sea salt and carbon monoxide, more tropical yet more urban than it had been in Homosassa and Georgia.

Roche's outer office was nothing like Dr. Cho's—no soothing fountains or bamboo benches here. Everything had been made of dark, gleaming metal, and the room was lit by recessed ceiling lights. Even the receptionist seemed metallic, her copper-colored hair fitting her head like a cap, her features as perfect and polished as those of a bronze statue.

She led me into an adjacent office, this one as glaringly bright as Dr. Cho's examination room, with a black upholstered steel chair as its centerpiece. The chair itself seemed massive, broad and heavy. At its top, a skinny metal tube supported a black rectangular cushion meant as a headrest.

She told me to sit down. "You are extremely lucky to have been given a chance to meet the doctor," she said. "Most patients wait for months and months."

I didn't feel especially lucky. I felt nervous.

On the wall facing the chair hung a large framed certificate, whose gilt letters read: "The Xavier Prize for Innovation in Medical Research has been awarded to Dr. Godfried—"

Before I could read the rest, the doctor strutted in. He reminded me of a bird. A small man, shorter than me, he had a thin neck and legs, a round belly, and a large, bald head. His nose was beaklike, his eyes dark and small. His lab coat was black, not white, and it zipped up the front.

Dr. Roche took short, quick steps to reach the chair, and as he moved, his eyes scanned me, darting from left to right. Was it a turkey vulture he most resembled?

"Ms. Montero." His voice sounded unusually reedy. "You've come here for Septimal. Tell me why."

He preened himself as he spoke, his fingers stroking his throat with obvious affection. His long fingernails looked sharp.

"I've thought about this for some time," I began. As I talked, telling him why I wanted to be twenty-two, never mentioning Cameron, I had a sense that he was studying me, recording data. I told him how old I was. I told him I wanted the advantages that came with adulthood. I didn't tell him I was half-human, because then he might have turned me away.

He rested both hands on his paunch, seeming proud as a pregnant woman. He didn't seem all that interested in what I was saying, though. I couldn't hear his thoughts, and I couldn't tell for sure if he was one of us.

When I'd finished talking, he said, "You've come to the right place. CIN is dedicated to clinical research into the underlying biology of perception, memory, movement, emotion, and other aspects of consciousness and cognition in vampires and in humans. *I* was one of the first physicians in the United States to administer Septimal, and *I* am the foremost practitioner using Septimal today. Are you aware that *I* am the recipient of the Xavier Prize?" He said it as if he were the *only* recipient.

"I've heard that."

He stroked his left arm with his right hand. "Septimal is truly a kind of miracle drug, better than anything else on the market. One treatment will take you from adolescence to maturity, adjust the gray matter in your brain, and prune your neural connections, simulating the normal aging process. *I* will make you into the woman you want to be." He extended his arms, waved his small hands. "Look around you. *This* is where the magic happens."

"So you'll give me Septimal?" I felt a little lost among his extravagant claims.

"Of course." He grinned, as if my question was unnecessary.

"When?"

"Does right now work for you?" He laughed, a kind of birdlike titter. He picked up a clipboard from a table and handed it to me, along with a pen.

"Standard consent form. Sign here," he said, pointing at a line on the paper.

The print was so small I could barely read beyond the words *I hereby authorize.* I signed and handed it back.

Then I noticed a gleaming silver tray on top of one of the black metal cabinets. The tray held a single hypodermic needle filled with red fluid.

Before I could speak, he'd picked up the needle and returned to the chair. "Now you might feel a slight sting, nothing worse than a pinch."

He thrust the needle deep into my inner arm. I thought, *He never asked if my parents approved. He never asked me to pay him. And how did he know I wanted Septimal before I mentioned it?*

Then the world went away.

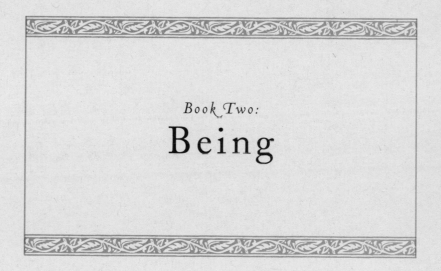

Book Two:

Being

Twelve

The first difference is a sense of spaciousness. Inside and out, I have more room to move around.

If my mind was a well, the well is deeper now. I don't speak as quickly, and I don't ask as many questions. Ideas take longer to digest. This is to be expected.

I woke up in a white room. They haven't told me how long I'll be here. Dr. Roche says they're preparing me for reentry.

Every morning they run tests to see how much my brain remembers. Some questions I couldn't know the answers to, but then they tell me, and later that question is asked again, and again, until I get it right.

Diana gives me lessons in the afternoon. She's the receptionist. She taught me new ways to walk and talk and how to use my eyes so that a man can't look away from them.

She asks me what I think about politics and shows me a magazine photo of Neil Cameron. "He's a fascinating man," I say.

"Yes, he is," she says. She approves of my answer, I can tell.

Once, she leaves the room to make a telephone call. In a folder on her desk I find drawings labeled "Ariella Montero," each one numbered. The doctor must have made them. They are paper-clipped in two groups: Ari at thirteen and Ari at twenty-two. The older Ari's waist is more defined, and the hips and legs are more shapely. The face is more angular, the nose slightly longer. And the eyes look more self-aware, more confident.

I hope I can take these drawings with me when I leave.

⚬⚬⚬

"No, do it *this* way."

Diana isn't a patient teacher. She says I have a habit of grabbing objects. Instead, I should approach them, consider them, bend toward them, lift them lightly. "Like this," she says, and walks across the office to her desk, leans toward it, and picks up a pen.

"Now you try."

She says we need to spend this much time because small gestures reveal character. Picking up objects is more important than I would have guessed.

So I cross the room, bend over the desk, pause, and slowly lift a pencil.

Diana perches on a chair, her long legs crossed. "Better," she says. "Do it again."

The afternoon lessons are more fun. She takes me shopping.

Shopping in Miami means sauntering through malls and South Beach boutiques filled with glittering jewelry and incredible shoes, surrounded by women and men who look and move like models. They never smile. Shopping with Diana means trying on armloads of clothing selected by her, posing in mirrors while she makes the choices. She buys thousands of dollars' worth of clothing, accessories, and a winter coat she says will be essential in New York. She even gives me a fancy new cell phone.

Then she takes me to a salon. My hair is styled. Makeup is applied, and I'm shown how to re-create the results on my own.

"You need to emphasize those eyes," the stylist tells me, and Diana says, "Make them pop."

The afternoon stretches into evening by the time our taxi reaches the Delano Hotel. I begin to get out, but she stays in the cab. "Dr. Roche will meet you in the bar and take you to dinner," she says.

I walk into the hotel lobby, which doesn't look like a lobby so much as a Hollywood mansion. Billowing white curtains fall from cathedral ceilings to polished wooden floors. Twin gargoyles support a bench, and metal bears climb an umbrella stand. Diana insisted that I wear the clingy black chiffon cocktail dress. People stop talking to watch me as I come in.

I don't stop to ask where the bar is. I walk straight on, past the beautiful people gaping at me, as if my feet know exactly where they are going, even though they're wearing unfamiliar high-heeled shoes.

Dr. Roche sits at a round table in a bar area edged by rose-colored curtains and mirrored walls, lit by tea lights. He sips a rose-colored cocktail, which he sets down the moment he sees me. His dark little eyes flicker over every inch of me as I make my way to his table. He stands up.

"Ms. Montero," he says, extending his hand.

The name makes me smile. I shake his hand in the brief, emphatic style Diana taught me. "It's a pleasure to see you," I say.

He laughs. "Oh, the pleasure is all mine, believe me."

He summons a server and orders me a drink—something red, in a frosted glass, smelling faintly of strawberries and roses. I reach for my purse, in case the server needs to see my new driver's license with my new birth date, but he never asks.

The drink matches my lipstick.

The doctor asks about my day. I tell him about the shopping, but he doesn't seem to be listening so much as studying me, measuring me, assessing me.

"And you're looking forward to your internship?"

I don't remember telling him about that. "Yes," I say. "I will like living in New York."

"It's a setting that will suit you," he says.

We finish our drinks and move on to dinner. The restaurant is called Blue Door, yet almost everything in it is white, except for two high-backed red leather chairs against the curtained wall. I think I'll sit in one of those fancy chairs, but Dr. Roche takes it and beckons to me to take a low-backed one opposite him. A server pulls out my chair, hands me my napkin and menu. We order Chilean sea bass and a bottle of white wine.

While we wait for the food to arrive, I excuse myself to visit the restroom. Like everything else in the hotel, the room has high ceilings and sculpted fixtures.

A woman in a tight red dress half lies across the marble sink, her face upside down, while a blond woman in green drinks from her throat. When she notices me, the blond one raises her head and lets me see her fangs and a trickle of blood at the corner of her mouth. She licks it away and bends back to her feeding.

The Delano is quite a place, I decide. Mortals and immortals mingle freely, unabashed about their natures. Plus, everyone and everything look so perfect.

When I walk back to the table, Dr. Roche is speaking into a cell phone. He puts it away when I arrive. "Nice dress," he says, and I thank him.

After dinner we stroll outside, past a long swimming pool with tables set in the shallow end. Couples dine there, candelabra on their tables, clothing tucked up to stay dry. Others sit in poolside cabanas, partially visible through parted white curtains, their silhouettes romantic, mysterious. This is the world I want to live in.

Dr. Roche talks as we stroll, telling me how pleased he is with my "results." I think I've passed his examination.

He says that tomorrow I'll be leaving them to go to New York. But instead of going to a hotel, I'll be living in an apartment he owns in the Meatpacking District. "I keep it there for business trips," he says. "It's empty, so you might as well use it."

Again, I thank him. "You're like a fairy godfather," I say.

"I'm a magician," he says. "That's why *I* won the Xavier Prize."

Next morning, Diana ushers me to my car. Inside, I see the bags of clothing we bought yesterday.

"You'll drive safely, of course," she says. "And if you have any questions at any time, call or text me. My number is programmed into your phone—just press two."

I don't think I'll have any questions. I'm so impatient to be on my way that I never ask her about the drawings in her file.

I drive twelve hours that day, stop at a motel in North Carolina, and drive nine hours the next day. At a diner near the exit ramp, I notice a newspaper headlined, CAMERON GATE-CRASHES NEW HAMPSHIRE PRIMARY. The article says it's the first time a third-party candidate has received a significant number of write-in votes on the primary ballots of both major parties.

I feel an urge to call and congratulate him, but of course I don't. Our time will come soon enough.

❦

It's exciting to see the lights of the city wink through a veil of snowflakes. I make my way to the Blackstone building without any problem and park in the garage underneath the apartments.

Dr. Roche's place is a loft—an open layout in which one room flows into the next, reminding me a little of the Delano. Even the bathroom is an open cubicle without a door. But there are no curtains here. The furniture is modern and minimal: white sofas, black chairs, a huge white-sheeted bed mounted on a black pedestal. Everything looks new. I never dreamed of living in a place like this.

I open my suitcase, noticing how perfectly it has been packed. Each item is folded precisely. My Peruvian dress is wrapped in tissue paper and my shoes placed in cotton bags. My journal is the only item that looks used, even bruised, its blue cover beginning to tear. I need to buy a new one. I spend the evening unpacking, putting each item in exactly the right place.

Next morning I take a taxi to the NetFriend office in an anonymous building in Midtown. My new boss is named Chelsea. She has straight, dark hair and dark-framed glasses.

"So you're the new intern," she says. "You dress like a fashion model." She's wearing jeans.

"Thanks," I say, not sure if it's a compliment.

"Too bad we can't put you straight into sales. But you have to go through orientation and the usual intern duty first."

She stares at me, admiring my outfit.

There are ten other interns, all wearing jeans, sitting in a conference room waiting to be oriented. Orientation means a series of presentations about NetFriend—a bit about its history and a lot about its present. NetFriend is booming. Its money comes from advertisers and marketing companies, who pay for information about users in order to target certain audiences.

I'm the only person in the room who doesn't have a Net-Friend account, a fact that seems to shock the others. During a break, Chelsea helps me set up my profile online. She uses the computer camera to take my picture and loads it onto the profile page.

"Everything you post, we have access to," she says. "As a result, the ads you'll see on the right of your page will be targeted to your age group, gender, and preferences in music, movies, clothes, and other products. We pay attention to what you say. A few users think we're invading their privacy, but we're really saving them time and money by informing them about the products they'll like best."

I choose the user name AriVamp. That way, I figure, I'll be sure to get the coolest ads. And I upload a photo Diana e-mailed me. Taken after my afternoon makeover, it shows me wearing the black chiffon dress. My hair and makeup are flawless.

As an intern, my job is not going to be glamorous, I'm told. But if I work hard, I might be invited to apply for a full-time job after I graduate.

I don't think I'll need a job then.

We're given a tour of the office, whose largest room is called the Trend Room. A computer projection of a world map fills one wall, with tiny points of light flickering in clusters across it. Trend is a partner company of NetFriend, and each light represents someone sending a text message, or buzzing, from a cell phone or computer.

"Spain is busy today." Chelsea points at the map. "But look how quiet China is."

I notice a cluster of lights in southeast Georgia. Hill-house students are busy buzzing their way through the spring semester, completely unaware that each of them is a dot on a map in New York.

Next to the Trend Room is a door leading to another suite of offices, but we don't go in. "You have to have special clearance to go in there. That's where the Security Team works," Chelsea says. "They handle cybercrime investigations." She says sometimes cyberpunks hack in to NetFriend accounts, access their e-mail, and steal their identities.

"Sometimes they e-mail their NetFriends asking for loans," she says. "Other times they find links to bank accounts and credit cards and hack them, too."

I wish I could see beyond the Security Team's unmarked door. If I have to work, that's where I want to be.

Instead, Chelsea sets me up in a cubicle and gives me administrative access to a NetFriend page dealing with user complaints. NetFriend users have to provide Social Security numbers when they file their complaints. My computer's desktop features a file of stock responses, so basically my job will be saving the Social Security numbers, matching the key words in the complaint e-mail with the same words in a response file, and sending off the reply.

"Isn't there a program to do this?" I ask.

"We tried that, but it wasn't infallible. Our users prefer the personal touch." Chelsea laughs. "Our users are like insecure teenagers, Ari. They need to be told they're okay, over and over again."

The response files confirm what she said. Many of the complaints come because users' accounts could be deleted if they don't follow the NetFriend Code of Conduct, which prohibits obscenity, nudity, death threats—that sort of thing. In fact the code is enforced only if another user complains about the content of a particular page. NetFriend doesn't check out the complaint, they simply send offending users e-mail that their accounts have been disabled.

Most of the e-mails I have to answer ask why their accounts aren't accessible. The stock response is: "We understand your concern. Your account was disabled because it didn't conform to NetFriend policies. Unfortunately, we are unable to divulge the specific nature of your offense."

Some of the e-mails I read sound desperate. One reads, "You cut me off from all my friends. How will they know what I'm up to now? Can't you tell me what I did wrong?"

I click my mouse and send her the stock response. Sinneca at omail.com will be isolated forever, unless one day NetFriend changes its mind and reinstates her. Sometimes that happens, thanks to an algorithm that randomly reinstates some rule breakers weeks or months after they've been banished.

Chelsea says, "The process isn't logical. But who said life should be logical?"

"Why do you ask for the Social Security numbers?" I ask.

"That's part of our security operation." Chelsea shakes her head, telling me not to ask any more questions.

⌁

A group of interns is going out for after-work drinks, and I'm invited to join them. I say thanks, but I can't tonight. I want some time alone. I put on my new winter coat and walk home, savoring block after block.

A tall man with blond hair stops and asks me what time it is. I'm wearing my diamond watch, a gift from Dr. Roche, and I'm happy to tell him. He smiles and thanks me. He says, "Don't you remember me?"

His face is familiar, but I can't think of his name.

"That's okay," he says. "We'll talk again. Meantime, do be careful. You're too valuable to lose." He walks on.

On a corner kiosk newspaper headlines say that Cameron has won another endorsement. When I arrive home that night, I go online and find Cameron's NetFriend page. He has nearly two million friends already. He probably isn't even monitoring the page, but just in case I add him to my friend list.

Again, I have an urge to call him, but I don't. I can bide my time. The New York primary is only a few weeks away. We'll be together then.

Thirteen

That weekend I go shopping—this time, for a gift. Diana told me what to look for, and she texted me a list of stores where I might find it.

I work my way down the list and end up at an antique shop on City Island. The cab ride to get there costs a fortune, but, after all, I have all the money I need.

City Island is a funny place, a small town in the Bronx that reminds me of upstate New York, but the antique shop owner has what I'm looking for: an antique sextant in a polished mahogany box. A sextant is a navigational instrument that measures the altitudes of celestial bodies. Diana taught me that. She said Cameron has a long eBay record of bidding on sextants but so far hasn't bought one.

I pay the asking price, counting out more than three thousand dollars in large bills. The seller says, "You shouldn't walk around carrying so much money. You'll get mugged."

"No, I won't," I tell him.

I carry the box out of the shop, feeling hungry. There are a few restaurants on the street, specializing in oysters and lobster, but I'm in the mood for a cheeseburger. I hail a cab and head back to the city.

Chelsea has a way of coming up behind me without making a sound. "What are you doing?"

I've been writing in my journal. "I'm on my lunch break," I say.

"Is that a diary?"

When I tell her it is, she says, "You come from another planet or what? Why don't you keep a blog?"

She leans over me to reach the computer keyboard on my desk. Within seconds she's opened my NetFriend page and, pressing a few keys, created a new page called AriVamp's Blog. "You can give it a new title if you want," she says. "Now you can share your experiences with your friends. What's the point of keeping a diary that only you can read?"

I close the journal and as I slide it back into my purse, a yellow tag falls from its pages. "Ocala National Forest Recreation Resource Management," it reads. I toss it into the trash can.

When I open my blog page, I think of writing about what I saw the previous afternoon in the break room: Chelsea drinking from the neck of one of the other interns. Other employees must have seen them, too, but nobody paid any attention except one older colleague.

"That's odd," he said. "Chelsea usually takes her lunch break at noon."

～

My cell phone keeps ringing. The "missed calls" list shows that Dashay and Jacey are determined to talk to me. But I don't want to talk to them.

My new phone has an application that can place any call I make directly into voice mail, and I use it to leave messages for each of them. I tell Dashay's phone that I am swamped with work and enjoying life in the big city. I promise to call again soon. Jacey gets a different message: New York is dirty, my job is boring and time-consuming, and my apartment is a pigsty. She wouldn't want to visit, and I have no time to come to Pittsburgh. I say I look forward to seeing her back in Georgia.

I go to work, come home, bide my time. The newspapers are full of Cameron now. He already has his party's nomination sewn up, though it won't be official until the summer convention. A surge in voter registrations has been noted nationwide. The new voters are of all ages and come from all economic brackets. Political analysts are having a hard time finding any pattern to his popularity.

None of them even considers that one reason for the surge might be vampire voters.

The night that Cameron speaks in New York, the line of hopeful attendees stretches for blocks. A thousand or so tickets to the event have been issued, but when the doors open another thousand will be admitted.

I go to the head of the line, because I have a ticket. Dr. Roche mailed it to me. "I can't make it myself, but I know you'll enjoy the speech," he wrote.

That night a misty rain is falling. Temperatures are unseasonably warm. I wear a red trench coat and red lipstick, both selected by Diana, as well as the black chiffon dress. Scanning the seats, I see a single empty one in the center of the third row from the front. I make my way through the row, facing forward as Diana taught me.

Joel Hartman, Cameron's running mate, introduces Cameron. An older man with white hair, he probably isn't a vampire, I think. He's not much of anything. He doesn't interest me at all until he says, "I give you the next president of the United States, Neil Cameron!"

Everyone stands up, cheering, and I do, too. Cameron

comes out from the wings of the stage, shakes Hartman's hand, faces the audience, and smiles. His eyes run across the crowd as he waits for them to stop applauding. They stop when they reach me.

Diana had said, *Focus your eyes directly on his, as if you are the only two in existence. Focus your energy, feel it coalesce. Send it from the backs of your eyes into the depths of his. Open your mouth slightly, a quarter of an inch, no more. Don't move.*

Then I do something she didn't tell me, something I didn't plan. I put my right hand over my heart.

He stops smiling. His eyes look shocked, then full of wonder. He raises his right hand and places it over his heart.

All around me, people stop clapping and put their hands over their hearts. They are ready to pledge allegiance.

And so am I.

⤚ ⟨

What does he speak about? The usual things: the need for conserving environmental resources, for fiscal prudence, for unity. He tries not to look at me as he speaks, but his eyes return to me every other phrase or so. Later the media will report that he seemed so distracted that night that he wasn't in his best form. I think otherwise.

When he finishes, his eyes remain with mine, helpless. He manages to pull them away and leave the stage. The audience members begin to stand up, putting on their coats. I stay where I am.

A few minutes later, a young man wearing an ill-fitting suit and running shoes makes his way to my seat. He hands me a folded note, which I don't open.

"Tell him I'll meet him wherever he wants," I say.

He ushers me to a town car parked in an alleyway behind the hotel. No one except a driver is inside.

The car glides down the wide black avenues, gleaming silver from rain. Riding in that town car is as close as I've ever come to being a passenger on a ship. It stops, and I get out. I stand in the light rain, watching the car drive away, sad to see it go. I like being driven.

The restaurant has no name but is known by its street number: 410. It has a small dining area with a dozen tables in it. When I come in, the hostess doesn't even ask who I am. She leads me to an empty private dining room and shuts its door behind me.

A server comes in through a second door, carrying a bottle of champagne and an ice bucket. He takes my coat and leaves again, then returns with a pitcher of ice water and two goblets.

I send Diana a Trend message telling her how well her advice worked. She buzzed me yesterday, asking me to get back to her. Then I sink into the high-backed leather chair, sip water, and reapply my lipstick.

When the first door opens again, Cameron rushes in as if someone is chasing him. I rise, and he is in my arms. His camel-hair coat feels damp, and so does his hair. He kisses me, but when we separate, his eyes look surprised, then uneasy, then a bit frightened.

"What have you done to yourself?" he says, his voice low.

I smile and make my eyes command his. "I've grown up. I'm twenty-two. And I did it all for you."

He takes off his coat. He's wearing a dark blue suit with a barely visible silver stripe. He says he had a hard time getting away to meet me. His "handlers" wanted to know where he was going, but he told them he needed a break. He said he'd meet them at the airport in three hours to fly to Chicago.

I smile. I know he'll miss that flight.

We eat poached shrimp and lemon sole meunière and roast potatoes. We drink champagne. It isn't easy, keeping my eyes on his while we're dining, but I manage to keep my gaze steady, looking away only to glance at the food. Cameron eats less than I do. Even when we're finished, I feel hungry.

He orders a second bottle of champagne. We sip it slowly. I tell him about my job, and he talks about the campaign.

"We're under a lot of pressure from some of the Nebulists," he says. "They want me to rewrite our platform, make it more vamp-centric. I can compromise on some things, but their goals aren't mine, pure and simple. And we'll lose the Sanguinist support if we let them have their way."

"You have to be true to yourself," I say.

He looks as if he wants to ask me a question. Instead he says, "I switched off my cell phone. If I turn it on, there will be ten messages asking where in hell I am."

"Don't turn it on."

I stand up, walk around the table. He stands up, too.

"Kiss me," I say.

And a moment later, I say, "Kiss me again."

When we finish, he helps me put on the red trench coat. "Time to get back to reality," he says.

"Reality," I repeat.

We walk out onto the street. He walks to the curb to hail a cab, but I put my hand on his arm. "I live only a few blocks away. Walk me home."

And so we walk. I link arms with him, so that he can feel the shape of my hip. The streets are dark and mostly empty, only a few people moving through them. The rain has stopped and a winter chill returns. I look up and see a black bird perched on a ledge, watching us. The bird will be seeing a couple, a woman in red and a man in a tan coat, moving through the night with a purpose.

I know what's about to happen. We will arrive at my building and I'll invite him in. He'll say he shouldn't. I'll say I have a present for him, and he'll follow me inside. We'll step into the stark, immaculate loft, and I'll hang up our coats. I'll hand him the mahogany box, and he'll be thrilled by the sextant. I'll kiss him again, and I'll take his hand, lead him into the bedroom. We'll sit on the platform bed. Then we will make love.

In the morning he will act as if he's ashamed of himself. He'll say, "We should have waited. What would your father think of me?"

I'll tell him Raphael Montero would like him, that one day they will meet and become friends. But I'm not too sure about the last part.

When he leaves, I'll hand him the sextant. "Don't forget your present," I'll say. "It's what you've been waiting for."

Fourteen

Next day at the office I sent off a batch of replies to user complaints, saved all the Social Security numbers, then checked my own e-mail account. Jacey wanted to know what was up. Sloan said campus was quiet and the weather was cold. And Diana wrote, "How are things going?"

I wrote back. Nothing much up, I told Jacey. Weather also cold here, I told Sloan. And to Diana, I wrote, "Last night I became the woman I've always wanted to be."

I liked that sentence so much that I used it in my blog, too.

I expected that Cameron would call, in spite of what he'd told me—that it wasn't wise for him to be in touch, that during the next few months would come the campaign's most important segments: securing the popularity and endorsements that would help him and Hartman win the fall election.

I'd told him I understood. But I still expected him to call.

❦

On my last night in Manhattan, all the interns and most of the NetFriend administrators went to a Russian bar. They drank vodka mixed with Picardo, and I did, too, though I didn't much like the taste.

I sat next to two guys who worked in Security: Josh and Quibble, they said their names were. They were skinny guys wearing black pants and neon-colored shirts, and both wore dark-framed glasses. I'd seen them a few times in the break room, playing chess. They'd seemed afraid of me. But tonight the vodka made them less afraid.

"What do you do when you catch a hacker?" I said.

Josh, who seemed smarter than Quibble, said, "We don't do anything."

"What kind of a question is that?" Quibble said. "We work *with* hackers to solve problems."

"Our hackers are the white hats," Josh said. "The good guys who try to find bugs and worms."

"Who are the black hats?" I could tell this conversation wasn't going to go where I wanted it.

Josh looked at Quibble. "The ones we don't hire," Quibble said.

"Until next month," Josh added. They laughed.

Quibble changed the subject. He talked about a former girlfriend of Josh's. After she dumped him, Josh went into her NetFriend account and had all of her friends "unfriend" her. "She was so desperate for company, she took Josh back again," he said.

"Then I dumped her," Josh said.

They laughed.

I smiled. "How do you use the Social Security numbers I send you?"

"We don't use them," Josh said. "We sell them."

Chelsea joined us. She'd been standing behind me, talking to some other admins. "What's with all the questions?"

"I only asked three," I said. "I might want to be a hacker someday."

"You aren't the type," she said.

Leaving New York in March to return to college was like leaving a party as it hits its peak. I walked around the apartment in the dim early morning light, saying good-bye to style and sophistication, then packed my suitcases. When would I wear the black chiffon dress again? Or the black stiletto heels with deep red soles?

But I packed them, just in case. Then I put on jeans and a T-shirt, the uniform of Hillhouse students, closed up the apartment, and carried my bags to the elevator and the car.

I wished a town car had been waiting there to drive me, so that I could have lounged in the back seat. But the Jaguar would have to do. Heading south, I decided not to stop for the night, but to drive straight through. I had snacks to keep me company, and I took a bathroom break near Richmond. Fifteen hours after I started, the Jaguar rolled up the Hillhouse driveway.

When I walked into the dorm, a group of students in the lounge stopped watching TV to stare at me. When I got to my room, Jacey, lying on her bed, reading, sat up with a start.

"Oh my god," she said, her voice high with excitement. "Ari, you're famous."

She held up the newspaper she'd been reading—not the *New York Times*, but a tabloid called the *International Herald*. SENATOR HAS MYSTERY DATE, read the headline, over a huge photograph of Cameron and me, my hand on his arm as I told him we didn't need a taxi, he could walk me home.

I stared at the headline. It would be on newsstands all over Manhattan, and I wished I was still there, walking down the avenue, people noticing me and saying, "That's her! That's the mystery woman."

It wasn't a bad photo, either.

"Your hair looks different," Jacey said.

"I had it styled."

I took the paper and opened it to read the article. Three more photos, the first showing Cameron and me entering Dr. Roche's apartment building, the second showing Cameron coming out alone in daylight, carrying the mahogany box. He looked tired, rumpled, pensive. The article said, "Less than a week after Neil Cameron told *Time* magazine that he has 'no one special' in his life, the *Herald* spotted Cameron in the company of someone very special indeed. But who is the woman in red?"

The third photo was the same as the one on the cover, but it had been cropped and enlarged to feature only my face. My eyes did indeed "pop" that night with mascara and liner and shadow, but I suspected the paper had retouched them as well. They seemed to jump out from the page, enormous and deep, full of secrets.

The photo caption featured a line of question marks.

Jacey stared at me as I read. "*You* look different," she said.

I noticed her braided hair and flannel pajamas, thinking how young she looked. "I've grown up," I said.

The article said the Cameron campaign had no comment to make at this time.

I'd begun to unpack, Jacey nearly squealing with admiration at my new clothes, when my cell phone rang. It had a ringtone selected by Diana: "Anitra's Dance" from the opera *Peer Gynt*.

The voice on the other end wasn't familiar. It belonged to a man who said he was a reporter for the tabloid that published the articles. "Have you seen yesterday's edition?" he asked.

I said that I had.

"Someone sent us a link to your NetFriend page. You look like the woman in the pictures with Cameron."

I said that I had no comment and disconnected the call.

Almost immediately the phone rang again.

"I like your ringtone," Jacey said.

We sat and listened to "Anitra's Dance" over and over again, until we were so sick of it I switched off the phone.

⌒

Next morning, I blocked calls from that reporter, but soon others were calling. My incoming calls all came from unknown numbers. I couldn't ignore them completely. One might be from Cameron.

Jacey agreed to answer my phone and screen the calls. She took my phone with her and drove to the gas station in town to buy a copy of that day's *International Herald*.

"My parents would die if they knew I was reading this stuff," she said when she got back. "I was halfway home from Pittsburgh when I stopped for gas and saw your picture on the newsstand. Ari, I couldn't believe my eyes. And here it is again."

I sat in front of her vanity table mirror, stroking mascara onto my lashes. Even if I was back in the middle of nowhere, I wanted to look my best.

"Did anyone call me while you were at the gas station?" I asked her.

She said she'd taken calls from four reporters and told them all I had no comment. "And there was one from some woman named Tamryn Gordon. Weird voice. She wants you to call her. She said it's urgent."

Jacey handed me the *Herald*. On its cover was the photo of me from my NetFriend page.

MYSTERY WOMAN NAMED!, the headline read.

"Maybe you should get a different number?" Jacey came to read over my shoulder.

"The senator's office will neither deny nor confirm it, but the *Herald* has received anonymous tips that the new woman in his life is Ariella Montero, a twenty-two-year-old student enrolled at Hillhouse, a liberal arts college in Georgia." The article said *Herald* reporters had contacted Hillhouse, which confirmed that Ms. Montero was a student there and had recently done an internship in Manhattan, and that an unnamed resident of the Blackstone apartments said he'd recognized the woman in the photographs, having seen her in the building elevator.

"I didn't know you were twenty-two," Jacey was saying when my phone rang again. She answered it, then handed it to me. "It's him," she whispered, her eyes wide.

I said hello in my sexiest voice. Cameron said, "Can you talk?"

I motioned for Jacey to go away, and when she'd left, he said, "Are you okay?"

"Except for all the phone calls from reporters, I'm fine," I said.

"You've seen the pictures?" he asked, and I said I had.

"I can't talk long," he said, "but unless you say otherwise, I'm going public about us later today." He said his advisors had decided keeping quiet would do more harm than good.

"Does that mean I can talk to the reporters now?"

He advised against it. "Let me handle the initial questions, and then we'll see what sort of reaction there is. Oh, and Ari? Could you please delete your blog? It's very flattering, I guess, but it could prove embarrassing."

The blog hadn't said anything explicit. I'd simply talked about becoming a woman and quoted lyrics from songs I'd heard on the radio. But I told him I'd delete it. "Anything I can do to help," I said.

"That's the right spirit." His voice sounded not encouraging or relieved but resigned. He ended the call abruptly, saying he'd be in touch again soon.

I opened my laptop and found the blog. A pity to delete it, really. It had some of the best lines I'd ever written. Before I pressed the delete key, I copied all the entries and saved them on my hard drive.

※

Everywhere I went that day, people stared at me. A few made comments, just loud enough for me to hear. They were wondering why I'd lied about my age and why a twenty-two-year-old was an undergraduate at Hillhouse. They were wondering what my affair with Cameron was like and how long it had been going on.

I stared right back at them, until they looked away.

The dean of student life came by the dining hall at lunchtime and asked me to meet with him. I went to his office. He asked how I was and if I wanted counseling. I said I was fine, and no, counseling wasn't needed. He said he'd had the impression I was younger, that he'd been surprised when he checked my records and found out I was twenty-two.

I said I guessed I was a late bloomer.

At dinner that night Sloan stared, too. He didn't say anything until Jacey left us to get a second dessert.

"What'd they do to you?" he said.

I kept my voice as low as his. "They made me older."

He shook his head. "They did more than that. They did you no good."

Jacey returned, carrying a large bowl of strawberry ice cream. "My favorite thing in the world," she said.

For some reason it reminded me of the game we used to

play, Anything in the World. "If you could have anything in the whole world, what would it be?" I asked Sloan.

"I know that game," Jacey said.

"And we know your answer: strawberry ice cream. What about you, Sloan?"

His eyes had a faraway look to them. "The chance to rewrite history," he said.

"That's a good answer," I said. "I think that might be my answer, too."

Jacey said, "You forgot to take your tonic, Ari." I wished she'd stop nagging me. After all, she wasn't my mother.

As we walked up the hill toward the dorms that night, I asked Sloan when he'd finish my portrait. "Do you want me to sit for you tomorrow?"

"No," he said. "I can't do it tomorrow."

"Maybe Wednesday?"

He walked faster. "I'll let you know."

But when I ran into him the next day on campus, he said he'd put the portrait away for a while. "I'm doing other things," he said, "and besides, you're too much of a work in progress right now."

I didn't know what he meant by that. But I smiled and went on my way to class.

❧

Internships are supposed to apply your academic experience to the real world. As a result, interns are likely to make important connections between theory and practice and synthesize their insights.

That's what the Hillhouse catalog promised. But from what I saw, the internships mostly made the interns unhappy when they had to come back to school.

Jacey incessantly yearned for Pittsburgh. In only eight

weeks, she'd fallen in love with the city and with what sounded to me like an entirely thankless job tending tots at a day care center. But I understood what she meant when she said, "For the first time, I felt like a grown-up there. I was in charge of my own life."

Living in a dorm and going to classes didn't give us that feeling at all. We existed to please our professors, it seemed.

I was taking another creative writing class, this one a "mini course" on "writing about life experiences." In other words, we were supposed to write nonfiction, but we could use fictional techniques.

Jacey was the first one to workshop her essay, which was about a girl who had an abortion. The essay was painful to read and more painful to talk about, filled with fear and guilt and images of truncated trees and dying flowers. Even Professor Warner seemed at a loss for words. She hadn't handed out a list of prohibited topics for this course, but now she looked as if she was having second thoughts.

Jacey sat silent, not meeting anyone's eyes, as we critiqued her essay. I said something about the images needing to be more subtle. Sloan said the images were too subtle already and the essay needed stronger ones.

After the workshop we all walked to town for drinks at a bowling alley, but we didn't talk as we went. Richard didn't come. He hadn't been in class, either, and I expect we were all thinking the same thing: since he was the only boyfriend Jacey had ever had on campus, he must have been the father.

It felt odd to have everyone's attention directed at Jacey instead of me. But that didn't last long. The owner of Leo's Bowl, leaning on the glass counter where he rented shoes, was reading the *International Herald*. Cameron's photo topped the left page, and mine topped the right. The headline read: SENATOR ADMITS AFFAIR WITH MYSTERY GIRL.

The owner seemed oblivious to the fact that the mystery girl—excuse me, woman—stood right in front of him, trying to read the article upside down.

We were walking back to campus when a passing car slowed, then stopped. A man jumped out of the car and began taking photos of us.

Sloan grabbed my arm and began to run. I had no choice but to run, too. His grip was strong. We took off through the woods that bordered the road, and even after the photographer was far behind us, we kept running. We didn't stop until we reached the art barn.

"Better come in," Sloan said. "They've probably got your dorm room staked out by now."

We climbed the ladder to the loft. In his studio, Sloan motioned for me to sit on one of the rattan-seat chairs. He took the other one and sat facing its back, his elbows along its top edge.

"I want to hear your story," he said.

"Which one?"

"I want to hear *your* story, from the beginning," he said.

And so I began to tell it: growing up in Saratoga Springs without a mother, homeschooled by my father, running away to find her after my best friend was murdered. "She was killed one night for no reason at all," I said. "She worshipped my father and me."

I told the rest of it: hitchhiking south, fighting off a rapist by biting him, becoming *other*. Then finding Mãe in Florida and coming to Hillhouse.

When I'd finished, he said, "What color are the words?"

"What?"

"The words of your story. See there, they're hanging there between us." He gestured at empty space.

I didn't have an answer for his question. Was he trying to trick me?

He answered it himself. "Rose madder. A color similar to alizarin crimson, wouldn't you say?"

"Yes," I said. "Exactly."

⁓

When I got to the dining hall the following night, no one was eating. Everyone stood around in little groups, talking in low voices. And they weren't talking about me.

Apparently someone posted Jacey's abortion essay on her NetFriend page, next to a photo of her. And someone commented on it: "Way to go, Richard."

Apparently Richard heard about it and took an overdose of sleeping pills. An ambulance had taken him away.

Late that night I was awoken by the sound of Jacey weeping. She made a deep, rhythmic noise, as regular as the sound of the tide striking the beach. I might have offered her some comfort, talked about heaven, that sort of thing. Instead I let the dull sound of her despairing lull me back to sleep.

Fifteen

acey stopped answering my phone after that, and we no longer drove to town to find the *International Herald.* The paper must have moved on to some other hot topic, because a few days later my phone stopped ringing, except for the occasional call from Dashay. I left innocuous replies on her voice mail.

Richard's stomach had been pumped, and he was expected to be okay, though he wouldn't be finishing out the semester. Apparently he hadn't taken enough pills.

∼

A registered letter arrived for me from Ireland. Inside were plane tickets to New York and on to Dublin, the flights leaving in less than a month. Exams ended the third week of April, and then I'd be gone.

Really gone. I didn't plan on returning to Hillhouse. The coursework was too boring, the company too juvenile for my tastes. I wanted to take my place in the world, beside Raphael Montero.

And the Hillhouse professors were ignorant, I decided, after Professor Warner trashed my personal essay. I'd written a variation of "The Little Match Girl," a fairy tale by Hans Christian Andersen. On a cold winter night, I wrote, a girl is huddled outside on the pavement, lighting matches to keep herself warm. As each match explodes into light, she has a vision of the life inside the houses, where families gather around holiday trees and banquet tables while logs blaze in fireplaces. The girl's last vision is of her dead grandmother, who's come to take her soul to heaven. The girl dies, frozen to death, smiling.

A boy across the room made the first comment: "Why would she use matches? Everybody carries lighters these days."

He seemed inclined to go on, but Professor Warner held up her hand to stop him.

"This is a class in nonfiction" she began, "and retelling fairy tales is simply not appropriate. Not to mention a kind of plagiarism."

"But the story is true," I said. "It didn't happen exactly that way, but the spirit of it is true. I've always been on the outside, looking in."

In a flat voice, Sloan said, "I believe it."

No one else spoke. Professor Warner set my essay facedown on her desk and moved on to another student's work. Class droned on. We didn't go to Leo's Bowl that day.

~

When my phone rang that evening, I instinctively looked around for Jacey to answer it. But she wasn't in the room, so I said, "Hello?" in an imitation of her voice.

Cameron's voice said, "Ari? Is that you?"

This was the call I'd been waiting for. "Congratulations," I said. "You're making history."

"And there's talk we may be endorsed by some major Democrats. Can you imagine that?" He sounded exhausted but more optimistic than he'd been in a long time. He said his staff would be calling me. They needed details for a biography of me they were putting together for the media.

So I would be in the limelight now, not in the shadows. "I'll help any way I can," I said.

"They're planning some events for us—you know, first official picture of us together, first time out in public. It won't happen until sometime next month."

Next month I was going to Ireland. "Okay," I said.

"The skies seem bluer every day," he said. "Are they gray where you are?"

"Sometimes," I said.

"Gray with an *E* or an *A*?"

"I don't know," I said. "It's all the same color, isn't it?"

⌁

My last weeks at Hillhouse? They're a jumble of memories: taking exams, eating boring meals, writing papers. Cameron's staff sent a photographer to take my picture and Tamryn Gordon called, in that grating voice, to ask me questions. Before she hung up, she said, "I hope you're pleased with yourself."

I said yes, I was pleased.

The next day they issued my official biography to the press. It was much duller than my real life. A few reporters telephoned me, but I made it clear I wouldn't be talking to anyone until Cameron made the arrangements.

Jacey's laptop was stolen right out of our dorm room, and then someone took all the money out of her checking account. It wasn't much, maybe three hundred dollars, but from the fuss she made you'd have thought it was a thousand. "That's what you get for keeping a file on your desktop labeled 'Passwords,'" I told her.

She didn't say anything. She'd pretty much stopped talking to me by that point, which was a relief. I looked forward to having a room of my own at my new home in Ireland.

Cameron called me twice a week, like clockwork. He

sounded polite and distant, as if he was playing a part he didn't enjoy. I made my voice warm and seductive, to shame him.

In the lounge I found a new magazine article about him, talking about his love life. And there was my name, Ariella Montero, right next to his. He told the reporter that he didn't think I was too young for him. "She's twenty-two," he said. "She knows her way around the world."

I smiled at that.

Packing up at the end of the semester was easy. I left most of my stuff for the campus Free Store. I didn't want to carry much, because I'd be getting new clothes in Ireland—new clothes for a new life. I was throwing sweaters into a box when the cell phone rang, and for once the caller ID said it was Cameron.

But the voice was one I'd never heard before. "How could you do that to me?" It was Cameron's voice, but it sounded harsh, bewildered, and angry.

When I began to reply, the phone went dead. When it began to ring again, I switched it off and returned to sorting through my sweaters. When that became boring, I simply threw a bunch of stuff away.

❧

The next morning I rolled my suitcase outside to wait for the taxi. Dashay and Bennett would come later to pick up the Jaguar. Everything had been arranged via e-mail.

I'd planned to carry my laptop in my shoulder bag, but it was too heavy. So I left it behind. Jacey could have it. My family could afford to buy me a new, more up-to-date one.

Spring had made the grass pale green. I wore a light coat that almost matched it.

"You're off, then." Sloan stood behind me, his hands in the pockets of his jeans.

"Yes. I'm off."

He watched me critically, as if he didn't like my hair and makeup. But I knew they looked perfect.

"When are you leaving?" I said, to be polite.

"Tomorrow. Going to work at a supermarket in Atlanta."

It sounded dreadful. "I'll tell Ireland you said hello," I said.

"You do that." His eyes finished their scrutiny, and he began to walk away. He didn't even say good-bye.

Then he stopped and turned toward me again. "Tell me one thing. Remember that day in class when you turned invisible?"

I smiled.

"Why did you do it?"

I didn't have the answer. Finally I said, "It was a joke."

"A *joke*." He said the word as if it were an obscenity. Then he spun around and strode off, his shoulders hunched high and square.

⁓

At the airport I had two hours to kill, but the shopping options weren't exciting. I was browsing through magazines at a shop when a man said, "You're the one. You screwed Neil Cameron."

He held a copy of the *New York Times*. The lower right side of its front page displayed my photograph—the official one released by Cameron's aides—next to a photocopy of a birth certificate. The headline read: SCANDAL MAKES CAMERON QUIT RACE ABRUPTLY.

I said, "You must be confusing me with someone else," and walked away.

At another shop I bought a copy of the newspaper. The birth certificate on its front page said that Ariella Montero had been born only fifteen years ago.

The tabloid covers had harsher headlines: CRADLE-ROBBER! JAILBAIT! CAMERON DATING TEENAGER. CAUGHT BY HIS OWN

LIES. They featured photo after photo of the two of us, my hand on his arm.

I hadn't known how things would end. It might have been fun to be the first lady.

But I didn't mind so much. My heart was set on Ireland.

⌇

"It's my first time on a plane," I told the attendant.

"Are you nervous?" He was a small, agile man in his thirties, with wiry hair. "Because if you are, just push that button." He gestured toward the ceiling panel. "I'll come and tell you a joke."

I liked that. "Can I have a drink?"

"Honey, you're in first class," he said. "You can have three."

I had two, gulping down the first. The attendant seemed amused. As I sipped the second, leaning back in the plush leather seat, I used my phone to text Diana, telling her I'd made the flight safely. Then I sent myself an e-mail about the events of the day, so that I'd have all the details later to use in my blog. When I got to Ireland, I wrote, I'd tell my side of the story. I wouldn't talk to all of the reporters, only the ones who paid the most. Maybe I'd be offered a book deal. I tried to think of a good title, but we took off before I came up with one.

⌇

The plane was reportedly cruising at thirty-five thousand feet when the explosion happened.

Envision it: the passengers screaming, the attendants stumbling, then chaos as the plane nosedives into the Atlantic. Everyone in a panic except for the girl in seat 2A, who sits motionless, pressing her face against the cabin window glass, peering out into a rush of nothingness. Then, hearing voices thin as water, silver as mercury, calling her name.

Welcoming her home.

Book Three:
Knowing

Sixteen

I awoke in a white room. Where I was, who I was, didn't seem too important. What mattered was the cat.

It sat in the middle of the white-tiled floor, a silver cloud, washing itself. Then its head lifted; its empty eye sockets turned toward me. Told me it was time to go.

Even in the fluorescent glare from the ceiling lights, the cat had patterns of grey amid its silver coat. "Marmalade," I said.

I slid out of bed, shook the skirt of my blue dress to lose its wrinkles. The cat crossed the room and disappeared through a shut door. It wasn't locked, and I followed. The cat moved down a brightly lit, empty corridor. I walked quickly, keeping close to the wall.

Marmalade led me to another door, then down a concrete stairwell. I saw her tail disappear through a steel door at its bottom and I ran down the last flight, trying to catch up.

The door sprang open, and I was outside, underneath a night sky. The wind smelled like Miami. And Marmalade was gone.

I moved through the darkness between two buildings, looking for her, but saw nothing, not even a wisp of smoke. A streetlight ahead showed a sidewalk, and the sidewalk bordered a street full of slow-moving cars. Like a sleepwalker I followed the empty sidewalk for blocks, realizing with each step something I lacked: money, form of identification, car keys, phone.

Then I saw people: tall women made taller by high-heeled shoes, wearing bright colors and drinking cocktails, surrounded by slender men in their shirtsleeves, smoking cigarettes. I thought the place must be some sort of court-yard café, with a brass fountain shaped like an urn and white chaises surrounding it, big as beds.

The smells of the women's perfumes mingled with ciga-rette smoke, making me feel weak. I had no idea how long it had been since I'd eaten or been fed.

I walked through the crowd, trying to find a restroom. A wall of glass blocks glowed and changed colors, and I moved along it slowly, following its curve, until I saw a muscular man leaning against it, drinking deeply from the throat of a red-haired woman. His shaved head lifted, and his eyes flicked over me, as if he recognized me.

"Little sister looks hungry," he said.

My hands made the open-mouth Mentori sign.

He held out his left arm, the other one still holding the woman, who seemed to have fainted. "Come and eat," he said. "I have more than enough."

᷈᷈᷈

After I'd bent my head to his wrist and drunk my fill, energy swept through my body, steadied my nerves, made me feel grounded again. I said thank you, but the man's attention had already returned to the redhead.

Finding the restroom, I washed my hands and face, wish-ing I could take a shower, wondering how long I'd been wear-ing the blue dress, afraid to ask a stranger what month it was. I combed my hair with my fingers and went back to the courtyard.

The women reminded me of flamingos as they stalked from the chaises to the bar and back to the fountain area again. Their voices sounded much too loud. Even the fountain's plashing seemed exaggerated, as if someone had turned a volume switch up as high as it could go.

I stood still and breathed deeply, scanning the place, until I saw a cell phone on an empty table. My heartbeat sounded loud to me as I swept past the table, lifted the phone, and went out to the street again.

Dashay. The name came to me easily. I knew that I knew her phone number by heart, but somehow I couldn't think of it. *Relax*, I told myself. *Don't panic.* I stood very still, willing myself to remember.

I tried to visualize this *Dashay*. A hazy image of a woman came to mind, as indistinct as my face would be in a mirror. I looked at the phone's keypad, imagining myself making a call, but I couldn't think where to begin. When I was about to give up, I remembered a single digit. Then I saw the entire area code, hanging in an orange cluster beneath the streetlamp. I pressed the keys. The rest came back just as slowly, one number at a time. Finally I had it all and tapped the last number into the keypad. The call went through. Each ring made my head hurt. No one answered.

A couple with their arms wrapped around each other sauntered along the street, headed toward the bar. I waved at them. "What's the name of this street?" I asked. Each word sounded too enunciated, as if I were trying to speak a foreign language.

The man smirked. He thought I was drunk. "You're on Southwest Fifty-eighth, sweetie."

"Southwest Fifty-eighth." I repeated it slowly, twice.

They kept walking. I pressed the redial button. *Please,* I prayed.

On the fifth ring a sleepy voice said, "Who *is* this?"

"Dashay?" I said.

"*This* is Dashay," she said. Then she must have recognized my voice. "Oh my madda. Ari? For real?"

I said, "For real." I was thinking, *Ari. So that's my name.*

"I knew it," she said. Her voice came out like a sob. "I knew it all the time."

⤙❦

I read her the name of the café from its awning. She told me to go back and stay there until she arrived. "Sit down and don't move. Don't move one inch. And don't you go talking to strangers, now," she said. "Miami is a *bad* place."

After I hung up, I went back to the courtyard and managed to slip the phone back onto the empty table. Then I figured I might as well sit there myself, unless someone asked me to leave. The cell phone said the time now was 9:10. I hoped I'd be on my way home before the bar closed.

Meantime, I would people-watch. More likely, vamp-and-people watch. Hard to tell which of those around me were *others.* Everyone seemed a little larger than life.

The man wearing gold chains who said, "Lookin' good, mama," had to be human. He paused at my table, took in my lack of reaction to him, and said, "Okay, okay," as he walked away.

The man with the shaved head—my donor—came around the corner, patting his lips with a folded red handkerchief that he returned to the pocket of his black jacket. He went to the bar, ordered, and carried away two red glasses. Then he came to my table and set them down.

"You look as if you could use a drink," he said. He took the chair next to mine.

Only then did I realize how thirsty I was. I clinked his glass and took a sip. "Thank you. For everything."

"No problem." We sat back in the white upholstered chairs. For some reason I felt very comfortable around this man, with his blunt-featured face and enormous muscles. His strength itself soothed me, made me feel protected. I sensed he would bring me no harm.

Maybe he sensed the same about me.

"I wish I could buy you a drink back," I said. "But I don't have my wallet with me."

He looked thoughtful. "Somebody took it away, right?"

"How did you know?"

He sipped his Picardo. "I'm a regular here. A few years ago some poor vamp wandered in here looking like a lost puppy. Like you. I don't know what happened to you, what happened to him, but he came in here all drained and hungry and a little slow in the head. Without his wallet."

"That kind of sums it up." My speech was coming more easily now, though it still didn't sound normal to me.

"I talked to the guy. He said that he felt like his brain had been taken apart and put back together again."

I felt like that, too. "Could you tell me what month it is?"

When he said late April, I nearly spilled my drink. Last time I'd seen a calendar, it was January.

I wondered what I'd missed.

❦

His name was Miguel, he said, and he'd been born in Little Havana, a neighborhood west of downtown Miami. These days he lived in Coconut Grove.

The names sounded more musical than the sounds of the fountain, which didn't seem quite so loud now.

Then I thought about Dashay's warning. "You aren't in a gang, are you?"

"Everyone's in a gang," he said, "even if it's a gang of one."

We ate platefuls of oysters and olives, and the food's saltiness hurt my tongue. But I kept eating.

"You remind me a little of my sister," Miguel said. "Where do you come from?"

I had no idea. He must have seen the confusion in my face, because he said, "Hey, no big deal."

"My name is Ari," I said.

Someone began to play a piano—a grand piano, glimmering at the end of the courtyard like a white ghost. Small white candles flickered on the tables. The breeze smelled like exotic flowers. I sipped a second glass of Picardo and sent a thank-you to Marmalade for leading me back to the land of the living.

~

Dashay didn't walk into the bar, she sailed—her caftan wafting, braided hair flying behind her. When she spotted me, her face brightened, then turned sour when she saw Miguel.

The first thing I said when she reached our table was, "I'm okay. *He's* okay." That quieted her long enough for me to add, "This is Miguel. He saved me from starving." I turned to Miguel. "This is Dashay. She doesn't like Miami."

Dashay wouldn't even sit down. "Happy to meet you," she said, her tone contradicting the words. "The truck is waiting, Ari. We need to get you home."

Miguel stood up. Dashay glanced at him and said, "Oh my." In spite of her reservations about Miami strangers, she was impressed by his build.

Miguel gave me a quick hug. "I'm always here on Saturdays," he said. "If you ever need me."

I surprised myself, and shocked Dashay, by giving him a kiss on the cheek. Then Dashay took my arm, led me out to the street. "Since when do you kiss strangers?" she hissed into my ear.

I didn't know, so I didn't answer.

A truck was parked at the curb, its motor running. In its cab sat a man who looked familiar.

"That's Bennett," Dashay said, her voice softer. "You remember him?"

I said yes, but he seemed a stranger until he smiled.

Bennett was in the driver's seat. I sat in the middle, and Dashay climbed in next to me. She turned toward me, took my face in both her hands, looked hard into my eyes.

"You're all right," she said, as if willing it so.

"I feel strange," I said.

"Anything hurting?"

I said no. "My brain feels kind of"—I struggled to find the word—"spacious."

Dashay looked puzzled, then turned away and strapped us both in. "We'll deal with that in the morning." She rummaged in her purse and handed me a tissue. "You need to clean up. Your mouth is bloody."

"Her bad blood got the better of her, maybe," Bennett said. He pulled the truck away from the curb.

My head rested on Dashay's shoulder. She went to sleep as soon as the truck merged onto the interstate, but I felt wide awake. I watched the highway roll toward us in the truck's headlights as Bennett drove us home.

◁≺

"We're here."

Bennett's voice woke me. The truck's motion must have rocked me to sleep, after all. Beside me, Dashay still slept.

While I stirred and stretched, Bennett walked around the truck, opened the passenger door, and lifted her out. He carried her inside a blue-painted house that seemed to sprawl in all directions.

I looked at its windows, yellow-tinted from the lights inside. I knew I'd been there before, but the place seemed familiar only in the way a landmark glimpsed in a postcard might. I made my way toward the house and stepped warily inside, looking around me for clues.

Bennett walked into the living room. "Ariella?" he said. "Don't you know where your room is?"

I turned around slowly, looking for something I knew, finding nothing. Then I began to cry.

He crossed the room, enfolded me in his arms. "Don't be worried, child," he said. "I came back. You can come back, too."

The room he led me into—blue walls, white bed—smelled of lavender. I felt so pleased to recognize the scent that I said the word out loud: "Lavender." The blue violet letters of the word shimmered as I spoke it.

After Bennett left, I walked around the room three times. Every object in it stood out, as if outlined by a child using thick pencil strokes. Nothing but its scent seemed familiar to me. I stared at the books, the clothing in the drawers, the charcoal sketch of a girl propped against the dresser mirror. All the mirror gave me was a blurry face, edged by strands of dark hair. I looked from the sketch to the mirror, willing the images to marry.

Finally I went to bed, because I didn't know what else to do. Seconds after I'd turned out the light, I heard soft footfalls on the bedroom floor. Then the mattress moved, and something made its way toward me. A cold nose sniffed my hand, then a furry form molded itself against my left side.

I didn't know it until later, but Grace had arrived. After that, I drifted toward sleep, floating in the dark room. Where I was, who I was, didn't seem too important. What mattered was the cat.

Seventeen

I awoke to the sound of a voice, low pitched yet urgent, coming from another room. Straining to pick out the words, I heard another voice, this one in my head: *Please don't tell me you're eavesdropping again.*

Both voices belonged to Dashay. I wondered, *Am I a chronic eavesdropper?*

In the days to come I heard her urgent voice often. She was telephoning my parents in Ireland, making plans for my disappearance.

She explained the reasons on my first morning home, simply by leaving a folded newspaper by my breakfast plate.

NO HOPE OF SURVIVORS, read the main headline, and in slightly smaller type beneath it: "NY-to-Dublin flight disappears with 230 on board." Even smaller letters read: "Cameron's Mystery Girl among the missing."

Cameron. The name made my heart contract.

And there, above my captioned name, was a photo of me.

Except it wasn't me. Even though I had no distinct reflection in a mirror, and only hazy memories of how others had described me, I knew I wasn't the girl in the picture.

"I knew that wasn't you." Dashay lowered herself into the seat opposite me, slowly, as if she were a much older, heavier woman. Worry seemed to add weight to her actions. "I could tell by the eyes."

I stared at the grainy black-and-white photo. The young woman had on too much makeup. She wore a trench coat— something I'd never owned.

"There's a drawing of me," I began, but Dashay had been listening to my thoughts. She stood up from the table and left the room, suddenly seeming much younger and lighter, and came back holding the charcoal sketch. I looked from it to the newspaper photo.

"She's almost identical," I said.

"But not the eyes." Dashay rested her index finger lightly on the photo and tapped it, as if summoning it to life. "Look at them. Look how dead they are. Those are duppy eyes and no mistake."

"What's a duppy?"

She said she'd told me about duppies before. They were Jamaican ghosts who could be summoned from the grave and made to do the bidding of an obeah man. "You might call him some kind of magician, I guess," she said. "*Shaman* is a better name."

Dashay poured us large cups of tea and set a bowl of oatmeal on the table before me. "Eat your breakfast, please. Then I have some questions to ask you."

Obediently, I ate my breakfast. But I had no answers to her questions. My head felt as if it were full of marshmallows. I didn't know how I'd ended up in Miami or why I'd gone there. Whatever had happened to me seemed as mysterious to me as it must have been to her.

꘎

Patience was not one of Dashay's virtues, I learned. Yet I sensed how hard she strove to be patient with me during my first crazy days back in the land of the living.

That first day she explained to me why I mustn't go off the property: I was presumed dead, so in the eyes of the world I must stay dead.

She could have saved her breath. I had no desire to run away from home or even to go out for a walk. I was afraid I'd forget how to get back again.

Dashay began the same explanation a second time. "It would be too risky for you even to go down to the gate to get the mail," she said, enunciating each syllable.

I said, "I may be slow, but you don't have to talk to me as if I'm an idiot."

She tried to look indignant at my sassiness, but I could tell it actually pleased her.

Bennett was much easier to be around, all in all. He took me horseback riding around the property, and the gentle rhythm of the horse's trot brought back a flood of memories—of places we'd ridden before, of the sounds and smells of horses in other seasons.

Dashay had supper waiting when we returned. My appetite seemed insatiable, that first night after we'd been riding.

After we'd cleared the table and washed up, Dashay went off into her room to make and answer phone calls. Bennett taught me a card game, Crazy Eights, which I enjoyed, even though I knew he let me win the first few times we played.

We were in the middle of a "rubber" game—the tiebreaker after we'd each won one—when Dashay burst in, holding her cell phone. She handed it to me without speaking.

"Hello?" I said.

"Ari?" A woman's voice, soft and flustered. "Do you know who this is?"

And those few words unlocked something in me. "Mãe?" I said.

"That's right." The woman on the other end began to sob.

I handed the phone back to Dashay, shaking my head. Then I began to cry, too, without knowing why.

"No, no, no." Bennett's voice was as gentle as the arm he put around my shoulders.

Dashay left the room. When she came back a few minutes later, she no longer held the phone. "I'm sorry," she said. "That was my idea. She didn't want to talk to you. She knew she couldn't handle it. After all, she thought that you were dead. But listen, Ari. She can't wait to see you."

The conflicting emotions confused me. "Where is she?"

"She's way across the ocean. In Ireland, with your father."

Father. The word conjured no image, no feelings.

Bennett broke in. "Did you book a flight?"

Dashay shook her head. "Sara's superstitious. She wouldn't let Ari get on an airplane, not after all that's happened. No, we're going to take a boat."

"A boat." Bennett sounded skeptical. "All the way to Ireland."

"A big boat." Dashay's voice came fast now, as if she was excited. "A ship. So big it has movie theaters and restaurants and shops and swimming pools and a spa."

I thought, *Isn't a spa a kind of bathtub?* I didn't think that was anything to get excited about.

"We leave in two weeks. That's the first transatlantic crossing I could find, and lucky for us, it leaves from Florida."

Lucky for us. I had no sense of what those words could possibly mean.

～

On the day after Dashay announced her big plan, a rectangular box addressed to Sara Montero arrived. After a bell rang, Bennett went down the grassy path to collect the package at the gate.

When he came back, Dashay looked at the address label. "Everybody knows Sara goes by her own name, not Montero," she said. The return address was a box number at Hillhouse College.

Dashay tore open the box. Inside, encased in bubble wrap, lay a laptop computer.

"I think it's yours, Ari," she said.

I was more interested in the note inside the box. The cursive handwriting seemed familiar. It read: "Dear Ms. Montero, I am so sad to hear about Ari. I can't even imagine what you must be going through. She left her computer behind. I hope it brings you some peace of mind. We all feel terrible." It was signed, "Your friend, Jacey."

I had a momentary image of hair—thick, wavy blond hair.

Dashay read the note over my shoulder. "Poor thing," she said. "I feel sorry for her."

Yes, *sorry*. That feeling accompanied the image of the hair.

Bennett said, "There's something else in the box."

I pulled out a small mound of Bubble Wrap, bound with duct tape. *This Jacey person must be cautious,* I thought as I unwrapped it. *The sort of person who anticipates that things will be broken.*

Inside the package lay half an oyster shell, and in it rested a small dull pearl. Bennett seemed unimpressed and Dashay, downright disappointed. "What *is* that thing?"

I cupped the pearl in my hand, awed by its beauty. "Mãe," I said. The word came to me from nowhere. "My mother. She gave this to me."

Dashay's face softened. Bennett took the empty box away. I held the pearl for a few more minutes, then returned it to the shell and carefully carried them to a safe place on the bookshelf in my bedroom.

Later that day someone, probably Dashay, set up the computer on a desk in my room. I glanced at it from time to time, in passing, having no desire whatsoever to turn it on.

～

Dr. Cho arrived on my third day home. Dashay met her at the gate and drove up to the house with her, and they walked in together, talking.

The doctor set a leather satchel on the kitchen table. She looked familiar to me, the way a character actor you've seen in more than one film looks familiar. "Hello, Ari," she said. "How are you feeling today?"

I looked into her dark eyes and envied their alert intelligence. "I'm not sure," I said.

She examined me in my room. She listened to my heartbeat and stared into my eyes and ears and every other part of me, it seemed. Then she said she needed a blood sample. The sight of the needle made me nauseous. I had to close my eyes.

She didn't ask me a single question until all her tests were done and the tubes of blood had been packed into her bag. Then she asked seven.

No, I said, I didn't remember what I'd done after I left the house in January. I had a vague recollection of holiday celebrations, of food and gifts, nothing more. Miami? Yes, I must have driven there, but I didn't remember that, either. (Did I really know how to drive?) Yes, since I came home I'd been taking my tonic. Before that, I didn't know how I'd been fed. Yes, my appetite was strong. Yes, my body felt healthy. Yes, I slept soundly. My mood? That was a question I couldn't answer. I didn't know how I felt.

"I'll give you an injection to boost your immune system," Dr. Cho said. From her bag she removed a syringe and a vial.

As the syringe filled with dark fluid, I bent over, clutching my stomach. She set the syringe down and came to me immediately. She put her hand on my forehead and knelt to look deeply into my eyes. "It's all right, Ari. It's all right."

I was breathing hard, nearly panting, and my body was shaking. She wrapped her arms around me. "I won't give you an injection. It's all right. You're safe here." She was thinking, *Funny, she's never reacted that way before.*

Sometime later, after she'd left, I played the scene over in my mind, ashamed of my reaction. Whoever I might be, I didn't want to be a coward.

～

Every day I ate three meals and went horseback riding. I didn't talk much, and I liked that Bennett and Dashay didn't, either. We created an impromptu play of a small family devoted to keeping quiet about our worries.

But in the background, Dashay was up to something, I could tell. More discreet phone conversations, more scurrying from room to room while I lay on the living room sofa, Grace by my side, reading anything: comic books, cookbooks, old novels. I would have read the dictionary, but Bennett had taken all three copies to the guesthouse, for reasons no one seemed to know. I could have asked him to bring me one, but it seemed too much trouble.

One afternoon I heard singing coming from the kitchen. A strange scent wafted into the living room—rich and sweet, and somehow familiar, promising something impossibly delicious. Grace and I left our sofa to investigate.

The oven door was open, and the smell in the kitchen made my mouth water. Dashay lifted a narrow pan from the oven shelf and set it on the counter. I looked at the golden loaf and said, "Honey cake."

Dashay kissed me. And she let me eat half of it, right then and there.

～

"Don't you have anything better than that?" Dashay looked critically at my blue dress. It had been washed and pressed, but it was tight at the shoulders, chest, and hips.

I tried on the few other clothes in my bedroom closet, and none of them fit me. Dashay shook her head, then left. She returned carrying a white chiffon dress. After I'd put it on, I noticed the thin, yellow panels set into its skirt. "It's like an iris," I said.

She smiled. "It looks good on you. Your form has filled out this year."

"Do you mean I'm fat?"

She laughed. "No, no. But your chest and hips are fuller. More womanly." She looked thoughtful. "Must be the human side of you, growing up."

She'd made me dress up because we were expecting company. A boy called Sloan would be coming in on a bus from Atlanta, and Bennett had already left to pick him up in Crystal River. She said I'd met him when I was back at college.

"How do you know him?" I asked.

"He's your friend, Ari. The one who drew that picture of you. He was here for Christmas. We stay in touch every few weeks or so. Poor boy has been working in a supermarket. He can use a break."

When Bennett arrived, the young man with him did look familiar, in the way that Dr. Cho had: someone I'd seen before, someone who could most likely be trusted. He came over to where I sat in the living room. "No, don't stand up," were his first words to me.

He sat beside me on the sofa, and we eyed each other. His

long hair made him look romantic. I liked that word, *romantic*. He smiled as if he'd heard it and liked it, too.

"It's amazing to see you," he said. "Ari, you have no idea. It's deadly."

"Deadly?"

"In Ireland it means awesome. What a relief!"

∽

Dashay cooked us a feast that night: ackee, a kind of fruit that actually tasted a little like the scrambled eggs I'd had for breakfast, mixed with salt fish and spices, along with rice and red beans and fried sweet plantains.

Sloan asked for Scotch Bonnet sauce, and Dashay said, "I knew I forgot something."

When I tasted it, I knew I'd had it before. I had no trouble remembering the flavors of foods.

Afterward, as Bennett and I cleared the table, Dashay and Sloan went off for a walk. "Better enjoy the spring before it turns to summer," she said. But I sensed they were going off to talk about me.

Bennett was beating me at Crazy Eights by the time she came back, alone. She went straight to her room and slammed the door. Sloan trailed in afterward, looking forlorn.

"She's vexed and no mistake," he said.

"Sit down." Bennett patted the chair next to him. "She's like that, sometimes."

"Ari, I told her." Sloan sat down and folded his arms across his chest. "About you going to Miami for the Septimal."

"What's a Septimal?" I asked.

Eighteen

Sloan didn't tell me everything at once. He gave me information in small vignettes, manageable doses of my past: the meals we'd shared in dining halls; the class where we learned to dance Butoh; the winter break we spent at Blue Heaven; the portrait of me he'd never finished.

Within three days of his arrival I had a much clearer sense of the Ariella Montero I had been and might become once again. And Dashay finally forgave him, after saying several times that she could not fathom why he'd kept quiet all those weeks about my trip to Miami.

"I'm no snitch," Sloan said. "It was pretty plain to me that Ari hadn't told you, and if she didn't want you to know, why should I play the squealer?"

Dashay's face lost its animation. "I should have known all along," she said slowly. "Ari told me last Thanksgiving. She wanted to be older so she could have that politician man."

Sloan winced. They all looked so morose that I felt I should apologize. But it's hard to say you're sorry for things you can't remember doing.

Bennett said, "You know, you didn't need to try to be older. You were doing fine the way you were."

I looked down at my hands in my lap. "Thanks," I said.

Dashay spent more hours on the phone, consulting Dr.

Cho and my parents. She wanted to call Dr. Roche's office, or better yet, drive down to Miami and confront him in person. Dr. Cho had never heard of Godfried Roche, she said.

Then my father took charge. He told Dashay to stay away from Miami, that he would handle the inquiries from now on. He pointed out that we didn't know for certain that I'd ever kept my appointment. For all we knew, I might have fallen in with one of the vampire gangs that roam Miami. In any case, he would investigate the possibilities himself.

Reluctantly, Dashay went back to making preparations for what she now referred to as "our cruise."

"You really don't remember meeting Dr. Roche?" Sloan asked me later.

We sat outside in the shade of a water oak tree near the river. It was the first of May, a fragrant freshness in the air. Summer humidity would soon follow, but that afternoon, coated with sunscreen, we were celebrating spring.

I picked a pink flower and studied its star-shaped blossom. Later, Dashay told me it was sea purslane, delicate in appearance but surprisingly sturdy. "I have utterly no memory of any Dr. Roche."

"I'm the one who put you onto him." Sloan's dark eyes looked guilty.

"Don't worry about it."

He had a pencil in his hand and his battered sketchbook on his knees. I peered over his arm, but he flipped back the page before I could see what he was working on. "Remember this?" he said.

It was a detailed sketch of a landscape: hillside, trees, and a stream. Yes, I remembered it, and I remembered walking down that hillside. I said, "You captured it perfectly."

"You didn't think that way before," he said. "You've changed."

"Possibly." The landscape had a strange power: it made my optic nerves vibrate. Yet it took real effort to pull my eyes away.

"I wonder: did you actually keep the appointment? Did Roche give you the Septimal? Are you older now?"

I put the daisy behind my ear. "Dr. Cho says I'm maturing, but at a slower rate than humans. Remember, I'm only half-vampire."

"But you *are* aging?" He shook his head. "Does that mean—?"

"Does it mean I'll die?" That question had haunted me since the doctor called with her report. "I'm not sure. Neither is Dr. Cho. I'm hoping that maybe my father will know."

More and more, I felt comforted by the idea that I had a father, and a mother, and possibly answers awaiting me, even if they all were far away.

～

The daily newspaper was full of articles about Joel Hartman, considered likely to be the next president, and about how his platform had changed since Cameron dropped out of the race. For instance, Hartman advocated mandatory vaccination and sterilization of homeless people. And he went on and on about threats posed to the U.S. by China.

About Cameron himself, I found only two lines: "The former front-runner, whose scandalous relationship with an underage girl ended his campaign, is reportedly on an extended sailing trip. He remains unavailable for comment."

Sailing. The word brought me a sensation of freedom and lightness, almost of flying. And that sensation gave birth to the curiosity, which grew into a burning necessity, to discover what had happened to me.

When Sloan met me in the moon garden that day, he carried something instead of his sketchbook, but it was equally battered: a bound notebook with a blue cover. "It's your old journal," he said, handing it to me. "It turned up in the rubbish-sorting at the recycling center."

The book fell open on my lap. I stared down at its handwriting. It did look familiar. "Have you read it?"

"Of course not. I was planning to send it to your parents."

"Thank you. For not reading it. And for bringing it back to me."

He leaned back on his elbows. "Did you know I used to smoke cigarettes?" he said. "That's a habit I don't miss much, except sometimes, when I can't figure out what to do with my hands."

It was his way of changing the subject.

And so my reconstruction began with Sloan's anecdotes, continued with the journal, and grew more complex when we turned on the laptop computer. But that didn't happen until we were at sea.

Dashay, thrilled with even our initial small progress, asked Sloan to come with us to Ireland. At first he declined. Although I could tell he wanted to go, I now knew him well enough to understand and respect his need to not be beholden to anyone. And at times, I thought he might be frightened of being around me.

But Dashay overcame his reluctance by telling him he was essential to my "makeover." Since my physical appearance might be recognized, I had to dye my hair, change my eye color with contact lenses, and assume a new name.

Choosing the hair color—Sloan took charge of that. He and Bennett drove to the local pharmacy and returned with a box of dye. The color was a deep, vibrant red. He and Dashay ordered contact lenses via the Internet. When they arrived and I saw their color, I said, "Viridian."

Sloan smiled. "You remembered."

The transformation took place in Dashay's bathroom, which she referred to forever after as her salon. When I came out to the living room, Bennett said, "Wow."

Sloan didn't say anything at first. Then he stood up and left the room.

My father told Dashay that I could remain a Montero if I became a distant cousin named Sylvia. Dashay took my new passport photo and sent it to the wizards in the vampire underground, who corrected its blurriness and produced the passport. I doubt anyone would have mistaken Ari Montero for the woman in the photo, who had green eyes and glossy red hair, and a look of worldly sophistication.

Dashay took us shopping for *cruise wear,* as she called it, in a local thrift store. Sloan got into the spirit of shopping. He found me a vintage halter dress and himself a musty tuxedo jacket that had to be dry-cleaned. He insisted on paying for his clothing himself, using some of his summer savings. I worried about him quitting his job, but Dashay let me know that my parents intended to pay him for "tutoring" me about my own past. Whether Sloan would accept payment remained an issue to be settled later.

When it was time to say good-bye to Blue Heaven I had a strong sense of déjà vu. Bennett and Grace, the bees and the horses, and the safety of the blue bedroom were much harder to leave than I'd imagined. Bennett promised to send us regular e-mails, and he and Dashay said their good-byes privately the night before we left. The next day, they showed no emotion as he drove us to Fort Lauderdale in a third-hand station wagon he'd acquired while I'd been away.

That was the phrase I used: I'd *been away,* and now I had returned. Or at least some semblance of me had.

～

On our third day at sea, Sloan confided in me that he'd never been on a vacation before. *On holiday* is how he phrased it.

Most of the other passengers seemed to know how to enjoy themselves rather too well. Drinking and dancing and eating all night seemed the norm on our ship, the *Marco Polo.* Each meal featured a long menu, and we were urged to sample everything. A few hours later, the Fountain of Fudge buffet on the promenade deck would be thronged. Every time I sat in a deck chair, a smiling server offered me a pink cocktail with a paper parasol stuck in it, and every night drunken revelers cascaded from one deck to the next, lurching from side to side as they navigated the endless staircases. The cruise seemed designed to make passengers forget everything.

But ours was a working holiday, dedicated to remembering. Every morning after breakfast, Dashay went on deck to read, and Sloan and I sat at a table in the corner of our cabin. (Dashay and I shared a suite with a balcony, while Sloan had a tiny cabin with no windows, the only one available at the last minute. He assured me it was "deadly.")

At times, as we traced a timeline through the events, I thought of Marco Polo himself, setting off with his father and uncle on a voyage into unknown territory. He must have been as excited, and at times as frightened, as I was now.

But my voyage charted a different path, toward what should have been familiar. Someone had become *me.* That much was clear from the start. How and why it had happened, who planned it and who played my part: these questions we couldn't answer. All we could do was map what had occurred.

Our reconstruction work would have been impossible had

my substitute (I thought of her as my doppelgänger, a sort of ghostly double) not kept such copious notes. At first she'd used my journal. My own entries, written in a script that I now recognized as my handwriting, ended abruptly with the beginning of the new year. The entries thereafter were prone to right-slanted loopiness, all written in the present tense.

We worked in tandem; Sloan read an entry, then passed it to me. While I read it and took notes, he read the next one and made his own notes. Sometimes, when I took a break, I visited the NetFriend page for AriVamp and stared at her face. Now I knew all too well what I looked like.

And there were other revelations.

"Jacey had an *abortion*?" I set down the journal.

Across the table, Sloan stopped reading. "She wrote about it, in the creative writing class," he said. "And Richard took sleeping pills. I guess he was the father."

"I never even knew she'd been pregnant." A flood of memories came back to me: Jacey brushing out her hair, laughing with me in the cafeteria, telling me I was special, unlike anyone else she knew. "Poor Jacey. Poor Richard. What an awful thing to go through. I don't think I could do it."

He looked at me sharply. "Are you joking?" Then he said, "Ari, vampire women can't get pregnant. Didn't you know that? Or had you forgotten?"

I hadn't known. Or had I? "*You're* forgetting something," I said. "I'm a hybrid. Who knows what I can do?"

"Who indeed." His voice was so low I barely heard the words.

Later, when I was alone with Dashay, she confirmed what Sloan had said.

"That was the saddest thing the doctor told me, back in Miami when I was vamped," she said. "No children. You see, at that time I thought I might want a big family one day." She looked wistful, but only for a second. "So I have to make do with substitutes, like you." She grinned at me, touched my hair. "Pretty color, yes?"

~

When the journal entries stopped, we turned to the laptop, where the doppelgänger had copied long notes apparently posted earlier as a blog. The writing quality seemed to deteriorate as she went on, becoming gushy and embarrassingly sentimental. She'd wanted the world to know she'd lost her virginity—no, that Ariella Montero had lost her virginity. That was the hardest section for me to read and the only one that Sloan and I didn't talk about. The irony seemed even more cruel, since Dr. Cho had assured me that I remained a virgin. (I'd asked her when she examined me. Anything might have been done to me those months I wasn't awake.)

As Sloan and I carefully constructed my past, and the past of my pretender, all the while I felt a mounting sense of outrage. She'd stolen more than my name and appearance—she'd appropriated my dreams. She'd lived my fantasies. She'd managed to seduce Neil Cameron, the man I wanted. Worst of all, she'd been the ruin of him—not only of his political aspirations but of his personal ones. *Our* personal ones.

But had she known what she was doing? Was she accountable for her actions?

One night, after another meal of endless options, I walked around the deck alone. I leaned on the rail and stared out into the dark ocean, wondering if somewhere out there, Cameron and the *Dulcibella* were looking my way. *So on the ocean of life we pass and speak one another . . .*

But even if they had been, I could only imagine what Cameron might be thinking of me. Then I remembered: he thought I was dead.

If only I hadn't gone to Miami.

Then Sloan was there, standing at the rail next to me. "If they hadn't used you, they would have found some other way to bring him down," he said.

As usual, he had arrived at the truth of the matter before I did. With that one sentence, it all became plain: what happened hadn't been about me at all. The entire plan must have been designed to stop Neil Cameron from becoming president.

We stood side by side, facing the darkness. I knew he was wondering how I felt about Cameron, but I knew he wouldn't ask—any more than I'd ask if he planned to see Delia or his family. We respected each other's damage too much.

※

Sloan couldn't dance. Dashay gave him waltz lessons in our cramped cabin, but his feet couldn't follow her instructions. After an hour or so, Dashay gave up and went out for "some recovery time."

Sloan and I ambled out ourselves. Even with the balcony, the suite felt a bit claustrophobic at times. We ended up in a dance club/lounge called Orpheus, drinking Picardo. The club's deejay played industrial music—Sloan told me that's what it was called—with strong bass and percussion lines and incoherent lyrics. A machine sent clouds of smoke across the crowded dance floor. Sloan wore a vintage Hawaiian shirt that made my eyes hurt, and I had on the green halter dress he'd found me at the thrift store.

Two people came in, dressed in black. They had dyed black hair and heavy black lines drawn around their eyes, and their skin looked as if it had never seen the sun. They glanced over at us, then stared.

Sloan's mouth was open, exposing his fangs.

Good grief, I thought. And that reaction brought me a memory: I'd been taught to never let the world know what I was.

Sloan closed his mouth. "Sorry," he mumbled. "Sometimes my inner demon-child gets the better of me."

The couple in black came to our table. "Wanna dance?" one of them asked Sloan.

And it turned out that Sloan *could* dance, like a maniac. He simply couldn't waltz.

The three of them spun in a circle, moving through the smoke like dervishes. Ariella Montero probably never danced that way, I thought. But Sylvia Montero was ready to try, and she joined them on the floor.

After so many days of trying to make rational connections, it was bliss to simply move with the music.

In a break between songs, the woman introduced herself as Lilith and her friend as Ramon. "You two are amazing," she said, wiping her forehead on the sleeve of her shirt. "It must be a hundred degrees in here. How do you stay so cool?"

Sloan said, "Vampires don't sweat."

We outdanced Lilith and Ramon. Exhausted, they retreated to our table and sat watching us. Sloan and I barely made eye contact as we moved around the floor, never touching yet responding to each other's motions, letting the noise propel our bodies as if we'd made a pact to stop thinking about the past and begin to live again. We danced until the music ended.

⁓

Dashay had brought along cases of tonic, more than enough to keep the three of us nourished through the voyage. I noticed that Sloan wasn't drinking much of it.

When I asked him why not, he said that artificial blood

supplements were all very well, but they couldn't compare in taste to the real thing.

"So you bite people?" We were alone in the cabin when I asked these questions.

"Occasionally." His voice was flat. "Back at Hillhouse I used the supplements. But out in the world, I never seem to have trouble finding willing donors."

And I recalled the previous night, when he'd disappeared after dinner and not been seen again until this morning. "Those goth kids we met at Orpheus?"

"They're more than willing." His mouth had a curious half smile on it. "Aren't you tempted yourself?"

Ariella wouldn't have been, I thought. Sylvia might be.

⁓

During the next few days we entered rough seas. Most of the passengers stayed in their cabins, and Sloan and I had the ship pretty much to ourselves.

Many vampires suffer from motion sickness and vertigo— even Dashay spent most of those days in her bunk—but for some reason Sloan and I weren't affected. A growing sense of restlessness drove us out of the cabin, around the decks, up and down the internal stairways.

One night, Sloan and I went back to Orpheus. The club was deserted. Not even the deejay wanted to play music while the ship pitched and rolled. We moved on, to a lounge on the top deck where a lone barman poured us glasses of Picardo, and as an afterthought poured one for himself. "Nice weather," he said by way of a toast.

We sat at the bar and watched the ocean, grey and silver waves with whitecaps, roil beneath us. After we finished our glasses, the barman set the bottle on the counter. "I'm turning in," he said, and walked out.

"Are you sleepy?" Sloan asked.

"You know I'm not."

We refilled our glasses and carried them to a booth overlooking the foredeck. The ship plowed into the waves, sending spray so high it hissed against the lounge's windows.

"We're heading straight into the storm." Sloan leaned back against his chair. He didn't sound concerned. And any anxiety I felt had nothing to do with the weather.

Then he turned his face toward me. I don't know if I bent forward or if I sat still. Our lips touched, as if by accident, then pressed together fiercely. His arms went around me. Where were mine? I think one of my hands grasped a piece of his hair and the other cradled his ear. Our mouths burned against each other.

We fell back against the seat, hungry, thirsty, starved. Inside me my blood sang, celebrating this moment, wanting more, wanting all of him.

When he pulled away, his face looked haggard, as if he'd been in a battle and nearly lost. My fingers still clutched his hair.

"Why not?" My voice sounded hoarse.

"No," he said. "No, Ari. Not until you're put back together again."

✦

Next day the weather turned calmer. For days we'd seen nothing but water, and now, across the water ahead of us, loomed a dark shadow of land. The ship sailed into France at dawn, and the dim shapes of stone buildings and a lighthouse set along the coastline thrilled me. For the first time I let myself imagine what sort of house my parents might own, what sort of room might await me in Ireland.

The *Marco Polo* would stop briefly in France before head-

ing to Ireland and then on to England. We'd leave the ship at
Cobh, the port city of Cork.

Dashay and I decided not to go ashore in Brest, since we'd
be in port briefly, only long enough to see tourist shops. We
sat on our balcony, sipping tea, watching the shoreline pass.

Someone knocked at the cabin door. Dashay opened it,
and Sloan stepped in, wearing a backpack and carrying his
duffel bag.

"I came to say good-bye," he said.

"You're joking," I said, coming in from the balcony.

"Not this time." He set his bags on the floor. "Ramon
and Lilith are getting off at Brest, doing some hiking around
France. They invited me along."

Dashay said, "Who?" and I said, "Those are his goth
friends." *Willing donors.*

"You're on your way back to yourself now," Sloan said to
me. "The rest will come when you're with your folks. I don't
want to be in the way of that."

I began to protest, but Dashay held up a hand. "Let the
boy do what he will."

"But I thought you wanted to meet them," I said to him.

"I do. Someday. When you're all of a piece again." He
looked at his feet. "I want to thank them. They paid my way
over, and Dashay gave me money for a plane ticket back to
America."

"That money came from the Monteros, not me." Dashay
had her hands on her hips, looking a little bewildered at what
he was saying.

"I thank you, and them." He gave her a sudden, quick hug.
"Fair play to you."

Then he came over and gave me a brief, clumsy hug. "And
to you, Ari. Uh, Sylvia. You've worked hard, coming into
being." He sent me a thought: *The broken bowl is glued together.*

It wasn't enough. *Kiss me,* I thought.

He stepped backward. "I'll be back at Hillhouse in the fall. The scholarship, you know." He picked up his bags. "Won't you be coming back to school?"

I said I hadn't the faintest idea. Would Hillhouse welcome Ari's older cousin?

"Almost forgot." He set the bags down again, unzipped the duffel, lifted out his sketchbook, and ripped out a page. He handed the sketch to me.

This me looked different from the one in the sketch propped against my mirror at Blue Heaven. She held a star-shaped flower. Her eyes were fresh and full of wonder, her mouth slightly open. She looked as if she'd just awoken from a long sleep. I felt him watching me as I studied her, so I set the drawing down on a table and looked at him instead.

He turned away and gathered up his bags again.

Then we went on deck to watch Sloan, in the company of Ramon and Lilith, stride down the gangplank.

I felt jealous watching them go. "That was sudden," I said to Dashay.

Three dark shapes disappeared into the foggy morning.

She shook her head. "Me, I kind of expected something like this. He didn't feel ready to see Ireland just yet. Nobody wants to go back to the place that broke your heart." She sighed. "Besides, I think he's scared of how he feels about you."

Nineteen

The next afternoon, we sailed into Cobh. Bags packed, Dashay and I stood on deck in the rain and said hello to Ireland.

Through the mist we saw row after row of brightly painted houses, red and blue and green and yellow, and on a hill above them a soaring cathedral. The air smelled different than it had in Brest—earthier, mossier scents beneath the prevailing odors of engine fumes and brine.

The ship slid toward a long quay, where clusters of people stood under umbrellas, waiting. My eyes scanned them once, twice, but could make out no one familiar.

"They're not here," I said. I felt nervous, almost relieved to not see them.

Dashay said, "Be patient."

Ropes thumped and chains clattered ashore and were made fast to huge iron cleats. The engine groaned and went silent.

Then a couple emerged from the terminal building, both walking briskly. Her long auburn hair flew behind her. He was buttoning his raincoat as he walked.

I saw my parents for the first time.

They easily were the most elegant figures on the pier. They seemed unconscious of the rain as they moved through the crowd to a spot near the gangplank and tilted their heads to look up at the ship. Then they waved at us.

We waved back. I felt shy, exhilarated, anxious, all at the same time. For a moment I felt too scared to move.

Dashay took my arm and propelled me firmly through the crowd, down the gangplank.

How do you say hello for the first time to the ones who've known you all your life?

With awkward hugs. Smiles and kisses. Platitudes about appearances, the ship, the weather.

And all the while, our eyes asking for mutual assurance that yes, we *are* who we think we are, in relation to one another.

Before anything else, my mother insisted on feeding us. A squat yellow hotel along the pier wore a banner promising Fresh Local Oysters & Murphy's Irish Stout, a combination that apparently appealed to her, because within minutes we were sitting at a table in the hotel restaurant. My father stowed our bags in his car, and by the time he joined us, the edge of strangeness wasn't quite so sharp for me.

Mãe sat next to me at the table, holding my hand. As my father walked in, the other diners stopped talking to watch him. Tall, graceful, his dark hair damp, face glistening with rain, and utterly unconscious of the effect he had on others, he slid into a chair opposite mine.

"It's what the Irish call a soft old day," he said.

I must have looked confused, because he said, "That means we'll have a fine Atlantic drizzle with us all afternoon."

His voice, with every syllable it spoke, brought me a sense of peace and well-being. Later, when I considered it further, I realized that his had been the first voice I ever heard, as a baby. And now, it became the first to acknowledge my adulthood.

To my mother, I would always be a child. I learned that within minutes, my first day in Ireland. She hovered over me, ever protective, as if terrified that I might be snatched away from her. Dashay watched us, her eyes full of sympathy mixed with amusement.

After inhaling platters of oysters and pints of Murphy's—surely the most restorative food in the world—we climbed into my father's car, another vintage Jaguar. This model was dark green. Dashay and I sank into the back seat's tan leather upholstery. My mother half turned in the front seat to talk to us.

"I love your hair," she said to me.

"That was my doing." Dashay stretched out a hand to touch it. That day, she or my mother seemed to touch me every other minute or so. Later, they brought out a tape measure and recorded my physical dimensions, as if they needed to verify that I was real. "She looks like a different young woman now, doesn't she?"

My father's eyes met mine in the rearview mirror. He let me know that I was the same Ari he had rocked to sleep in his arms, years ago. He sent me that image as ballast, I think.

"What happened to your amulet?" Mãe asked.

I didn't know what she was talking about. Her face fell. "It was an Egyptian cat," she said. "You wore it around your neck, for protection."

"They must have given it to the other one," I said. I didn't like the thought of her wearing my mother's gift. Had it given her any protection?

The long car seemed to purr along the narrow country roads, and I leaned my head against the back seat. It had been one of the most important days of my life, I realized. But with reunion came a degree of exhaustion.

I perked up as we came into the city of Cork, its streets crowded with pedestrians and buses and cars.

Dashay said, "Why are there so many vamps here?"

How she knew—without sun, without telltale absent shadows—impressed me.

"Ireland is cultivating a sizable vampire population," my father said.

We stopped at a traffic light. He glanced out at the street, where four young women in a group noticed him and began making rapid Mentori signs in his direction. He looked away and drove on.

"After the collapse of the Celtic Tiger—that's a name for the economic boom years in Ireland, Ari—the government had to be creative in its recovery strategies. Beginning in 2007, they began offering significant tax breaks and other enticements to immigrants—especially scientists."

I would have listened to his voice no matter what he was talking about. "Is that why you came to Ireland?" I asked.

"In part. The government offered me start-up funds to build the lab."

"Wait until you see the house." My mother's eyes glowed. "Can you imagine what it's like to live in a castle?"

Dashay said, "Cold, I would think. Damp."

"Not this one."

The castle was somewhere in County Kerry, I'll tell that much. Outsiders couldn't find it if they tried. It stands on a hillside overlooking water, not far from a town that has three pubs. Good luck to anyone trying to track it down.

As we drove into Kerry, the air changed yet again, growing fragrant with clover and cows. I opened the back window to breathe it in deeply. "Mãe? Am I Irish?"

She smiled at me. "Yes, my grandparents on both sides came from Tipperary and Kerry. Why do you ask?"

"Because of the air. It smells like home to me."

～

The Jaguar swept up a long driveway. Then we truly were home.

I won't describe the castle's exterior, except to say it had turrets and stone walls partially covered in moss. But inside, my mother had outdone herself. She'd painted the walls of each room in rich, jewel-like colors. The living room walls looked like malachite, deep green with black veins. My room, in a turret, had been painted to look like chrysocolla, a wonderful blend of blues and greens. I raced from room to room, touching the glossy walls, knowing the names of the gems they emulated: yellow jasper in the kitchen, bloodstone in the library, moonstone in my mother's room, pale green beryl in my father's. He watched me run up and down the narrow stone staircases, heard me say the crystals' names.

"When you were younger, back in Saratoga Springs, you memorized a chart of crystals from a plate in our old dictionary," he said. "Do you remember that?"

I didn't remember. But I felt grateful that I recalled the names.

He gave me a brief tour of his laboratory, which occupied rooms in a long wing adjacent to his study. Here the walls were unpainted stone, lined with tables and equipment. Beige metal boxes—the DNA sequencing machines—and computer screens were prominent. Technicians in white coats looked up from their work to greet us.

"We have six research assistants working here," he said.

I couldn't be sure, but I suspected all of them were vampires. One, a young man with long hair, reminded me a little of Sloan. I wondered how his adventures with the goths were going.

The wing ended in a wall of glass. Beyond it lay green hills and a violet mountain range, their colors muted by drizzle. *That's Ireland*, I thought. *Color rising to meet the rain.*

～

To have a quarrel in such a beautiful place was close to sacrilege. Even though the kitchen was silent when I came in the next morning, I knew that my parents were in the middle of a disagreement. Words recently spoken had left a dull reddish tinge in the air, which smelled reassuringly of geranium oil and lavender, mixed with peat smoke from the fireplace that occupied most of one wall.

And somehow, I knew that I was the cause of their fight.

"You may as well tell me," I said.

My father kept silent, but Mãe said, "He's going to ruin everything."

"I hardly think that's a fair way of stating it." My father passed me a rack of toast and a plate holding a slab of the yellowest butter I'd ever seen.

"How many years have I waited for this." My mother wasn't asking a question. "Finally I have my family together, and he wants to take it apart again."

"I don't see how you arrived at that conclusion." My father took a bite of his slice of toast and chewed it quietly.

"You want to interrogate her." She folded her arms on the linen tablecloth.

"I want to ask questions about what has happened, yes." He drank some coffee, as if this were a typical breakfast conversation.

"And then you'll leave us."

For the first time, he looked surprised, even confused.

"Sara, the way you leap to such dire conclusions—I find the process more than a little alarming."

"But you will leave," she said. "I know you. You'll find out who's responsible for what happened, and then you'll go off after them."

"No," my father said. "I plan to talk to COVE."

The Council on Vampire Ethics is an advisory council that serves as a congress and court. Its decisions aren't enforced; they carry such great influence that the sects always abide by its rulings. Even the Colonists curbed some of their most barbaric practices in deference to a ruling from COVE.

Mãe didn't like the idea of him talking to the council, either. The rest of breakfast featured her playing variations on the theme of division and desertion, my father and me chewing toast.

"If you tell them what happened, her new identity will be destroyed." Her eyes looked wild.

"COVE proceedings are kept confidential," he said.

"How can you be sure of that?"

She predicted that his testimony would make us a target for whoever had engineered my identity theft. We'd have to move again, and she didn't want to move, she loved being here—

"Sara," he said. "We won't have to move. I won't let that happen. I love being here, too."

Although part of me felt I'd known him fewer than twenty-four hours, I believed him.

⁕

It was nothing like an interrogation, really. I brought into his study the notes Sloan and I had made on the cruise. We sat in leather armchairs, and I read him the story we'd assembled. From time to time he stopped me to ask questions.

Midway through the morning, Dashay joined us, carrying a cup of tea. She looked at my father, who beckoned for her to sit in the corner chair.

"So," he said when I'd finished. "Someone made a replica of you to carry out a course of action that you would never voluntarily have undertaken."

"Is that even possible?" I asked. "To make an exact—well, nearly exact—duplicate?"

"Yes, of course." He leaned back in his chair, his elbows on its arms, hands clasped. "With synthetic hormones and artificial DNA, new life forms can be created in a laboratory. Using nuclear transfer, clones can be made. There's a fellow in Dublin who's been doing it for years."

"But that's creepy."

He flinched. I knew he didn't like words that were vague or emotive. "Certainly the procedures raise ethical questions that no one has sufficiently addressed yet. In any case, I don't think you were cloned. The process takes years. I think some other science was employed."

From her seat in the corner, Dashay said one word: "Duppy."

"What's that?" my father said.

"Spirit you call from the grave to do your bidding. That other Ari, that was a duppy. I saw it in her eyes."

He looked skeptical. The scientist in him had never quite come to terms with the existence of ghosts. Yet, to my knowledge, he'd seen at least two: the spirit of James Wilde, who'd haunted my mother's apartment in Savannah, and the ghost of my old friend Kathleen.

And that's when it came to me, a memory that became speculation that became certainty, all in less than a minute. "I think I know who she was," I said. "She was Kathleen."

Dashay said, "Who?" and my father said, "Ari's friend

in Saratoga Springs. The girl whom Malcolm killed."

I opened my journal, turned to its last entries. "This handwriting, look at it. I knew I'd seen it before. It's hers. It's Kathleen's. The same as the writing in the notes she used to write me."

My mind, suddenly flush with remembrances, raced now, putting the pieces together. It made sense—the girl who had wanted to be me had actually *become* me. I looked down at the journal. A sentence jumped out at me: *I want to take my place in the world, beside Raphael Montero.*

I shuddered. What other horrors might she have provoked, had she lived?

But my father's mind raced ahead, faster than mine. "The physical approximation, that's the easy part. With plastic surgery they could make any body of similar height and build look like yours. The spiritual animation—Dashay's duppy theory might explain it. But the replication of knowledge, of memories—that's the part I can't answer yet."

"I've read about drugs that can block memories," I said. "Could there be drugs that transfer them?"

My father stood and walked over to his desk. He gave it a questioning look, as if he'd forgotten why he'd approached it.

"It might be done," he said slowly. "Imagine your memory cells mixed with a drug that could cross the blood-brain barrier, then say the drug was injected intravenously into another. Or injected into her spinal fluid. In the brain, the cells might proliferate and connect to preexisting neurons. Similar methods are used in the treatment of degenerative disorders, such as Alzheimer's disease."

It was too much information for Dashay and me to comprehend.

But this line of thinking visibly entranced my father. "Yes, I see how it might be done," he said. "Of course, the ethical issues associated with such an experiment are profound. It's one thing to use technologies to cure or mitigate diseases, but quite another to use them to create duplicate beings or to bring back the dead. After all, who has the right to play God?"

Then I asked the question that my mind seemed to have been framing for weeks: "Do you think that whoever made her also destroyed her? Caused the plane to crash?"

My father rested his hands on his desk. "The authorities are still investigating the cause. The plane's black box hasn't been found."

"Or maybe *she* caused it? She didn't mention anything like that in her writing, though. Maybe someone put a bomb in her suitcase?"

"I need more coffee." Dashay left the room.

My father turned to me and held up one hand. "It's pointless to speculate about the cause until mechanical failure is ruled out."

I changed the subject. "Mãe said that you're doing genetic work."

Then he told me about the Vampire Genome Project, aimed at determining the sequences of the base pairs that make up vampire DNA. Researchers were using the information to understand the causes of weaknesses—for instance, the genes that make vampires susceptible to sunlight and fire.

"The potential benefits of the research are vast," he said. "Not only for vampires. We're also looking at the genes that make us resistant to death and disease, hoping to develop therapies that will treat human diseases and extend human life spans."

He stayed by his desk. Suddenly his expression darkened. "And you, Ariella? How are you?"

I leaned back in my chair. "Dr. Cho said I'm fine."

"What does Ariella say?"

I shrugged. "Do I seem different to you?"

"You seem older, somehow." He picked up a stone used as a paperweight on his desk, looked at it instead of at me. "It's not the red hair or the green eyes—which, I admit, become you. It's something about the way you move and speak. There's depth in your eyes I didn't see before."

"Do you think I was given Septimal?"

He set down the paperweight. "Not likely. Dr. Cho told me she didn't see any evidence of Septimal in your blood sample. Only a trace of anesthetic, she said."

I kneaded my skirt with both hands. "So, what changed me, then?"

"I don't know for certain," he said, "but I'd bet that your brain has matured. Brains aren't static in mortals. The volume of gray matter changes. Neural connections are pruned."

The idea of my brain being pruned struck me as disgusting. "Are you saying it's the mortal part of me that's caused the change?"

"Most likely." He looked away, toward the window. "And the stress you've been through. The experience of stress generates hormones that affect the limbic system. Stress hormones affect memory, too."

Even though he was blocking his thoughts, I knew what he was thinking. If I *was* aging, at whatever rate, it meant that one day I would die.

"Not necessarily." Once again, I'd forgotten to block mine. He turned to face me again. "Who knows what sort of therapies may be available to you? Research in antiaging technologies for mortals has made enormous progress in recent years, and the genome project is very promising. It may be that your vampire nature will protect you. We simply don't know."

"And you don't know if I could have a child?" I'd been waiting for the right moment to ask him that question.

He folded his arms, as he always did when he felt uncomfortable. "No, I don't know. The vampire/human combination is relatively rare, and not enough study has been devoted to it. I suspect it would be a risky thing to attempt."

Dr. Cho had told me the same thing. One thing was certain: I was a complex being, all right.

"We've talked enough for one day." My father came over to me, put his hand under my chin. "You're back with us. That's enough for now."

I let the big worries slide away, then replaced them with smaller ones. "I need new clothes. Cruise wear doesn't seem warm enough here."

"I've already contacted Gieves & Hawkes. You'll have metamaterials gear in ten days or so. Sara gave me your new measurements. As for the rest, she'll take you shopping in Killarney. She enjoys that sort of thing."

From his voice, I knew that he had no interest in coming with us. I was leaving the room when he called me back.

"About your mother," he said. "See if you can talk some sense into her. You know I have to do something about Roche. Dr. Cho will come with me to testify before COVE. And your journal and notes will be invaluable."

"I'm going with you, too," I said.

"Your testimony would no doubt be useful." He crossed his arms. "But your mother will not approve."

Twenty

If Mãe had been upset before, the news that both of us would be leaving made her livid. She burned the bread she'd been baking, and the fumes of her fury spread through the castle.

She threw the charred loaves into the rubbish bin, then stormed off to her bedroom and tried to slam its door. The heavy oak door had a mind of its own and shut with a quiet click.

Mãe did not appear at dinner, a pasta dish cooked by Dashay with her usual flair. Dashay carried a tray up to her. My father and I sat at the kitchen table, twirling bucatini around our forks, not talking.

When Dashay came back, I said, "Is there anything—"

"No." Dashay sat down heavily. "You've done enough."

And I realized that, not for the first time, I'd driven my parents apart.

～

I found Mãe in the garden the next morning. She was weeding a bed of wild irises and calla lilies, flinging the uprooted plants behind her as she worked. I sidestepped a clump of nettles and said, "Good morning, Mãe."

She nearly hit me with a thistle stalk.

I took a deep breath before I spoke. "I think you're being childish," I said. "After all, we'll be gone only a few days at most. And we have to let COVE know about Roche. If we don't, others will suffer. It's an acceptable risk." The words seemed familiar to me, as if I was quoting someone.

She stopped weeding, straightened, and turned to face me. Her eyes had tears in them.

"You should remember: my parents died when I was five," she said. "My sister and I were raised in a foster home. I never had a sense of being part of a family, until now." She brushed away her tears, leaving a streak of dirt across one cheek.

"Forgive me." I went to her side, reached out my hand, brushed away the dirt as best I could. "I didn't remember. My memory is spotty."

She took my hand in hers. "Ari, when the airline called—" She shook her head, swallowed hard. "When we thought we'd lost you—" Her eyes filled again, but this time the tears were for me. We hugged each other. I tried to tell her not to worry, but I was crying, too.

We went back inside, up to my room in the turret, and sat side by side on a cushioned seat. All of the furniture in the room had rounded backs to sit flush against the curved blue green walls. We sat there, holding hands, listening to each other breathe. After a while I dropped her hand to go to my suitcase. I unzipped an inner pocket, pulled out the tissue-wrapped package, and carried it back to the seat. Then I unwrapped it and placed the pearl in her hand.

"The pearl brought you back to me," I said. "Now let it bring me back to you."

Later that morning, Mãe drove us into Killarney, and we bought some warmer clothes for me. Even the sunny days in

Ireland felt chilly. And buying me cashmere and wool seemed to soothe my mother.

Dashay came along, making fun of my mother's driving all the way. We caused something of a stir as we walked through the city, which seemed more like a village, really. Dashay said, "Haven't they ever seen a black person before?"

"Possibly not," Mãe said. "Although they might be staring at your clothes."

Dashay was wearing a billowing summer dress and a huge woolen cardigan borrowed from my mother—not her usual chic attire. But I sensed she was right—it was her skin that drew the stares. We didn't see another person of color all that day.

We lunched on smoked salmon sandwiches in the library room of a quiet hotel, and we talked about jealousy. My mother owned up to the fact that another reason she resented the COVE trip was that Dr. Cho would be there.

"That woman has always flirted with Raphael," she said. "Even when he was ill, and she came to doctor him, she wore *lipstick.*"

It seemed a flimsy reason for such a strong reaction, but I knew better than to say so. I might question my mother's judgment at times, yet I had to concede that her feelings had their own kind of validity. She existed in a world different from the one my father and I knew, where logic and reason tempered intuition and feeling.

"I'm jealous, too," I heard myself saying. "A man I thought I loved was stolen by someone I thought was my best friend." Then, for some reason, I thought of Sloan. *He* hadn't been stolen—he'd been eager to get away from me. And what had I felt for him, anyway, aside from that wave of jealousy as he left the ship?

Dashay said, "*Thought* you loved?"

"Who knows? I never had time to find out for sure."

"Well, don't waste the time you do have having regrets or being jealous." She squeezed a lemon slice over her water glass. "Jealousy is a sign of weakness."

Mãe winked at me and said to her, "Last time I saw you in Georgia, jealousy was your constant companion."

Dashay sipped her water calmly. Then she said, "Oh, I am so over that."

After lunch, we gathered our bags and walked down the hotel steps toward the street. Out of nowhere a large black bird swooped down, its wings brushing Dashay's hair. She didn't even duck.

A group of tourists on the sidewalk stared at her.

Dashay gave them a regal wave. "Guess it's time for me to go back to Blue Heaven," she said to us.

❧

The Council on Vampire Ethics doesn't hold regular meetings. It convenes as needed, always in a different setting. My father let us know at dinner that night that the next meeting had been called for June 16 in Dublin.

"Bloomsday," he said. He looked warily at my mother, but she was meekly eating her share of the pasta left over from the night before. She seemed resigned to our leaving.

We'd all read *Ulysses*, the novel by James Joyce that traces one day—June 16, 1904, to be exact—in the life of Leopold Bloom. It's become a favorite book among vampire scholars, who interpret the book's six vampire references in all manner of ways.

I'd found *Ulysses* a challenge to read but richly rewarding, its prose as lyrical as music. More than the vampire references, I recalled its description of a dead mother come back to haunt her son, smelling of wax and rosewood, her breath carrying the scent of wetted ashes. The pleasure of remembering was ruined. Perhaps Kathleen had smelled that way, too.

I shivered. Whatever anger and jealousy I'd felt toward Kathleen left me, and in their place came sadness. Sadness, and bitter regret that she'd been with Cameron, known him in ways I never would. But forgiveness? Not yet.

"Better go put on a sweater," Mãe said.

Dashay left us two days later. She said Bennett was feeling lonely.

I didn't know when we'd see her again. And two weeks after that, my father and I were off to Dublin. *Another round of good-byes.*

My mother showed unusual restraint during this time. She didn't ask to come along because she knew she'd be in the way, and she didn't cry once. She was trying to create future memories of a happy family, I thought, safe and intact inside a shadow box. The morning of our departure, she came to my room and handed me a velvet box. Inside it lay a tiny silver pendant in the form of a triple spiral:

"It's a Celtic symbol called a triskele," she said. "To me, the spirals stand for our family."

She fastened it around my neck and I thanked her. Neither of us cried.

But later, as the Jaguar rolled down the driveway, I looked back through its window and saw her resolve begin to crumble. Her shoulders hunched forward and her hand rose to cover her eyes.

"We'll be back in three or four days." My father's voice sounded gruff.

I turned and faced the road ahead of us, clearing my throat. "Have you been to a COVE meeting before?"

He'd been to several, he said. He told me the reason for the first one. "I'd been on a research trip in Argentina. I was working with two colleagues in Buenos Aires on developing artificial blood that could also be used in human transfusions. Then I spent a weekend in the countryside and saw first-hand one of the Colonists' ranches. They breed humans, milk their blood, keep them in pens like cattle. The place was more depraved than anything I'd ever imagined."

So he and one of his colleagues had contacted COVE. "And in due time, we were summoned to the meeting. We gave our testimony, showed them photographs. Then we were dismissed. A week later, we were told the council voted to shut the ranch down."

"So you did a good thing."

"I suppose so. Yes. Some lives were spared." The Jaguar barreled down the narrow lane. He drove much faster than my mother did. "But other ranches remain in operation. When one is shut down, another one opens somewhere else. Sometimes I wonder if there's a constant quantity of evil in the world."

I didn't understand. "How could evil be measured?"

He grinned, as if he'd embarrassed himself. "Indulge me for a moment. Let me be as fanciful as your mother. Have you ever looked down at earth from an airplane?"

"Once."

"And have you thought what a reasonable place it seems? I imagine it's even more so when seen from space, judging from NASA photographs. Landscape has its own logic, its special symmetries. Ocean and land, they appear to be precisely as they should be, all in beautiful balance. *Bella Gaia*—Beautiful Earth.

"But when you get closer—when the plane lands or the spaceship touches down—the world rushes back at you in terrible, inconsistent, overwhelming particularity. It makes no sense at all. And evil lives in the details, embedded everywhere. You might root it out in Argentina, only to have it rise up in California."

His words made me think of Sloan's landscape sketch—of being pulled deep into it by unsettling details.

"Talking to you sometimes makes my head hurt," I told my father.

He apologized and turned the car radio on. The station was playing a piano concerto. As I listened, I admired my father's malachite cuff links, grey shirt, black cashmere coat. I tried to fill my mind with pretty things, to not imagine what the ranch near Buenos Aires must have looked like.

～

Although I'd found some lovely cashmere sweaters and skirts in Killarney, I mourned the loss of my Peruvian dress. Another thing I loved that the other one had stolen. It would have been the perfect thing to wear in the oyster bar of the Shelbourne Hotel.

My father and I dined on oysters from Galway, Carlingford, and West Clare. We sipped champagne. Then we strolled through St. Stephen's Green, its paths and pond reminiscent of a Monet watercolor in the cool twilight that bled greens into blues—as my Peruvian dress had.

Later, alone in my hotel room, I admired its pale green walls and overstuffed furniture: a king-sized bed, two armchairs, and a chaise longue. I realized that my father had designed the evening to fill my mind with beauty, to erase the horrors he'd described earlier that day.

~

The Council on Vampire Ethics met the next morning in the hotel's George Moore Suite. I wore my new metamaterials suit, since it was the most professional-looking outfit I owned. As we were ushered in, I had a momentary impression of silk wall coverings, an ornate ceiling, a crystal chandelier, and a round mirror on the wall at the end of the mahogany conference table. The air smelled faintly of old wood and furniture polish.

I braced myself and met the eyes of the men at the table.

Yes, all ten of them were men. Most wore suits and ties, but three had on more colorful shirts or robes. Each sect had two representatives on COVE, and the other four were independents. Existing members nominated new ones, and they served ten-year terms.

The faces around the table seemed vaguely familiar to me, except for those of two independent councilors who must have joined since my last appearance, when I testified during COVE's hearings into the source of opiates found in water distributed from a Miami bottling plant. The chair, also an independent, introduced us and named the men at the table. I felt too nervous to remember the names, but I never forgot the expressions on three of the faces: a Sanguinist representative looked gravely concerned; one of the Nebulist representatives seemed amused; and one of the new independents, a short man with red hair, stared at us with eyes so hostile that they looked threatening.

My father went first. With his customary poise, he moved around the room as he spoke, making them follow him with their eyes. "We have come to inform you of a travesty," he said.

His voice clear and unemotional, he laid out the case against Dr. Godfried Roche. He told the story of a girl who contacted the doctor because she wanted to be old enough to date Neil Cameron, the aspiring presidential candidate; the doctor said he would administer Septimal but instead rendered her unconscious and used her DNA to create a replica that took her place.

The faces around the table grew even sterner. The Sanguinist councilor I'd noticed earlier, who wore a collarless white shirt buttoned at the neck, nodded emphatically, as if urging my father on.

I'd known he was going to do it, but nonetheless I felt embarrassed when my father produced my journal as evidence and passed it around the table, along with photographs of Kathleen. But he never mentioned Kathleen's name or Dashay's duppy theory. In his version, the replica became a soulless automaton bent on destroying Cameron's career. He stuck to the facts that we knew for certain, based on the evidence of the journal, the blog, and Sloan's memories.

Only at the end of his testimony did he show a hint of feeling. "As someone who has worked on the Vampire Genome Project since its inception, I find it deeply disturbing that a fellow scientist would appropriate our research in such a cavalier way. I can only speculate as to Roche's motivations or affiliations. From what my daughter heard in Miami, she's not his first victim. I ask you to stop him. His activities go far beyond identity theft. He's in the business of making monsters."

There was a moment of silence when he'd finished. Then the questions began. My father handled them effortlessly, even the ones from the man with red hair.

"Don't you yourself profit from your DNA research?" he asked. His nasal voice had a Midwestern American accent.

"To some extent," my father answered. "I live in the building that houses the laboratory. But any profits that might be generated from the research will go to the nonprofit institute we created last year."

The man seemed not to listen. "Dr. Roche has been at the very forefront of neuroscience. Yet you dare to call his character into question." His voice bristled with indignation. "Dr. Roche is, after all, the recipient of the Xavier Prize."

"I beg your pardon, Mr. Truckler, but the Xavier Prize is a dubious distinction at best. Dr. Sandra Cho will speak to that this afternoon."

Truckler grimaced. He stood up, as if he were about to deliver a speech, but the council chair motioned for him to sit down. "We need to move on," he said.

Some questions were directed at me, and I answered as best I could. No, I'd had no contact with Cameron since November. No, I had no memories of the weeks between early January and late April. No, I didn't know how I'd managed to escape from the Center for Integrative Neurosciences—I'd simply awoken and walked out of the building.

Truckler made a derisive noise deep in his throat.

That was the only time I'd lied. My father had asked me not to mention ghosts, thinking it likely that the councilors shared his skepticism.

But an odd thing happened in the George Moore Suite. As the hearing went on, I began to think about the ghosts more than anything else. I remembered seeing them in my car in Savannah, and along the path at Hillhouse on Halloween, and in my dorm room, trying on my clothes. The spirit in my Peruvian dress—that had been Kathleen. I was certain of it. But who was the other one? Her understudy?

Twenty-one

After we were dismissed, we stood in the carpeted corridor outside the suite. Inside, the council was discussing the case we'd made. We'd been asked to wait, in case they had any additional questions.

I asked, "Where's Dr. Cho?" I'd been too nervous before to even think of her.

"Her plane was late." My father, elegant in a charcoal-colored suit, leaned against the embossed wallpaper. "She left a message for me this morning. I didn't mention it, because I didn't want to make you any more anxious. She'll give her testimony this afternoon."

Dr. Cho would corroborate that I was the real Ariella Montero and that I'd talked with her about Septimal. "Will we get to see her?"

"Tonight," he said. "At dinner."

I hoped she wouldn't have lipstick on. Mãe would be sure to ask.

"Do you think it went well?" I asked him.

"As well as it could. I don't know some of the newer councilors. The fellow named Truckler seemed set against us before we said a word."

"What happens now?"

"I expect it will go like this: When the council has heard

from Dr. Cho, it will move to investigate Roche or to dismiss our case. A team may be sent to Miami to look into CIN's operations. Its report will determine whether or not Roche is called to defend himself. Ultimately, he may be censured. And if he is, he will be finished. Whatever reputation he has in the vampire community will be ruined."

I ran my hand across the velvety wallpaper. "I don't understand. How can his reputation be hurt if the proceedings are kept confidential?"

He stood away from the wall then, put his hands in his pockets. "COVE's decisions are sent out to the international vampire community via thoughts, the same way we let each other know about collective threats. We're all part of a connected network, even the independents. The councilors never disclose how they arrived at a decision. They don't have to. A COVE dictum carries enormous weight. Since the very early history of vampires, the council has acted to protect our interests." He sighed. "COVE endorsed your friend Cameron, early on. That's one reason they agreed to hear our case."

"Why didn't I know about that?"

"Because you're half-human, Ari. You're not part of the network."

I slumped against the wall. *Half-breed.*

My father put his hand under my chin, raised it, and met my eyes with his. "It's a mark of great respect that COVE agreed to hear your testimony. Not once, but twice."

The same man who had led us into the Moore Suite came out and told us that we were free to leave. My father asked what I'd like to do: Sightseeing? Shopping? Touring the National Gallery?

I said it didn't matter, and he chided me. We ended up at the National Gallery, looking at an exhibit of portraits.

As we moved through the room, I barely glanced at the

paintings, still deep in my own self-pity. Then one sketch made me gasp. It showed a young man with tousled hair, a high-bridged nose, large, dark eyes, and a beautifully curved mouth. He looked exactly like my father.

The wall placard said the sketch was of William Butler Yeats in his youth. John Singer Sargent had drawn it.

"Yes, apparently there's a close resemblance." My father seemed embarrassed. "I've been told that for years. It explains the way people stare at me sometimes. Haven't you noticed?"

I had noticed, but I didn't think the Yeats resemblance was necessarily the reason they stared.

~

That night in the hotel oyster bar, Dr. Cho wore crimson lipstick and a dark red silk sheath with matching jacket. Her long black hair fell loose, and it shone in the candlelight. She greeted us with hugs.

"How did it go?" I asked.

She raised her eyebrows.

"Let's order first," my father said. He turned to Dr. Cho. "I particularly recommend the oysters from Galway Bay."

Even the server seemed impressed by the quantity we ordered.

After the doctor had sampled six or so, she said, "All right. That's how it went. Just all right. I answered their questions, most of which were perfectly reasonable. That Sanguinist rep, Anook Sharma, seemed exceptionally nice. Then that independent guy, Truckler, went after me as if I'd defamed his mother. How *could* I disparage the sterling character of Dr. Roche? And the illustrious Xavier Prize, which I pointed out is the concoction of the pharmaceutical company holding the patent on Septimal?

"Truckler suggested that the whole case is based on professional jealousy, yours and mine," she said to my father. "Who is he, anyway?"

"I made a few inquiries this afternoon, but I didn't find out much. Apparently he practices law in the States." My father refilled our wineglasses. "William Truckler. Goes by the name of Billy."

"Down with Billy." She raised her wineglass and waited. He looked rueful as he raised his. She clinked his glass, then mine.

Was she flirting with him? I thought so. Just a little. Was he flirting back? No. My father was equally charming with everyone.

"Of course I said this was a matter of professional ethics, not jealousy." Dr. Cho took a sip and set down her glass.

"Do you think the council was convinced?" I asked.

"I can't tell. All those men around the table had blocked their thoughts. Incidentally, what's that about? Why aren't there any women members?"

My father said he supposed COVE was something of an old-boys' network. "I agree with you, Sandra. It's high time a woman took a seat."

"Maybe one day I'll see if I can be nominated." Dr. Cho lifted another oyster shell to her lips and drained it. "Or maybe Ari here will do it."

The idea of joining the group of men at the conference table appealed to me about as much as the thought of having to tell my mother how beautiful the doctor looked. Maybe my spotty memory would excuse me from doing either.

꿍

When we'd finished the food, my father and Dr. Cho began talking science. They were deep into the merits of gene-replacement therapy using viral vectors when I said good night. I told them I felt tired.

In fact, I had restless energy in abundance, thanks to a day spent mostly sitting and listening to others talk. As I walked through the lobby toward the elevator, a young bellman said to me, "Surely you'll not be hitting the hay so early as this? It's Bloomsday, after all."

I hesitated. Who knew if I'd ever be in Dublin on June 16 again?

Then someone walked past me, talking rapidly into his cell phone: "No, that should do it. That should take care of the whole thing. I'm on my way now to pick it up." The red hair and nasal voice identified him: Billy Truckler.

I followed him down the stairs and into the street, eavesdropping.

"What's the name of the place?" he said. "Okay. Must be a classy hotel if it doesn't have a name. Oh, apartments. Yeah. Okay, Godfried, I'll be there in five minutes."

How many Godfrieds might there be? That's when I decided to turn invisible.

But my concentration was interrupted, first by the street noise, then by a memory of my father's voice saying, *Use invisibility wisely, if at all. Only when it's absolutely necessary.*

Surely this circumstance met his criteria, I thought. If Truckler was working with Dr. Roche, we needed to know what they were up to.

Invisibility always brings me a rush of exhilaration, a great sense of freedom. Of all the vampire's special talents, it's my favorite.

I moved lightly along O'Connell Street, which was crowded with Bloomsday revelers who didn't seem to notice when they brushed by me. We passed boisterous pubs. From three of them came amplified voices reading portions of *Ulysses*. In passing, I must have heard Molly Bloom say *yes* a hundred times.

Coming toward me, a blind man navigated the crowd, tapping a white cane from side to side as he walked. He wore a dark suit, dark glasses, and a fedora hat. I'd seen him before. He was my harbinger, my shadow man. Like Dashay's black bird, he showed up when a major change loomed ahead for me. He'd also appeared to my father. I dreaded the sight of him.

As I hesitated, Truckler began to walk faster. I made myself keep moving. The blind man drew nearer. I tried not to look, but as he passed me, I did. His lips curved into a smile.

Was he really blind? My mother had told me that harbingers represent what we most fear. For me, that meant someone with an absence of vision and an abundance of malice. I walked faster and returned my concentration to staying invisible.

Half a block ahead, a man singing on a street corner jostled Truckler, who flung out his elbow and kept moving. At the next corner he turned off the busy main road in to a narrow side street, and stopped to study the numbers on the buildings. I hovered near the curb, waiting.

Truckler scanned the street, looking twice at the spot where I stood. The hardest part of staying invisible is maintaining concentration when someone stares at you, but I managed it. He shook his head and turned away.

He entered a red-brick Georgian building through a green-painted door, and I slipped inside behind him. Up a flight of stairs we went in tandem, me grateful for the crêpe soles on my shoes. When he stopped on the landing, I nearly ran into him. Finally we arrived at a white door with a brass number 3 on it. He knocked.

The door opened. A woman with long blond hair said,

"Welcome. My husband has been expecting you. My name is Elizabeth Roche."

She had a voluptuous body and perfectly symmetrical features. How had Godfried Roche managed to attract someone like that?

I stood near the door as they went into an adjoining room, wondering if I should follow them. Then someone made the decision for me. Another knock sounded at the door, and out from another room walked another Elizabeth. She opened the door and said, in the same syrupy voice, "Welcome. My husband has been expecting you. My name is Elizabeth Roche."

"Delighted, I'm sure." I knew that voice.

Malcolm walked inside.

~

There were three Elizabeths altogether.

The third one carried in a tray of dark red drinks. We were all in a kind of sitting room now, me close to the wall near the doorway, the men sitting on leather chairs, the Elizabeths standing in a row like patient attendants.

Dr. Roche looked plump and birdlike, wearing a black shirt with zippers that ran diagonally. He sat like a king on a throne, his beaklike nose high in the air, introducing his wives.

"Elizabeth I is the nurturer and social organizer." He gestured toward the woman standing closest to me. "She's a marvelous cook and an immaculate housekeeper. Elizabeth II is the brainy one. She handles the accounting, and I can talk to her about work. And Elizabeth III is all about passion. Need I say more?"

All three Elizabeths wore identical low-cut black dresses that clung to their curves, and black stiletto heels. They stood still as mannequins, glossy blond curls cascading past their shoulders, their eyes opaque. When I tried to hear their thoughts, I heard only static.

Malcolm slouched in his chair, his elbows bent, hands pressed together. "You've outdone yourself, Godfried."

Truckler looked confused. "Why did you make three?"

"Isn't it obvious? I'm a very important man. No one model could take care of my needs. While Elizabeth I is planning dinner, Elizabeth II is investing my money, and Elizabeth III is in bed with me."

Truckler said, "The perfect marriage. But why did you make them all look alike?"

Roche's mouth spread into a grin. "I'm something of a connoisseur of the feminine physique. I've studied beauty through the ages. I used the golden ratio to create a model of the perfect woman. Besides, I've always loved blondes." He laughed, and the other men joined him. The Elizabeths smiled dutifully.

The sickeningly sweet smell of stargazer lilies in a vase behind me seemed appropriate to Roche's little kingdom of the grotesque. Clearly he'd never heard of wabi-sabi—if he had, he must have considered it a poor joke.

Truckler said, "But when you travel, don't people stare?"

"No more than they would at any set of triplets." Here or elsewhere, Roche clearly didn't mind being the center of attention—he relished it. "I don't call them my harem, except when we're at home. I'm building a new house for us in Miami, nearly twenty thousand square feet. Each Elizabeth will have her own wing."

As if on cue, they simultaneously nodded and smiled.

Malcolm watched them closely. "When you made *them*, where did you find the S factor?"

"I had an old friend who spent many years in India and learned how to communicate with the dead. He summoned my first wife." Roche turned to Truckler, who still looked confused. "The S factor animates simbos."

"Supplied by real spirits!" Malcolm said.

"It's a very complicated process." Roche crossed his arms over his protruding stomach, as if it were a giant egg that needed protection.

"Yes, there were some problems with the last one." Malcolm sipped from his glass.

"She was *almost* a perfect replica." Roche sounded defensive. "She had a few vestigial memories and personality traits that I couldn't quite erase. She liked the limelight a little too much. And I couldn't translate the prototype's synesthesia or ability to hear thoughts—those traits are triggered by brain activities incompatible with eidolons." He looked at Truckler. "That means ghosts."

"So when you said spirits, you meant actual *ghosts?*" Truckler's face was more ugly when incredulous than it had been earlier, in anger. *Nasty little man.*

"Think of it as the transmigration of souls," Malcolm said. "Or, as Joyce called it, *metempsychosis.*"

"Malcolm handles that aspect, now that my old friend is gone," Roche said. "Which allows me to focus on the real work: making the bodies and building the brains."

Malcolm shrugged, as if he disagreed but wouldn't debate the issue. "Like Godfried, I take pleasure in my work. Particularly in the last one, as it happens. It allowed me to correct a mistake, in a way. She died too young. I brought her back, gave her the chance to experience being grown up, the way she wanted to be."

"*We* gave her the chance." Roche didn't like Malcolm, I could tell.

What they were saying confused me less than it did Truckler. I knew they were talking about Kathleen.

The men were on their third round of drinks, and the purpose of their meeting still wasn't clear. Roche and Malcolm traded boasts of the "simbos" they'd made. Some of them were well-known Hollywood actors.

Movie directors prefer simbos to humans, they said. They named a star less known for her acting than for her perfect appearance and tendency to seduce all her leading men, whether they were married or single. Like most vampires, I didn't go to movies—only humans are drawn to theaters, to savor the rare experience of feeling safe in the dark—but even I had heard of that notorious star. She made me wonder how many other modern-day femmes fatales had been manufactured by CIN.

And I hadn't known until now that vampires worked in the film industry. But the conversation didn't end there. Malcolm said Nebulists ran two social networking sites: Facebook and NetFriend. Roche talked about sports and music. CIN-created simulations headed two successful rock bands and were active on several athletic teams, in particular the New York Yankees. Humans and even most vampires couldn't compete with them, he said.

Truckler listened to all of this with nearly as much surprise as I did. "What about crime?" he said.

"Colonists run the vampire mafia, and it still controls most of the human criminal world," Malcolm said. "Which is as it should be. As for simbos, they're employed in minor roles, but they don't head up the mob families. They make excellent hit men and women."

"I created a simbo last week to assassinate the president of Mexico." Roche flinched at the look Malcolm shot him, telling him he shouldn't have revealed that. But he went on.

"My simbos hold important roles in the courts, the banks and brokerage houses, dot-coms, organized religion, and politics. They'll be invaluable to us when the next war comes."

His words sickened me as much as the smell of the lilies. Like most humans, and most vampires for that matter, I'd lived my life never suspecting the machinations and manipulations of power going on all around me. What I'd just heard reminded me of Sloan's landscape and of my father's remarks about evil in the details.

Roche said, "The work is far too valuable to be interrupted by trivial annoyances like a COVE hearing."

"I agree totally." Truckler drained his wineglass, and an Elizabeth came to refill it. "I want you to know, I made a lot of noise during the vote last week to call you to Dublin. But some councilors are pretty upset about what happened to Cameron. And that guy Montero is well respected. Even the Colonists are scared of him."

How fitting that Truckler equated fear and respect, I thought. So my father's scenario had been wrong—COVE had summoned Roche even before we gave our testimony. Why, then, did Roche seem not worried in the least about their decision?

Twenty-two

Elizabeth I asked if anyone was hungry.

"Leave us alone until we're finished," Roche said. She smiled as if he'd paid her a compliment and left the room.

"In fact, I did COVE a service," he said to no one in particular. "If Cameron had been elected, he wouldn't have helped our causes one bit. He's all about compromise and compassion. Fair Share Party, my foot." He glanced at Truckler. "Now, with Hartman, we have someone we can rely on."

Truckler sat forward, resting his hands on his knees. "Hartman's a simbo?"

"He's a mortal," Malcolm said. "Easy to control. He likes money. And he's gullible. He's completely in sync with the Nebulist agenda. We'll have no trouble with him."

"And if we do"—Roche's index finger and thumb simulated a gun—"bang!" He laughed.

I'd been nervous ever since I entered the house. Now fear pulsed through me, centering in my chest. More than anything, I longed to leave, get back to the hotel and my father.

Malcolm's eyes, trained on Roche, had contempt in them. "Tell me, Godfried. I'm curious. How did the Montero girl manage to escape?"

"Who knows?" Roche stroked his belly absently.

"The prototypes are kept sedated," Malcolm said. "So how did this one get away?"

"Once in a great while, one of them disappears. It's happened only twice. I can ramp up the building security, I suppose." Roche looked angry then. "But I don't see the problem. So they escape. So they go out and get lost in the world. Flotsam, jetsam. Dust in the wind. So what? They have no memories, no way to reconstruct what happened to them."

"The Montero girl does." Truckler told them about the testimony the council had heard. "The girl's journal is pretty incriminating."

"And what if she's recognized by the media?" Malcolm said. "She's a public figure now. What if she talks?"

Truckler said, "The testimony this afternoon wasn't pleasant. This Dr. Cho made you look like a fraud."

Roche's face contorted. The two Elizabeths rushed to his side, but he brushed off their hands. "Betsy, bring me my briefcase," he said to one of them.

Briefcase in his lap, he opened it, pulled out a sheet of paper, and handed it to Truckler. I moved slightly away from the wall to read it. The heading was "Medical Consent." I had to move closer to read the small type:

I hereby authorize Dr. Godfried Roche, winner of the Xavier Prize, to inject me with the synthetic growth hormone Septimal. I understand that the diagnostic label of Growth Hormone Deficiency has been assigned to me.

I am aware that I will never be able to remove this diagnosis, or any other that will be added in the future, from my medical record. I understand that it is exceedingly difficult to determine what is brought about (both desired and unwanted) by a drug that has wide and diverse effects on the brain and other organ systems.

In consenting to take the drug as part of a research study, I understand that the researcher's primary interest and loyalty is not to me as a patient and not to my personal interests or welfare. I understand that the "needs of the research project" come before and have priority over my own personal needs.

I understand that the drug will have a wide range of effects on my brain, body, consciousness, emotions, and actions. My sleep, my memory, my judgment, my coordination, my stamina, and my sexuality are likely to be affected. I understand in particular that the effects of this drug may undermine my ability to accurately monitor and report upon just how the drug has affected me, even impaired me, perhaps in a dangerous direction (judgment, social perception, impulse control, etc.).

Having understood the above, I realize that the drug treatment may cause severe pain or discomfort, worsen my existing problem significantly, or even damage me permanently. However, most doctors or experts will never formally or informally acknowledge that the drug harmed me in this manner. I will have practically no chance of proving that the drug caused my damage and obtaining compensation.

I saw my signature at the bottom of the form.

Truckler read the document slowly. Then he looked up. "Brilliant!" he said.

Staying invisible requires energy as well as concentration. Even though I'd consumed two dozen oysters a few hours ago, when the aroma of food wafted into the room it distracted me. I willed myself to ignore it.

"Something smells good," Truckler said.

Roche petted his belly. "Elizabeth has cooked us a hare."

Now I could smell the meat beneath the scents of garlic and butter and cream. My stomach recoiled. *Concentrate,* I told myself. I took shallower breaths to avoid smelling the food.

But the men, thankfully, found it irresistible. They stood up and left.

I waited a few seconds, to make sure no one would come back. Then I inched my way to the end table where Truckler had left the consent form. If I was lucky, I could destroy it and leave before anyone noticed. But I debated: was it wise to destroy the document? It proved that Roche had injected me. Better to take it to my father and let him decide.

Paper in my hand, I'd nearly reached the door when Elizabeth appeared. Which one, I couldn't tell. She stared in my direction as if she could see me. But I remained invisible. I checked to be sure.

Then I realized: it was the paper she saw, apparently floating in the air.

Elizabeth didn't hesitate. She grabbed the form. But I held on, and it tore in two.

Enough of this, I decided. I turned and headed for the entryway. I was turning the door handle when I heard someone behind me. Something sharp stabbed into my back.

I whipped around. Elizabeth held a letter opener, a long blood-tinged blade with a crystal handle. She drove it into my chest.

Then I was dancing Butoh. I began to swoon but caught myself, twisted my body upright, only to spiral down again. On the ground, I moved involuntarily, in twitches and spasms, and then I stopped thinking at all.

A voice said, "No, no, no. Do you really want to add murder to your résumé?"

I opened my eyes and shut them immediately when I saw Roche and Malcolm standing next to me. Apparently I was lying on a bed.

Malcolm continued talking. "On the one hand, she's too unimportant to kill, since you claim to have a strategy to discredit all she said. On the other hand, she's too important to kill. She's one of the rare half-breeds. Her death would be a significant loss to vampire research."

"Well, if she *did* die, Elizabeth would take the rap, no problem." Roche sounded unconcerned. "Elizabeth would be phenomenal on a witness stand. And if she lost the case and went to jail, I'd just make another Elizabeth."

Malcolm looked at him, his eyes sharp and critical. "There's something sloppy about the way you think," he said. "You claim to be so precise about details, but I don't think you're paying enough attention to any of them. This is a real mess you've made."

"*I've* made?" Roche's lips pressed together tightly, and his head tilted from side to side. "*You* were the one who hatched this particular idea."

"And you were the one who botched it. But that's neither here nor there." Malcolm paused. "I'm taking her back to her hotel. I'll make sure she doesn't talk to the press. As for the rest, you're on your own now."

I felt arms go around me, lift me up, hold me firmly. The

wound throbbed. I couldn't have got away if I'd tried. I stayed limp, kept my eyes closed.

We were moving now. Behind us Roche was saying something, something about COVE. I heard a door open.

"Good luck with that," Malcolm said. "You can tape the form together again, but no one can read the part that's soaked in blood." The door clicked shut.

We were in a smaller space now, probably an elevator. *"Golden ratio,"* Malcolm said, his voice contemptuous. Then he sang, under his breath: "Bye-bye, Betsy, good-bye."

I lost consciousness, of a kind. But I could hear voices, murmuring, then singing. Then I began to see them. I saw two young women, ghosts, dancing in a silvery garden— dancing not with each other but separately. They beckoned and dipped, graceful as figures on a Grecian frieze, arms lifted high. The opposite of Butoh. They sang some melody I couldn't quite hear. Then they called my name. "Ari. Come and dance with us."

I knew who they were: Kathleen and my other friend Autumn. This was their heaven, a garden on the ocean's floor. Tall grey coral formations framed them. Sea lettuce the color of steel undulated beneath their feet. They were home, and I was lost, much too far away to join them.

～

I can only imagine the scene when my father answered the door of our suite and found Malcolm standing there, me in his arms, both of us stained with so much blood that my invisibility suit had to be destroyed.

Awakening in another bed, this time with Dr. Cho and my father hovering over me, I saw anxious concern in their faces. I tried to tell them not to worry. They told me not to talk, but later my father said I'd kept repeating, "Yes I said yes I will yes."

❦

Stab wounds heal almost immediately in vampires. Not so quickly for me, since I'm half-human. Dr. Cho told me how lucky I was—the blade had barely missed my heart.

Dr. Cho and my father took turns watching me those first few days. COVE had asked both of them to remain in Dublin until Roche's testimony was complete, in case the council had further questions. And that's how our prolonged stay was explained to my mother.

Everyone, perhaps me most of all, thought it would be a bad idea to tell her about my wound. Her initial rage over our decision to come to Dublin still terrified me.

On my third day of recovery, my father came in, wearing a midnight blue suit and carrying a breakfast tray. He set it on a table. Then he came over, put his hand on my forehead, and met my eyes. "How are you this morning, Ariella?"

"Better." I'd slept well, and the pain in my chest felt duller now. "Why don't you ever call me Sylvia?"

"You may have to use that name in the human world, but to me you are Ariella, always."

He helped me sit up, set the tray before me, sat in a chair by the bed, watched me eat oatmeal. When I'd finished, he said, "Do you feel up to talking? I need to ask you a few questions."

I'd been expecting them.

❦

Malcolm had already told him what happened in Roche's place, along with a few details I hadn't been privy to. The Elizabeth who'd stabbed me had been alerted not only by the sight of the consent form apparently suspended in air, but by my triskele amulet. I'd forgotten I was wearing it.

"Why didn't the others notice it?" I asked.

"Malcolm said they must have been too absorbed in their business or distracted by wine. Even he didn't spot it until you'd been stabbed. Besides, the amulet is very small." He sighed. "What troubles me is this: *you* didn't remember you had it on, when you made the decision to emutate. That was very careless of you."

"Put yourself in my place," I said slowly. "What if you heard Truckler, who's clearly not on our side, talking to someone named Godfried. Wouldn't you have followed him?"

"Perhaps." He frowned. "But not invisibly."

"But I remembered what you'd told me," I said. "I decided that following him was absolutely necessary."

"Did you remember my warning before or after you made the decision?"

When I hesitated, he said, "I'm disappointed in you, Ari. I thought you'd grown up considerably."

I winced.

"Because you acted on impulse, our case against Roche may be lost."

I sank back against the pillows. "How could it be lost?"

"He can accuse you of breaking and entering, and of attempted burglary. And for what? That consent form you signed—"

"That form can't hurt us. It's illegible. It has blood all over it." I realized it was the first time I'd ever interrupted him. "I'm sorry," I said. "For interrupting, I mean."

He said, "Didn't you think his office kept a copy?"

❧

While I convalesced, my father said, Roche had appeared before COVE to testify and answer questions. Anook Sharma had come to our suite the night before to report to Dr. Cho and my father about the case Roche was making against me.

Roche had told the council that he'd never heard of me until I made an appointment with him for a Septimal injection. I'd signed a consent form (a faxed copy of which was passed around the table), and he'd administered the drug. That was the extent of his involvement, he said. Yes, he had the means to make "models," but he'd never considered making one of someone as inconsequential as me. He told the council he was convinced that all of the actions I'd claimed were committed by a doppelgänger had been actually executed by me (possibly directed by my father, one of his professional rivals). I impressed him as an unusually competent liar, he said, capable of fabricating the journal and the related notes. And I was clearly a thief, evidenced by my attempt to steal the consent form from his flat.

"Pity my poor Elizabeth," he'd told COVE. "She's not accustomed to invisible burglars. Yes, she stabbed at whatever was stealing the form, and she was horrified when a bleeding woman manifested herself on our carpet."

Probably horrified at the thought of carpet stains, I thought.

"The shock has taken its toll on her, but she came with me today to tell you what happened."

Sharma said that Truckler had licked his lips when Elizabeth entered the meeting room. She'd worn a high-necked, semitransparent white lace blouse that drew all the councilors' eyes to her, and she'd dabbed at her eyes with a lace handkerchief as she spoke. She repeated her story twice, never changing a single word.

"A lace handkerchief?" I asked. *What a clichéd prop.*

"This fellow Roche doesn't know where to stop," my father said. "In any case, she seems to have most of the council convinced that she acted to defend her home and that she thought you might cause her and the others bodily harm."

"When do we get to tell our side of the story?"

"Dr. Cho and I have been summoned to appear tomorrow."

I was sorting through all he'd told me. "If I supposedly did all the things Kathleen did, then who died in the plane crash?"

"Someone you arranged to take your place." He rubbed his hands together, as if he felt cold. "He's thought it all out. He says the Septimal might have contributed to your psychosis but that the form you signed absolves him from any responsibility. He even suggested that you planted a bomb in that someone's suitcase to blow up the plane. He's painting a portrait of you as an amoral terrorist—a spurned teenager who lost her sense of right and wrong when Cameron tried to end your relationship with him."

I shook my head slowly. "But he has no proof of any of that."

"No," my father said. "All he has is a creative, malicious mind. He suggested that later, when you needed a new identity, you dyed your hair and came to Ireland." He sighed. "He's asking the council to censure *us*."

Twenty-three

That night, when my father brought in my supper, I said, "I've thought of a way to prove him wrong."

He set down the tray and looked at me. His green eyes looked grey in the light filtered through the lace curtains on the window. On those June nights in Dublin, the sky darkened gradually, staying light until nearly half past ten.

I said, "We can ask Malcolm to testify."

"No." His response came the second I stopped speaking. "That's unthinkable."

"But he was part of it. He's the only one besides Roche who knows all that happened."

"Malcolm isn't to be trusted."

My father turned to face the window. For the first time, I imagined what it might have been like to be him during the last four days—to watch his daughter ignore his advice and compromise the family reputation, be wounded and carried back to him in the arms of his old enemy, and recover only to challenge him again. What I'd done hurt him, more than the knife entering my chest had hurt me.

"Maybe Sloan would be willing to testify." I said it reluctantly. I didn't know how I felt about Sloan, even if we could manage to find him. "You know, the boy who helped me come back."

"I doubt any friend of yours would be considered a credible witness." His tone was as formal as if we were strangers.

I said, "I know how much I've disappointed you."

"'Parents,'" he said, "'are sometimes a bit of a disappointment to their children.'" He turned toward me. "Anthony Powell wrote that. Have you read Powell?"

I said I hadn't, and I admired how he'd changed the subject. I changed it again. "Father, we can't let Roche get away with this. Did Malcolm tell you all the dirty work he's done?"

"Probably not all of it." His voice sounded dryly amused. "He did ask me to be sure you didn't tell any humans what happened. I assured him that media attention is the last thing our family wants.

"We didn't talk that long, after we patched you up. He said he had to get back to his place in Sandycove."

I didn't know where that might be.

"By the way, Sandra Cho was magnificent that night. I don't know what we would have done without her. She went to a local hospital, brought back the equipment and supplies we needed for the surgery. We took a risk by not rushing you to the emergency room—but Dr. Cho said the wound wasn't life-threatening. The hospital would have notified the gardai, and once the police were involved, things would have been completely out of our control. Most likely you—that is, Sylvia Montero—would have been charged with breaking and entering, and Elizabeth Roche charged with attempted manslaughter. How the court would have treated you, we'll never know, thankfully."

He shook his head. "An utter shambles. All because you had a whim to turn invisible. I hope you'll never do anything so risky again."

Though I told him I wouldn't, I could tell he wasn't convinced.

"I forgot to mention one thing," I said. "Just after I turned invisible, I saw the blind man. Our harbinger. He was walking through the crowds, and he smiled at me."

He didn't seem surprised. "Yesterday I took a walk through St. Stephen's Green, and I saw him myself."

~

A memorable week, that one. I lost my father's trust that day, and my mother's the next.

I must have been dozing after lunch when a voice awoke me.

"Yes, of course, madam." An Irish voice outside the door. Then the door opened and my mother stepped into the room, carrying a travel bag, looking very businesslike in a black suit. Her face registered joy when she saw me, quickly followed by shock.

She rushed to my bedside, bent to feel my forehead. "You're ill!" she said.

"Better than I was," I said.

She gave me a sudden hug, so fierce that I gasped with pain.

"You're hurt!"

"I'm on the mend," I said, making my voice more cheerful than I felt.

"What happened?" She wanted to touch me, but she was afraid she'd hurt me again.

The prospect of telling her daunted me. I'd rather have testified before COVE again. "Well," I said, "it began this way."

I told her about the hearings and about overhearing a councilor's cell phone conversation. "So I turned invisible," I said.

"Ari." Her voice sounded defeated.

"And I followed him. His name is Truckler. And he met up with Dr. Roche. And Malcolm showed up, and they all were talking about the vampire mafia—"

"Tell me who hurt you."

It's rude to interrupt, I wanted to say. "Roche's wife," I said. "At least I think she's his wife. One of them."

My mother shook her head. "What did she do?"

"Um," I said. "Stabbed me in the chest." I didn't mention that her gift, the triskele amulet, helped Elizabeth locate me.

"What?"

"I'm healing really fast," I said. "Not quite as fast as a one hundred percent vampire might, but much faster than any human could."

She didn't say a word. Her silence frightened me more than if she'd burst into curses.

"Mãe, I had to do it," I said. "Roche had a consent form I signed that would have destroyed the case we made against him. I tried to steal it."

"So did you steal it?" Her voice was unfamiliar, low and terse.

"No. Roche's wife, or whatever she is, caught me. And now Roche is saying that Father and I are the liars, the ones who brought down Cameron and caused the plane crash. Our family's reputation is being destroyed."

"Can't your father do something about that?"

"Well, he could. But he won't."

I told her how Malcolm's testimony could save us.

"Where is Malcolm?" The pitch of her voice rose slightly, began to sound more like hers again.

I searched my memory, and the word came to me like a gift: "Sandycove."

"Sandycove," she repeated. "It's a Dublin suburb."

The bedroom door opened. My father stood on the threshold, Dr. Cho behind him. They both were smiling, as if they'd just shared a joke.

My mother looked away, toward the window. My father stared at her.

For several seconds we all seemed frozen, waiting for her explosion.

But it didn't come. She rose, picked up her travel bag, and headed for the door. Dr. Cho quickly stepped aside to let her pass, and my father turned sideways to watch her go.

⌁

"How did she find the right room?" Dr. Cho said. She and my father were inside now, sitting in chairs upholstered in vintage chintz. "The desk isn't supposed to give out the numbers."

"Sara has her ways," my father said. He looked morose.

"Don't you think you should go after her?" I asked him.

"No. Better to let her cool off. You told her everything?"

"Yes."

"Well, it had to be done, I guess. I should have told her the truth when you were injured. I thought it better to spare her the worry."

"You did exactly the right thing." Dr. Cho sat with perfect posture, looking unfortunately pretty in a yellow linen dress and pink lipstick. "She tends to be overemotional, doesn't she?"

"Sandra, please," my father said. "You're talking about my wife."

The silence in the room felt awkward, but I couldn't think of how to interrupt it. Then Dr. Cho abruptly stood up and left.

I said, "How's the hearing going?"

"Not well. Roche seems to have won over the independent councilors now, with the possible exception of the chair, and the Colonists as well. I'm not even sure we can count on the Sanguinists' votes, much less the Nebulists'."

"Can't you discredit Truckler?" I asked. "After all, he was working behind the scenes with Roche. Some independent representative *he* is."

"I intend to try."

"And I thought of something else I forgot to tell you before: Roche was bragging about making a simbo assassin to kill the president of Mexico. He said simbos will help his side win the next war."

My father frowned. "Malcolm didn't mention that. I can report it tomorrow, but it would be only hearsay. We have no proof, and you're the only witness."

He rested his chin on his hand and looked at me. "Are *you* angry with me, too, Ari?"

Actually, I felt sorry for him.

And, later, I felt sorry for my mother.

After I'd finished dinner and my father had told me good night, someone knocked at my door. Then I heard a key turn its lock, and Mãe came in.

She tried to smile at me, but it was a struggle—her face, even the way she moved, looked defeated.

She sank into the same chair Dr. Cho had left hours ago, and I tried not to compare them.

"I did my best, Ari," Mãe said.

She told me she'd taken the bus to Sandycove and tracked down Malcolm.

"It's a pretty village," she said. "Has your father taken you to visit the Joyce Tower yet?"

I said we hadn't had time for much sightseeing. "How did you find Malcolm?"

"It wasn't hard. I went into a few pubs. One of the bars had three bottles of Picardo on display, so I ordered a drink, talked to the barman. Sandycove's a small place. I told him Malcolm was my cousin. Once I'd described him, the barman told me the name of his hotel."

For some reason I hadn't expected my mother to be a good detective.

She went on. "It was a funny little hotel called Hennessey's. Malcolm wasn't in when I got there, so I sat in the lobby— more an entryway, really. The old woman who owns it told me he'd gone to lunch with a lady friend.

"Nearly an hour went by. We chatted. Then Malcolm came in. It felt strange; I hadn't seen him since—you know."

Since he'd made her a vampire. "It must have been hard for you," I said.

"I wanted to help." She rested her elbows on her knees and clasped her hands. "The woman with him was stunning, but something about her gave me the creeps. And no manners. 'Who's that?' she said to Malcolm. Her voice was like ice.

"Malcolm didn't look at all happy to see me. Mrs. Hennessey said, 'What sort of greeting is that? Here's your cousin, come all the way from America to pay a call.'

"'Cousin Sara!' Malcolm gave me a big fake grin.

"The other woman said, 'I'll call you later,' and left. We were never even introduced."

"Tell me more about what she looked like," I said.

My mother squinted, as if she were seeing the woman from a distance. "Tall. Thin. Dark, wavy hair. Beautiful, as I said. But so cold. And a voice like granite."

Her description brought me the name. "Was she called Tamryn?"

Mãe's eyes opened wide. "How did you know that?"

Maybe I wasn't such a bad detective myself, I thought

smugly. It was the first positive thought about myself I'd had for some time. But what would Tamryn want with Malcolm?

"She was one of Cameron's aides. So then what happened?"

Mãe stretched her arms, then wrapped them around herself. "We went out, sat on a bench across from the beach. I told him what you'd said: that he's the only one who could convince the council of your innocence. But he said I was wrong. He said he couldn't do it, even if he wanted to. And it's clear he doesn't want to. 'I might incriminate myself,' he said.

"Ari, I begged him." She hugged herself more tightly, and her eyes filled with tears. "It was so humiliating, to have to do that. He handed me his handkerchief, told me not to cry." She pulled a linen handkerchief from her pocket. Its edge had been embroidered with crimson initials: *MAL.*

"Malcolm Lynch," I said. "What's his middle name?"

"Albert, I think. Does it matter? He said he didn't have time to talk further, but he told me not to worry. 'Things are in good hands,' he said. What can that mean?"

I didn't know, but the words made me nervous. I wished I felt stronger and could go talk to him on my own.

My mother heard that thought. "Not a chance. You're staying in bed until you're completely recovered. Then I'm taking you home. Back to Florida."

To change the subject, I told her about the exchange between my father and Dr. Cho earlier that day. She didn't say anything, but I saw that my father's words pleased her.

⌒

Sometime in the night, I stirred and opened my eyes, sensing I wasn't alone.

Pale moonlight from the open window pooled on the carpeted floor. In the dim light, the chaise made a gray outline against the wall. It was empty.

I noticed a wisp of smoke. First, it eddied along the floor. Then it began to spin. I smelled mold and dead leaves. The room felt cold, but I didn't want to leave my bed to shut the window.

Then I saw her: a grey figure in motion, now a woman, becoming more distinct with each swirl. She wore jeans, a torn T-shirt. Her feet were bare. I didn't want to look at her face, but I did.

"Kathleen." I whispered the name. It sounded loud in the stillness of the room.

Her smile looked lopsided.

"Ari? You couldn't come to me, so I came to you." Her voice had a peculiar pitch, sounding soft and steely at the same time.

"I don't like the smell of you." I hadn't planned to say that.

Her smile disappeared. "Is it really bad?"

"Not too bad." I was lying, but quickly I became used to the odor. It wasn't that different from Florida air on a damp November night.

The smoke dissipated, but the form—the thing that was her—remained. She stood with her hands outstretched, her head tilted, watching me. "Do you hate me for what I did?"

"No."

Her smile returned. "I couldn't stand it if you did."

"I got over it." Suddenly I had a hundred questions for her. "Why did you do it? How did it happen?"

Her form became smoke again. What had Dr. Roche called her? *Eidolon.*

"They called me back. I had to come." Her voice sounded like a record played at the wrong speed. "First I haunted you. Studied the way you lived, watched you with your friends. I'm ashamed to admit it—I even stole your mail and read it, looking for clues.

"Then they gave me a body, taught me to be you. I loved that part." Her voice broke, as if she might weep. "Autumn wanted to do it, but they chose me.

"But I never *was* you. They lied to me. I did everything they said, but it didn't happen the way they promised. The whole time it was only me, acting. I never became you. And I wanted to, more than anything else in the world. Remember that game we used to play?"

I shook my head. "Who are *they*?" I felt like one of the COVE councilors now.

"Dr. Roche. Diana." She shook her arms, as if willing them to become real. "Diana texted me lots of instructions."

For a moment, I fantasized that Kathleen—this eidolon— could go before the council, give testimony, make our case. But my father had already told me that COVE didn't want to hear about ghosts. Even he wasn't comfortable believing in them.

I pulled the bedspread closer, around my neck. "Did you carry a bomb onto the plane?"

The question seemed to confuse her. Her image began to blur, vibrating slightly. "I don't understand." Her voice sounded faint.

"Don't you remember how you died?"

"Oh yes. I remember that." Her voice grew stronger now. "I was role-playing a game, outside, at night. A man came up to me. 'Why are you always around?' he asked me. I didn't know who he was, but I had my suspicions. 'I want to be a vampire,' I told him."

I shivered. She was talking about Malcolm on the night he killed her, back in Saratoga Springs.

"No," I said. I didn't want to hear that story now. "I mean what happened after you got on the plane to Ireland. Don't you remember that?"

Her substance began to settle again. "Of course I remember. It was my first plane trip. The attendant brought me drinks. He was cute."

"You don't remember what happened on the flight?"

"He brought me another drink. And he said he'd tell me a joke if I got scared."

"And then?" The room had grown uncomfortably chilly.

She moved her head from side to side, in a gesture I interpreted as denial. "Nothing." The pitch of her voice undulated between a scream and a sigh. "Nothing."

The door clicked. A key turned in its lock.

My father came in. His eyes went from me to her, and then he suddenly seemed taller.

"Go!" His voice was soft but powerful. "Go back to your grave."

Not yet! But no one was listening to my thoughts.

The smoke swirled rapidly. Already she'd begun to disappear. She was leaving, and I had so many more questions. And I hadn't had a chance to say good-bye.

"I forgive you," I said, hoping she could hear me.

And then she was gone. The room grew warmer. The scent of decay evaporated.

"*We* do not consort with the dead." My father's voice chilled me again.

A moment later, he left, shutting the door silently behind him.

Twenty-four

When I was awake the next morning, Dr. Cho brought me my breakfast tray. She seemed a little stiff and formal, as if things had changed among us. She said my father was in the Moore Suite, presenting his closing argument to COVE. And Roche would make his final statement at noon, she said.

Neither of us mentioned my mother.

Dr. Cho gave me my pills and tonic, cleaned the incision in my chest, changed the dressing, and watched me finish a bowl of oatmeal with strawberries strewn across it. Then she rose to shut the window. Light rain had begun to fall outside. My father might have called it another *soft old day*.

"When can I leave this room?" I asked her. Beautiful though it was, I felt I knew it much too well.

"Maybe this weekend," she said. "The wound is healing well. You're definitely getting stronger."

"Are you staying on in Ireland?" It felt odd, asking her, but I had to.

"No." She sounded disappointed, somehow. "I'll book my flight back to the States once we know the council's decision. Maybe as soon as tomorrow."

"Do you love my father?" I hadn't planned on saying it, but out it came.

Her dark eyes, full of emotions I didn't recognize, met mine. "I think everyone who meets Raphael falls a little in love with him." Then she stood up. "You know I have a partner back in Savannah."

⁓

When the doctor had gone, I eased myself out of bed and walked around the room. My only exercise during the past five days had been walking to and from the bathroom. Dr. Cho had promised that tomorrow she and I might stroll the hotel corridor together.

But I was fed up with being treated as an invalid and tired of spending long days mostly alone. My father had brought me books, but I felt too anxious to read them. If Bennett were here, we could have played Crazy Eights. If Sloan were around, we could have tried to put more of the puzzle together. Or if Grace were with me, I could have found some comfort simply in the sound of her purring.

I looked down at the shapeless cotton nightdress Dr. Cho had put on me. It fastened with snaps. I tore them apart and threw the gown on the rug. The white dressing on my chest reminded me that I should be cautious, but caution wouldn't help us get a judgment against Roche.

Slowly I pulled on a cashmere skirt and sweater, wishing I still had a metamaterials suit. I doubted that my father would present me with one ever again.

My feet slid into my shoes. I brushed my hair and washed my face, and picked up my raincoat and purse to carry before leaving the room. My mother might have failed to convince Malcolm to help us, but I had a plan.

In the elevator going down, I felt the first wave of vertigo. Two more came over me before it reached the lobby. Feeling weak and stupid, I didn't even get out, but stood there as the car began to fill again.

I'd planned to take a taxi to Sandycove, track down Malcolm, and make him an offer: in exchange for his testimony before COVE, I would agree to take part in his medical research. Any risks involved would be worth it if we could discredit Roche's testimony, put him out of business, restore the family's reputation. If you're likely going to live forever, the honor of your family name means a great deal.

But I couldn't risk leaving the hotel. I didn't feel strong enough. So I rode the elevator as it ascended again, and when it stopped I got out.

I'd been too dizzy to pay attention to the floor when the lift stopped, but now I recognized it. Ahead loomed the tall ivory doors of the Moore Suite. And, in the otherwise deserted corridor, there was my mother, sitting on a bench against the wall.

The shock on her face quickly turned to anger. "What are you doing out of bed?"

I sat next to her and leaned back against the wallpaper.

She placed her hand on my forehead. "I'm taking you back upstairs as soon as you catch your breath."

Finally the door opened. Dr. Cho stood there, looking poised. She had no makeup on. My father stepped out next, his face drained, as if he'd used every ounce of his energy. Nonetheless, he seemed astonished to see Mãe.

Then Dr. Cho noticed me. "What are you doing out of bed?"

My father closed the door and looked from my mother to me.

"I got bored staying in the room," I said.

"Well, at least you didn't leave the hotel," Dr. Cho said.

My mother, sleek in her black suit, said, "Why can't hotels make doors that lock only from the outside?"

They wanted to take me upstairs at once, but I convinced

them I needed a few minutes to regain my strength. I said to my father, "Please. Tell us what happened."

"I think it went rather well," he said, his voice emotionless.

"You were fantastic." Dr. Cho sounded elated. Then she spoke directly to Mãe: "I've never heard such an eloquent speech. You should be so proud of your husband."

"Oh," my mother said. "I am. Very proud of *my* husband."

The Moore Suite's doors both opened, and COVE members streamed out. Anook Sharma came over and shook my father's hand. "A wonderful presentation. You reminded us what COVE truly stands for. I think you may have changed some minds in there."

Truckler came out of the suite, walking fast, talking to no one. When he saw us, he scowled and kept walking. My father must have made one powerful speech, I thought.

"My, what a face on that fellow," Mãe said.

Sharma turned to my mother. "I do not believe I've had the pleasure."

"Anook, forgive me," my father said. "This is Sara Stevenson. My wife."

My parents exchanged a long look. Dr. Cho walked away.

More councilors came over. A Colonist patted my father's back, and three other COVE members shook his hand. Mãe stood by his side and smiled. Someone commented, "What a lovely family you have."

And we stayed lovely, the rest of that day.

❦

Because I meekly stayed in bed that afternoon, I was invited to join my parents for dinner downstairs that night. Dr. Cho had declined to join us; she said she had to pack, since she planned to leave the next afternoon. COVE's ruling was expected by noon.

We sat at a corner table in the oyster bar. My mother wore a pale yellow dress and an emerald necklace I'd never seen before. It glimmered in the candlelight. "It belonged to my grandmother," she told me. "And one day it will belong to you. I've decided that when I turn sixty in mortal years, I'll give away all my jewels."

"And what will you wear then?" my father asked her.

"A silver chain, perhaps. Nothing ornate. Older women need to dress their age."

This made no sense at all to me, or to my father—his eyes had a baffled look—but we knew better than to challenge her. Sara logic made its own rules.

After we'd ordered, I said to my father, "I want to hear your speech."

But he declined to repeat it and claimed he didn't remember much of what he'd said. Knowing the quality of his memory, I doubted that. He was being modest, as usual.

"I didn't prepare any speech," he said. "My comments came spontaneously. I simply reminded them of the facts we'd been able to verify and of the specious nature of Roche's arguments. Ari, your comment about the Mexican president proved prescient. He was assassinated about three hours ago."

"The poor man!" Mãe said.

"We can't prove that Roche was behind it, of course. But this morning I quoted what you'd heard him say about making an assassin. I'm sure he had to respond to questions about that when he testified."

I was about to ask if he'd heard anything about the testimony, but Anook Sharma had entered the restaurant and, after spending a few seconds scanning the room, headed directly for our table. He looked perplexed, and my heart sank. *Don't come over here,* I thought. *Let us have one night together without worries.*

Sharma said hello. "Have you heard the news?"

Our faces showed we hadn't.

"About Godfried Roche," he said. "He's dead."

~

Afterward, when I tried to remember how I'd felt when I heard that news, I couldn't precisely recollect the feelings. They were a jumble of surprise, apprehension, and—yes, I'll admit it, relief, even guilty pleasure, that he wouldn't be able to harm anyone further.

"Someone attached a bomb to the starter of his car," Sharma said. "He was with two of his wives, on their way here, when it happened."

So Roche never had to answer COVE's final questions. I wondered how that would affect our case. Then it sank in: we had no case. Its subject was gone.

"Do they have any idea who did it?" As usual, my father's voice and words betrayed no emotional reaction.

"The gardai are investigating. Apparently there are surveillance cameras in the area where the car was parked, so they're reviewing the tapes." Sharma moved from foot to foot, as if he felt nervous.

"Won't you join us?" Mãe said. "This news is so disturbing."

He said he was on his way to a dinner meeting with other councilors. "I wanted to tell you about Roche. After all you've gone through, I thought you should know." He turned to me. "Are you feeling better, Ariella?"

"Much," I said. In truth, I didn't know what I was feeling.

After Sharma left, I asked, "Is it wrong to feel no remorse about someone's death?"

My father looked across the table, to see if my mother wanted to answer. When she remained quiet, he said, "That's a wrong question to my mind, Ari. Only you can determine whether what you feel or don't feel is right."

I sighed.

"But I *can* tell you how I feel about it. Roche was no friend to you, or to me. I disapprove wholeheartedly of everything he did. And I can't say I'll miss him. It's likely the world will be better without his presence.

"That said, I wish he hadn't been killed." My father stopped talking as the server delivered plates of oysters on ice. When she'd left again, he continued. "No one deserves to be murdered. Whoever placed that bomb acted immorally."

"What will happen to his wife?" Mãe asked. "I mean, the one who survived."

My father said he had no idea.

I excused myself to go to the bathroom. As I walked toward it, I wondered which Elizabeth had survived and why she'd been left behind. What would happen to the twenty-thousand-square-foot house, and how would she use the three wings? If the widow was Elizabeth I, she might run the place as an inn or rent it out for parties, I thought. If she was Elizabeth II, she might set up a think tank there or decide to sell the building and invest the proceeds. And if Elizabeth III had survived—here my imagination failed me. I supposed she might open a massage parlor.

As I returned to the table, I saw something I wasn't meant to see: my mother's hand stretched across the table to touch my father's fingertips. She quickly withdrew her hand when she saw me.

What next? Then I realized: today was the summer solstice. Tonight was Midsummer Night. When the sun stands still, enigmatic events are certain to happen. Sometimes the whole world turns upside down.

Late the next morning, COVE telepathed a notice to all vampires: it had launched an investigation into the death of Dr. Godfried Roche. Anyone with useful information was advised to come forward. Meantime, operations had ceased at the Center for Integrative Neurosciences.

CIN might be gone, I thought. But Elizabeth would go on.

My father let me know about the notice as he was leaving for a business lunch with Sharma. Today was our last day in Dublin, he said. We'd drive back to Kerry tomorrow. My mother planned to spend the day shopping, and he assumed I'd be joining her.

"Have a nice lunch," I said.

A few minutes later, Mãe knocked on my door. But I told her to go shopping without me.

"I want to write in my journal." I showed her the green-bound notebook I'd bought at the National Gallery gift shop.

And that wasn't a lie, because I took the journal with me later when I left the hotel. I had someone to see before we left town.

A taxi took me to Hennessey's Hotel in Sandycove. The owner said, "Ah, you look like the other cousin," when I asked if Malcolm was in.

When he came down the stairs, he acted as if he'd been expecting me. "Have you lunched?" he asked. "Then let's go to the pub down the road."

Outside, he took a monogrammed silver case from his pocket, opened it, and removed a cigarette. "Forgive me," he said, and then he lit it.

I'd never seen a vampire smoke. Even though vampire lungs can repair themselves, we associate smoke with fire— the single greatest threat to our existence.

"It's an affectation more than a habit," he said. "A small flirt with the devil."

Malcolm kept up amiable chat as we walked down the beach to the pub. "What a treat," he said. "For years I thought I had no close relations, and now, this rash of cousins. And Montero cousins, no less."

His blond hair, a little long on top, and the loose stride of his walk reminded me of a schoolboy's. Hard to believe he was the same man who'd collaborated with Roche to bring Kathleen back from the dead.

We sat at a low, round wooden table in the lounge area of a village pub. Malcolm ordered sandwiches and ale—not a customary vampire drink, to my knowledge. "You must try one," he said. "Deamhan's Red Ale is a relative newcomer, but in the last few years it's grown enormously popular."

The barman poured out two pints of ale, which glinted deep red in their faceted glasses. I was going to ask what produced the color. Then I took a sip and recognized the familiar tang of artificial blood.

"It's on tap in most of the Dublin pubs now." Malcolm set down his glass. "Might take a while to reach your neck of the woods down south."

"You know where we live?"

"Somewhere in Kerry. Your mother told me." Malcolm smiled. "I don't know the address, of course. She must have forgotten to send me a Christmas card."

I wasn't sure how I felt about his style of humor. It certainly never made me laugh out loud.

"Will you answer some questions?" I asked him.

"Of course. I wouldn't have come out with you otherwise. But first, do try a sandwich. They do an excellent shrimp salad here."

So we ate the sandwiches, served on thick whole-grain bread, and salt-and-vinegar crisps. We sipped the ale. With anyone else, it would have been a very good lunch. With Malcolm, it wasn't a bad one. I'd begun to feel more at ease with the man who'd saved my life more than once. But my father had been right—I'd never be able to trust him.

"Did you kill Roche?"

"Of course not." He dropped a bread crust onto his plate. "I'd be insulted if anyone else asked me that. I make an exception for you, since, after all, I was responsible for the death of Kathleen.

"But I've tried to atone for that. I brought her back. You should have seen her when she was you, Ari. I met her one night in Manhattan. She truly enjoyed being you. Did she tell you about that last night?"

So he knew about Kathleen's visit. "You made her visit me?"

"I thought it might be useful. Just as when I sent the cat to bring *you* back."

My head began to swim, and it wasn't from drinking ale. "Wait a minute. I'd like to go back to Roche, if you don't mind. Do you know who did kill him?"

"I might." He took a swallow of ale.

I waited, but he picked up another sandwich. "Malcolm," I said. "Who might it be?"

Instead of answering, he went to speak to the publican, who turned and lifted a newspaper from under the bar. Malcolm came back with the paper and spread it before me. Under the headline BOMB SUSPECT SOUGHT BY GARDAI was an indistinct photo, probably taken from the surveillance camera.

"Recognize her?" He took a bite of sandwich.

The grainy print showed a dark-haired woman caught in profile as she walked away from a car. Even though its quality was poor, I could recognize that sharp-featured face. "Isn't it Tamryn?"

He swallowed. "Might be."

"Why did she do it?"

"Oh, she had a number of reasons. But the chief one should be obvious: Roche ruined things for her precious Cameron. That woman wanted to see Neil Cameron elected president more than anything else on earth."

"How did she know Roche was involved?"

He smiled. "I own up to that one. I let her know about the COVE inquiry. She flew over last week to check things out. Our friend Tamryn is quite knowledgeable about explosive devices, you know. She told me she used one to set a fairly large fire on your old campus."

"Why would she tell *you* that?"

"She's proud of it. She wanted to establish her credentials." He lifted his sandwich again. "My, you ask a lot of questions."

I'd lost my appetite. "Establish credentials why?"

"Why? So that we'd trust her to take out Roche. Isn't that what we've been talking about for the past fifteen minutes? We—and I know you're going to ask who *we* are, so let me just say some concerned Nebulists—were fed up with Roche's posturings. He wasn't a very good scientist, and he was a perfect model of indiscretion. For every useful thing he did, he made ten glaring mistakes, and he didn't much care if others knew about them because he believed he was incapable of making a mistake.

"In addition to all that, he had remarkably poor taste. Those *Betsies*." He turned back to his lunch.

"To you, killing him was okay?"

"Not okay." He finished chewing. *"Necessary."*

"And so you used Tamryn." I took a sip of Deamhan's Ale, which was much better than I'd expected, and tried to think it all through. "What will happen to her?"

"Nothing. The photo's not good, and she's a thousand miles away from here by now. And I hardly *used* her—I made her aware of an opportunity to do something she wanted to do. The same sort of favor I did for your friend Kathleen."

I shivered. "Some favor." Then I found myself saying, "How did you bring her back?"

"Oh, are you interested in necromancy?"

All at once his face changed. His eyes sank deeper, his nose grew longer, his mouth set in a stern line. The bend of his neck and the slope of his shoulders conjured a much older man.

The transformation frightened me, but I couldn't look away.

"I learned how to converse with the dead in Africa." His voice, deep and guttural, belonged to someone else. "The rituals date to antiquity. Homer knew them."

And to my mind came an image of Odysseus pouring blood into a pit to summon hungry ghosts.

"The ceremonies are more beautiful than you are able to imagine now." His eyes blinked very slowly. "But I could show you. I could teach you."

With all my heart, I felt, I wanted to learn.

The barman saved me by shouting, "How's them sandwiches?"

The spell was shattered. I saw rage flare in Malcolm's eyes, but a second later it disappeared.

He leaned toward me, himself again, bent his neck so that our eyes met on the same level. His were cool and gray. "It could all have been very different. If only you had come to me." His voice had resumed its normal pitch. "I would have made you older, as I promised to, back in Savannah. You could have had everything you wanted."

I shook my head hard, reminded myself why I'd come. "You let them turn me into a zombie."

"Not so." His eyes seemed grey, transparent at that moment.

"I didn't know you'd been sedated, or even that you'd been to see Roche, until after the fact, when he called me in to handle the S factor. Why did you go near a quack like that? You fell right into their hands."

"Wait." I tried to think it through. "You didn't know? You didn't plan the whole thing?"

"Ari, I've told you what I did. Once I found out what had happened to you, I agreed to animate the model, bring back Kathleen. By then it was clear that Cameron wouldn't do in the White House, and using a simbo to take him out of the race seemed a pragmatic solution to that problem.

"But I didn't write the script. Cameron had a number of enemies among the Nebulists and Colonists, you know, including some wealthy Colonist ranchers in South Texas who were afraid he would shut them down. Any one of them could have hired Roche to do the job. But why did *you* go to him?"

"On the advice of a friend's doctor." I wondered who Sloan's doctor had been. "Who may or may not have known who I was."

He pushed his hair back from his face. "You know, you're not stupid, by any means. Most of your questions are good ones. I'm glad you survived. One day, I predict, you and I will work together."

I said I doubted that.

He shrugged. "As you like."

Then it was time to ask the big question. "Do you know what caused the plane crash?"

"No," he said. "Not for certain."

"Could it have been a bomb planted by Tamryn?"

"I don't know. She didn't mention it. I didn't ask. I'll admit, the idea has crossed my mind." He finished his pint of ale. "You drink so slowly," he said, and beckoned to the barman for another. "Now I have a question for you. Why is it so important that you find out the answers? After all, *you* can't bring back the dead." Then he laughed, as if he'd made the best quip of the day.

Two hundred thirty lives were lost. And Malcolm finds it funny.

He heard my thought. "You're forgetting what we decided about acceptable risks." He pushed back his chair. "Now, do you remember what I asked you back in Savannah? About helping us with the hybrid physiological profile?"

I stood up. "You must be joking."

I dropped ten euros on the table and walked out of the pub.

Twenty-five

The season of risks ended in another summer of love. But this time I was a spectator, not a participant. My parents were about to renew their wedding vows.

How two people who disagreed and misunderstood each other so frequently had arrived at this decision—that was one more thing I couldn't figure out. But during all the weeks of worry, something had happened. I knew it that night when I saw my mother's hand stretch across the restaurant table to touch my father's fingertips. And the idea that my parents would reunite soothed me as much as it elated me.

The ceremony, that was Mãe's idea. She chose the date: a Saturday in late August that she claimed would be lucky. My father went along with it gamely. When he wasn't working in the lab, he helped her address the invitations and pretended to be interested in the menu planning.

But his heart and mind were more invested in his work. He spent ten-hour stretches in the lab, and he always looked preoccupied when he came out.

I helped my mother with the invitation list, sitting at the round oak table in the castle kitchen. Dashay would be coming, as would Bennett, and a variety of vampire friends I'd never heard mentioned before. In a phone call with Mãe and me one afternoon, Dashay suggested inviting Sloan Flynn.

"We don't have his address," I said. I wasn't sure I wanted Sloan around, in any case. He'd hurt my pride when he deserted us in favor of the goth kids.

"I have his cell phone number," Dashay said.

"Good," my mother said. "Invite him by all means."

"He's probably too busy with his friends," I said. I told myself that I hoped he hadn't charged his phone.

"Dashay?" I said. "Could you bring Grace with you when you come?"

She and Mãe patiently explained Ireland's policies about bringing in pets. They were kept in quarantine for six months to ensure they weren't carrying rabies. In short, Grace would not be in attendance.

That night at supper, my parents agreed to invite Dr. Cho, which surprised me. "Although I doubt she'll be able to come," my father said. "She's been appointed to COVE, to take Truckler's seat. She'll be busy."

Truckler had been removed from the council as a result of my father's testimony. It pleased me that Sandra Cho would take his place in future sessions.

Then Mãe said, "We should invite Malcolm."

In an instant the room's atmosphere darkened.

"No," my father said. The word hovered over the table, black as coal.

"But he saved Ari's life." She gazed at me, her lapis blue eyes warm, then at him, her gaze sharper, colder.

My father's eyes met mine. His asked for support.

"No," I said, my voice almost as emphatic as his had been. "It would be too risky to invite him here." I hadn't told them yet that he was a necromancer. Even the idea of talking about it frightened me—as if mentioning the word might somehow summon him and who knew what else.

My mother hated to lose an argument, but this time she

held her tongue. She rose to clear the table. I changed the subject, tried to dispel the tension that mentioning Malcolm always seemed to introduce.

But tension still lingered in the air when I told them good night and climbed the stone steps to my bedroom in the turret. I couldn't sleep, so I leaned on a stone sill and stared out the narrow window at the moon. Nearly full, it kept the colors of my mother's gardens alive, even in twilight.

Then I saw them: my mother and my father, in the courtyard below, dancing. They'd been practicing for their reception. The night before, I'd watched them waltz. They didn't need music to dance.

Tonight they were rehearsing a tango. I'd learn later that it was called the *milonguero* style. Their shoulders and upper bodies touched, and Mãe's left arm draped around my father's neck.

From my vantage point, high in the turret, they seemed to move as one person. Whatever kept them apart had disappeared. Perfectly balanced, their bodies swayed to an elastic rhythm, bending, sliding, turning across the stones—as if that one person had just invented the tango and was making up the steps as she went along.

Epilogue

My name is Ariella Montero, but you have to call me Sylvia.

There are some things I can never know for certain.

Someone used me to ruin a man's political career and my own reputation. Who and why, I don't know.

Someone found my birth certificate on file in an office building in upstate New York and leaked it to the media.

Someone is monitoring the movements of every person on every social network website and has nearly unlimited access to their personal and financial information—yours and mine included.

Why, and who they are, I don't know.

When I try to imagine them, I see no faces—only grey shapes moving through smoke. Behind them, above them, or beneath them, I sense a more powerful presence, pulling the strings.

~

At breakfast, on our first full day back in Kerry, my father showed me an article in the *Irish Times*. The item was very short, headlined, COAST GUARD SEARCHING FOR LOST SENATOR.

The U.S. Coast Guard is conducting a search for former senator Neil Cameron in an area some 1,200 miles off the mid-Atlantic American coast.

A sailboat registered in Cameron's name was found adrift in the area yesterday. The 25-foot sloop, called *Dulcibella*, was spotted by two passing tankers. The Coast Guard boarded the boat late yesterday. The boat was empty and apparently undamaged, a spokesman said.

Cameron, 31, gave up his senate seat and dropped out of the U.S. presidential race last spring after several media reports confirmed that his romantic partner was a fifteen-year-old girl.

I read it twice, my hands clutching my sides, feeling like a child again. My mother refilled my teacup.

"Are you all right?" my father asked.

I took a deep breath. "He might have survived," I said in the calmest, most adult voice I could manage. "And if he did, I'd bet he knows the answers to my questions."

I was thinking, *And if he didn't survive?* I made myself visualize the words: *what if Cameron is dead?*

In that case, I would have to go on, and the unanswered questions would remain—with me, and with Kathleen.

Note to Editor

When I came to write this book, I used the notes Sloan and I made to try to put the pieces together. Since I prefer to write in the past tense, I changed all the tenses in book 2, except for those in chapters 12 and 13. Some of the events they described felt too painful for me to recount. My mother later typed up those two chapters directly from Kathleen's blog, e-mail, and journal. She even kept copies of her text messages on my laptop.

And in chapter 15, when I wrote about Kathleen's final moments as the plane crashed, I found myself writing her a vision of heaven. If it exists, I hope that's where she is.

Acknowledgments

*H*ow is a fifteen-year-old different from a twenty-two-year-old? Is there a relationship between age and maturity?

When you're fifteen, you're convinced you know it all. At twenty-two you realize you don't know anything, and that reality is rather frightening. I think you're more vulnerable at twenty-two. You have far more responsibilities, and on some level you wish you were that fifteen-year-old all over again.

—Indigo Ravenwood

Indigo wrote what I considered the best response to my questions, posted on a blog called La Femme Readers (http://lafemmereaders.blogspot.com). I'm grateful to her, and to Eleni Xekardakis, who runs the blog.

Dr. Jack Ballantyne, professor and associate director for research at the University of Central Florida's National Center for Forensic Science, addressed some of my scientific questions related to age. So did my daughter, Kate Hubbard, a doctoral candidate in the University of Washington's School of Oceanography. Linda and Jay Foley graciously let me interview them at their Identity Theft Resource Center in San Diego.

The quotations about ZIP come from "Brain Power: Brain Researchers Open Door to Editing Memory" by Benedict Carey, the *New York Times*, April 5, 2009. The consent form Ari signed is adapted from "A Model Consent Form for Psychiatric Drug Treatment" by David Cohen and David Jacobs, published in *Journal of Humanistic Psychology*, Vol. 40, No. 1, 59–64 (2000).

Heartfelt thanks to Sheila Forsyth, Kate and Clare Hubbard, Nancy Pate, and Tison Pugh, who commented perceptively on an early draft of the book. And to Robley Wilson, who read several drafts and challenged nearly every comma— infinite love and gratitude.

Many others helped this book come into being. Cill Rialaig and Anam Cara, artists' retreats in southwest Ireland, gave me time and space in which to write the book's early chapters. Students in California and Florida, several of whom read the first two books in the series, had perceptive suggestions for *The Season of Risks*. Among them were Griffen Baker, Tyler Branon, Sammy Harvey, Rafael Quiroz, Elizabeth Starr, and Michael Wise. As I spoke to classes and book clubs, I met extraordinary teachers and librarians, including Linda Dean, Laura Maggio, and Tommye Reynolds. Thanks to all of them, and to all the readers who sent kind words and incisive comments to me at thesocietyofs@yahoo.com.

Kate Ankofski, Kelly Farber, Elmedina Siljkovic, Leah Wasielewski, Carol Manders, Chris Kridler, and Marcy Posner offered consistently excellent professional support. For soul saving, I'm grateful to the intrepid attendees of the Sunday Afternoon Revival Meetings at Port Canaveral.

While this book was being written, my family had to say farewell to three beloved cats, Buddy, Melba, and Bartleby. In their memory, I am donating ten percent of net proceeds received by me from the sale of the book to Alley Cat Allies.

SIMON & SCHUSTER
READING GROUP GUIDE

The Season of Risks

INTRODUCTION

In the latest installment of the series "combining the creepiness of Stephen King with the acute social commentary of the Beats, Philip K. Dick, and Don Delillo" (*The News-Press*), Ariella Montero continues her quest through a turbulent landscape where competing sects of vampires and their vulnerable mortal counterparts must coexist—or perish.

While the Sanguinists advocate peaceful coexistence with humans and nonintervention in mortal affairs, Nebulists favor genetic modification and psychological control of the human population—and they have taken a keen interest in one Ariella Montero.

Set in Florida, Georgia, New York City, and Ireland, the much-anticipated third book in the Ethical Vampire series centers on losing and reclaiming one's identity, as Ari weighs the possible benefits of change against its potential risks to everyone and everything she loves most.

QUESTIONS FOR DISCUSSION

1. Buddha is quoted in the epigraph with his quote, "To watch the birth and death of beings is like looking at the movements of a dance." In what ways does this apply to the various characters? Did this metaphor color your interpretations at any point in the book?

2. One of the vampire characteristics that Ari possesses is the ability to read thoughts—and to have her thoughts read. She notes, "Often, listening to thoughts strikes me as justifiable, sometimes necessary." Discuss the pros and cons of such eavesdropping, both for Ari, and for Cameron as a politician. In what situations would you want this ability?

3. We learn in the prologue that Kathleen wanted to be Ari. Based on what we eventually learn—and what you may already know from the previous books in the series—what reasons does Kathleen have for wanting to be Ari more than "anything in the whole world"?

4. Ari tells us that "Colonists seemed easy to despise, even though I'd never met any." In what ways do you see this attitude in your own world? At school? At work? In politics?

5. Cameron is more than two hundred and thirty years old. If human beings were capable of living that long, in what ways do you think relationships would change? Marriages? Friendships? Politics? Ethics?

6. Does Cameron seem too old for Ari? Why or why not?

7. Cameron asks Ari to wait for him. Discuss how you would have reacted in her situation. What if he had so many years ahead of him, but was not a politician? What if he had as many years as Ari, but his campaign forced them to keep their relationship a secret? In which contexts would you stay, and in which would you decide to let him go?

8. On the campaign trail, Cameron is willing to make Mentori signs—even on television. Discuss the pros and cons of taking such a risk when so much is at stake.

9. On page 61, Mãe remarks, "The season is changing, and the cottage knows we're about to leave it." What other inanimate objects are given human characteristics in the book? What significance do they have in Ari's world?

10. Dr. Cho prescribes tonic for Ari, and tells her to "celebrate your true nature." In your opinion, does she succeed in doing that?

11. How does the atmosphere of Saratoga Springs affect the story? Blue Heaven? Hillhouse College? Dublin?

12. When Ari's parents travel to Ireland, her mother in particular has trouble saying good-bye. Given Ari's nature as

a half-vampire, what unique concerns might her parents have for her while traveling far away?

13. What characteristics do Sloan and Ari share that make them good friends? Ari and Jacey? Cameron and Ari?

14. Malcolm Lynch uses the concept of utilitarianism—in which an action is deemed morally good or bad based on the extent to which it contributes to the greater good—in order to persuade Ari to consent to his experiments. In his example of the physician and the procedure, discuss your reaction—would you rather the physician didn't try the experiment? Come up with your own examples of utilitarianism. In what circumstances does group benefit outweigh personal risk?

15. On page 89, Dr. Hyman discusses the ethical issues of editing memories. Given the option to eliminate painful recollections, what would your decision be?

16. Describe what you imagine as the process of becoming *other*. In what ways is this process similar to becoming a teenager or becoming an adult?

17. When Ari decides to take Septimal to grow older, she chooses twenty-two as the perfect age. Under what conditions—if any—would you make the same choice as Ari? What would your 'perfect age' be, and why?

18. On page 125, Ari admits that "Every culture has its monsters." Do you find this statement ironic? What monsters exist in Ari's world, and in ours?

19. Sloan and Cameron are two very different men in Ari's life. Discuss what it would have been like if Cameron—instead of Sloan—joined Ari's family for the holidays?

20. The book is divided into three parts: *Becoming*, *Being*, and *Knowing*. Discuss the different ways these titles relate to the chapters within each section.

ENHANCE YOUR BOOK CLUB

❧ Ariella Montero is half-human, half-vampire. Together with your book group, come up with a list of other "half-breeds"—for example, mermaids—along with the complications of each. Then, go back and discuss how these complications relate to complications in the real world, such as becoming a half-sibling, or a step-parent.

❧ Ari writes about Victorian shadowboxes for a class assignment on page 110. Have each member of the book club design a shadowbox based on Sloan's suggestion to recreate her poem "from the viewpoints of the birds."

❧ On page 127, Sloan discusses his dream journal; in one of his dreams, Jacey's hair is bleeding, symbolizing "a kind of rebirth." Given that Ari is a synesthete—a person who can see words and numbers in color and texture—and given the difficulties she has as a half-human, half-vampire, create sample dream journal entries for her based on events in the book.

A Conversation with Susan Hubbard

How did you first become interested in writing? What made you decide to pursue it as a career?

My first memory is of hearing what I later called "the wall of noise." I must have been two or three years old, listening to the sounds of my parents' conversation, trying to decipher meaning. In a way, my desire to write began with those early impressions of the power of words and the importance of decoding them. Later, when my sister introduced me to reading, I became enraptured (there's really no other word for it) by books. And by the age of seven or eight, I knew I wanted to be a writer more than anything else in the world.

What writing skills do you try to instill in your students? Did any of your personal experiences result in your depiction of Professor Warner?

I teach students the art of close reading—of paying attention to every aspect of a story, from characters, theme, and plot down to images, diction, and punctuation. Language is a form of music that too often we tune out or take for granted. Learning how to hear the nuances is essential to writing, as well as reading.

As for Professor Warner, she's a composite of some aspects of professors I've known over the years, with a smidgeon of me thrown in. Teaching creative writing is a delicate dance of its own.

How do you relate with the characters you create? Are there any aspects of yourself that you put forth in your work?

Ari's voice first came to me in a dream, and three books later, she's still talking to me. I see elements of my sensibility in some of my characters, but none of them is essentially *me*. Some of them share my concerns about the way we live now. Watching my two daughters come of age, and being around students most of the year, helped shape the characters of Ari and Kathleen. Ari has the same sort of curiosity and vulnerability that I had when I was her age, and still have to some degree.

What is your writing regime like? Do you outline first or just go where the story takes you? Has your process evolved with the series?

The first book came as a gift, in that I had a sense of the whole very early on. I wrote a detailed outline based on that sense, but I didn't follow it as I wrote—I let my characters take the lead. Since then I've come to depend on a process that I call retrospective mapping: writing a brief summary of each chapter after it's written. Each chapter is summarized on a sheet of paper, and I stick the sheets up on a wall. The mapping helps me keep track of time, plot, images, setting, and characters, and the display gives me a visual sense of the book's dramatic arc, and allows me to rearrange chapters if necessary.

The writing process has grown easier as I've come to know my characters better. The secret to enjoying writing is to create characters with whom you want to spend time.

Was there any aspect of how *The Season of Risks* developed that surprised you?

Kathleen surprised me. Originally she wasn't going to be in this book! She turned out to be more manipulative than I once would have imagined. Cameron surprised me, too. I trusted him more in the previous book. By the way, the genesis of his character was a politician I met years ago, when I was a newspaper reporter.

And the plot took on a weird life of its own, ending up in a place I hadn't anticipated.

Your books underscore social, environmental, and moral issues raised by immortality. What inspired you to include these issues in your fiction? Are there any issues you'd like to flesh out in future books?

The issues you mention are ones we wrestle with every day. I can't imagine writing without exploring them. Mortals' actions can have immortal effects, and we need to take responsibility for them. And yes, there are several other issues I want to write about, among them the profound consequences of materialism and greed, and the extent to which humans truly exercise free will. I have already addressed the latter, but not as fully as I might.

You thank several people in the acknowledgments who helped you with your research during the writing process. Were there any fascinating new facts you learned that didn't make it into the book?

Yes, but I won't list them because they may turn up in the next book. Nearly every time I talk to a doctor or scientist, I find out something that astonishes me. For instance, I'd never heard of the blood-brain barrier (mentioned in chapter nineteen) until I was describing the plotline of the book to a physician during a routine checkup.

What made you decide to write books about vampires? Did you ever consider a different supernatural breed of characters?

You know, I never planned to write about supernatural characters at all. *The Society of S* began with a dream that became a preface that led to a chapter, and Ari was simply a precocious girl trying to figure out her family's true identity, in a somewhat Gothic setting. When she began to wonder about her father being a vampire, I thought, why not?

And from there it was a short leap to: *What if some vampires were the good guys?*

Given the supernatural elements, have you ever had any uncanny personal experiences that enhance these mystical undertones?

I've admitted before that I believe I met Evil in the form of the devil, or one of his buddies, in Glastonbury, England. Once, in Saratoga Springs, I was visited by a ghost. Several times, I've been in places that strike me as haunted—some benignly, others not. And nearly every time I hike, or explore a new place, I sense the presence of *others* inherent in the natural world. Oddly enough, I'm less unsettled by those experiences than by most of my scary moments with humans.

If Ari had been your daughter, what would your reaction have been to her decision to take Septimal?

I hope I would have intuited that decision long before it was made and talked in depth with her about the reasons behind it and its possible implications. Ironically, Sara, Ari's mother, most likely would have done the same thing, if she and

Raphael hadn't agreed to not listen to Ari's thoughts in order to allow her independence.

The book begins "There are some things I know for certain." What things do *you* know for certain?
Benjamin Franklin said that nothing is certain but death and taxes. Wittgenstein said that since we can't live through death, we don't experience it. So that leaves taxes.
But I prefer to believe, as Poe wrote, that "All that we see or seem / Is but a dream within a dream." In other words, I know nothing for certain, except uncertainty.

You've traveled to Ireland several times now; what about that setting made you choose it as a destination in the novel?
Ireland is magical, mystical, otherworldly, haunted, and haunting. Landscape and legend are irrevocably intertwined. What better place for vampires to settle, and to help boost the economy? My great-grandmother was born in County Tipperary, but even without that connection I suspect I'd feel the same way: going to Ireland is like going home.

Was it any easier to write from the twenty-two-year-old Ari's perspective than from the teenage Ari's perspective?
No, in most ways it was harder to write the older perspective. It was a tricky business, writing the second section of the book, because the narrator is essentially a different person.

Did any of the characters resonate with you in a particularly strong way after you were finished writing? Did any resonate with you differently than from previous books in the series?
One of the minor characters, Dr. Godfried Roche, was inspired by a loathsome person I met at a literary festival, whose unabashed narcissism demanded caricature. As much

fun as it was to write him, it was even more fun to kill him—but now I miss him, in a way. (To clarify: Miss the character, not the actual person.)

I've already mentioned being surprised by Kathleen and Cameron. Dashay seemed to mature in this book, and yet some aspects of her remain elusive. I see her so clearly, but from the outside in; she tends to keep her secrets to herself. Sloan came into being rather unexpectedly, and I want to get to know him better, too. Surprisingly, while I was writing the book I came to find Sara a bit annoying at times. Raphael is, well, Raphael—but it was fun to watch him lighten up a bit. And Ari, poor Ari. I feel sorry for her. She deserves an easier life than the one I've given her so far.

Cameron tells Ari there are "no happy endings in vampire tales." Is this something you had in mind when crafting the conclusion?

Not consciously. That's a perceptive question, though. Maybe my unconscious mind was helping me foreshadow the conclusion.

What are you working on next? Do you have plans for another novel in the series?

I'm already visualizing another Ethical Vampire novel, which opens with Raphael and Sara's vow-renewing wedding ceremony in Ireland. Imagine such an occasion, intended to be perfect, in which absolutely everything goes wrong. This summer I'm teaching a fiction workshop in Ireland, and I'll be doing some research then.

And I have ideas for two other books that are very different. One of them involves a fairly ordinary woman living in Buffalo, New York, who happens to be a witch.

About the Author

Susan Hubbard is the author of seven books, including the Ethical Vampire series: *The Society of S, The Year of Disappearances,* and *The Season of Risks.* Hubbard's short story collection, *Blue Money,* won the Janet Heidinger Kakfa Prize in 1999 for best book of prose by an American woman. Her first book, *Walking on Ice,* received the Association of Writers and Writing Programs' Short Fiction Prize. Coeditor of the anthology *100% Pure Florida Fiction,* Susan has had fiction translated and published in more than fifteen countries, and her work has appeared in *TriQuarterly, The Mississippi Review,* and *Ploughshares,* among other journals.

A Professor of English at the University of Central Florida, Susan received the UCF Creed Keeper Award for Creativity in 2010 and a College of Arts & Humanities' Distinguished Researcher Award in 2008. She has also received teaching awards from Syracuse University, Cornell University, the University of Central Florida, and the South Atlantic Administrators of Departments of English. Her artist residencies include Yaddo, the Virginia Center for Creative Arts, the Djerassi Resident Artists Project, and Cill Rialaig.

Susan lives in Orlando and Cape Canaveral, FL. Visit her online at www.susanhubbard.com.

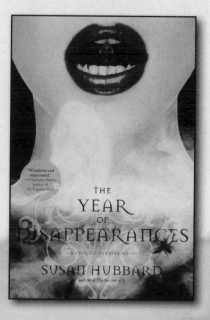